PRAISE FOR

The Coming Storm

"Ethereal and enchanting, this YA fantasy debut . . . tells an elegiac story about the complexity of sorrow. . . . Hansen's lyrical prose achieves stunning worldbuilding."

—*Shelf Awareness*

"This is a thoroughly enjoyable and suspenseful tale. . . . Readers will be drawn in by the haunting atmosphere. . . . A captivating historical ghost story."

—*Kirkus Reviews*

"Drawing upon maritime myth and Scottish folklore to weave an eerie story filled with magic and music, Hansen intertwines Beet's narrative with historical flashbacks as the mystery unfolds. There's a gentle subtlety to this atmospheric debut, with the ocean becoming a character of its own."

—*Publishers Weekly*

"The author's descriptions . . . create a spooky atmosphere that elicits a delicious sense of creeping dread. . . . An eloquent ode to the wild beauty of [Prince Edward Island] and a testament to the power of facing what confounds us."

—*BookPage*

THE COMING STORM

REGINA M. HANSEN

New York London Toronto Sydney New Delhi

An imprint of Simon & Schuster Children's Publishing Division
1230 Avenue of the Americas, New York, New York 10020

Also available in an Atheneum hardcover edition
Interior design by Irene Metaxatos
The text for this book was set in Fournier MT Std.
Manufactured in the United States of America
First Atheneum paperback edition June 2022
10 9 8 7 6 5 4 3 2 1
The Library of Congress has cataloged the hardcover edition as follows:
Names: Hansen, Regina Marie, author.
Title: The coming storm / Regina Marie Hansen.
Description: First edition. | New York : Atheneum Books for Young Readers, 2021. |
Audience: Ages 12 up. | Summary: Beet MacNeill, raised on tales of wild magic around her Prince Edward Island home, must protect her loved ones when the stories of a shape-shifting sea creature and the cold, beautiful woman who controls him begin coming true.
Identifiers: LCCN 2020026815 | ISBN 9781534482449 (hardcover) | ISBN 9781534482456 (pbk) | ISBN 9781534482463 (ebook)
Subjects: CYAC: Family life—Canada—Prince Edward Island—Fiction. | Supernatural—Fiction. | Shapeshifting—Fiction. | Prince Edward Island—History—Fiction. | Canada—History—Fiction.
Classification: LCC PZ7.1.H364328 Com 2021 | DDC [Fic]—dc23
LC record available at https://lccn.loc.gov/2020026815

To the memory of Isabel and Nelson Hansen
of Georgetown, PEI,
my beloved Banny and Bandaddy

Go to war, pray once. Go to sea, pray twice.

—PRINCE EDWARD ISLAND SAYING

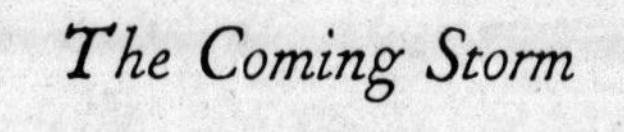

The Coming Storm

CHAPTER ONE

April 25, 1949

Beet MacNeill

I don't know what wakes me up first—Mom shaking me, or the screaming.

My heart's racing, even before I open my eyes. She's standing above me, her hair coming out of its curlers and her pink chenille dressing gown buttoned up to the chin.

"Come on, Beet. Sit up, let's go." Mom's talking a mile a minute, and her voice puts me in even more of a panic at first. Then I notice the look on her face. She's not panicking, just glowering, like she always does when she's on edge about something—and that right there's enough to calm my heart back down. A little bit, anyway.

There's a light on across the hall, and someone in there's shrieking to scare the sin out of the Devil. I'm sitting up now,

I can tell you, so quick I almost hit my head on the pail Mom's holding out to me.

"That's Deirdre! Is the baby . . . ?"

Mom drops the pail into my lap. It's made of aluminum and hurts like blazes when it lands. "The baby's going to fall out onto the floor if I don't get back in there. Now get a coat and go pump some water."

The grandfather clock in the hall is striking five as I set my feet down on the cold wood floor and head downstairs. It's not as frosty as it could be in April, but I'm still shivering like a dog in a wet blanket, or at least a dog in a yellow nightgown, which is what I'm wearing. Down in the kitchen, I grab Dad's mackintosh off the peg by the oil stove, step into a pair of gum rubber boots and there's Deirdre again, screamin' to high Heaven and above it. I let the door bang behind me, thinking how I don't ever want to have a baby, not if it hurts that bad. Especially not alone in some almost-stranger's house, poor thing.

Deirdre's my cousin Gerry Campbell's girl, and notice I *didn't* say wife. She's been living with us since she found out for sure there was a baby coming, three days after Gerry left for the Boston States to fish cod off one of those Georges Bank trawlers—him, plus Joe Curley and Newmie Myers, with not a brain between the two of 'em. The boats go out for weeks at a time, and Gerry didn't even know about the baby until last month. He was supposed to be earning the money for their wedding and for a house so that they wouldn't have to depend on Mom and Dad, or worse, go live with Gerry's not-so-poor widowed mother, Sarah (which would be a trial, let me tell you). Now Deirdre's parents have put her out, and she's staying here, in Gerry's old room.

Gerry used to live with us when I was little. Sarah left him with Mom and Dad two weeks after she had him; abandoned him and ran off south with some man nobody ever saw. Came back for Gerry a year later, but even then, she was no sort of mother to him—always dressed up like your aunt's spare room in her American catalogue clothes, while Gerry had to save his only shoes for school days. (At least that's what Dad says.) Gerry ended up staying with us off and on his whole life while Sarah was out running the roads, taking long trips to Halifax, or Boston, all down the coast, even New York City one time. So he's really more like my big brother than my cousin, especially since I never had any brothers and sisters of my own. Mom couldn't because she had such a hard time having me. Says I've been giving her trouble since the day I was born, and she never lets me forget it.

Gerry took care of me a lot in those days. We used to go on all sorts of adventures, stuff Mom would have hated to know about. He'd bring me out on the boats, the salt air and the thrum of the sea like a kind of magic, filling me up. We'd go walking in the woods looking for rabbits and foxes, creeping as quiet as we could, hand in hand as we hoped for a glimpse of any small creature. Mostly Gerry took me to hear music. Wherever there was music playing, we were there drinking it in, figuring out how the tune went so we could try it later, on Gerry's old fiddle. Sometimes we had to sit outside by the back door where the bootleggers came in, but I didn't mind. It was worth it, being there with Gerry, hearing the music. Besides, Gerry kept me safe, and I kept him out of trouble.

I was even with him the first time he saw Deirdre (or at least the first time he *saw* her saw her, if you know what I mean, since everybody around here knows everybody else). It was a summer day when we went to the Legion Hall in Montague to hear Jimmy Arsenault's band. We stopped at the new ice cream stand they have there, and Deirdre was sitting at one of the picnic tables in a yellow dress. Lorsh, did Gerry turn red, seeing her! Made me laugh to kill myself. He went right over to talk to her, though. Brave as brave, that's our Gerry. She looked up and smiled at him, and that was that.

At first, Mom got right tight in the face about the baby, the scandal of it all, but Dad brought her round. I'm glad, too. Deirdre may not be blood family, but the baby will be. Gerry's writing every week now since he's back on shore in Boston, saying he'll be home after the next trip out, with enough money for a family. Nobody in town believes him, except Deirdre, and me. I believe him. Gerry's wild (I mean, Deirdre didn't make that baby by herself, did she?), and he's not the brightest in some ways, but he sure loves Deirdre. We went out looking for sea glass just before he left for Massachusetts, and he told me how much he loved her. I know he meant it, too. Gerry always tells me the truth. I can trust him, and I don't trust just anybody.

There's that terrible yell again. I speed up, the pail banging into my legs as I head for the pump. Poor Deirdre. The baby must be hurting her like crazy. She sure is brave, though, I've gotta say.

Our farm is a mile outside of Skinner Harbour, some few yards back from Nelson's Point, a little knot of land looking out from Prince Edward Island across the Northumberland Strait. The pump is right by the back step, before Dad's rosebushes. They're bare now, but come June they'll take up three long beds right down to the green wooden fence that protects them from the worst of the winds we get out here. Just thinking about how pretty they'll be makes me believe I can smell them—above the dead seaweed smell of low tide, that is. Beyond the fence, through an iron gate, there's a dusty clay path that leads down over the bank to our rocky beach and then to our fishing grounds, called the MacNeill Grounds on all the maps. That's my name, Beatrice Mary MacNeill, but everyone calls me Beet for my red hair (and after my great-aunt Beet, who ran off to Bangor with a rumrunner).

The Strait's flat calm today, and the air's just as still as a funeral, which is good, because I'm cold enough without the wind. Across the water, I can see the shadow of Nova Scotia all rimmed in orange light. The sky's pinking up, but there are still a few stars to be seen, all the more pretty for their being so dim. Soon they'll wink out, disappear like magic, but there's no time to stop and watch them. There's a baby coming, a brand-new baby to live in my house! I can't wait. I stoop down and hold the pail beneath the old iron pump, give the handle a push, then another, up and down until the water flows freely. That's when I catch that whiff of roses again and see a sight that makes me drop the pail for joy. It's joy at first, anyway.

Now, if you were to take that narrow dusty path beyond the gate down to the beach, and then walk south, in about a half a mile you'd reach Poxy Point, where the Campbells have their land. Gerry has been living back with his mother the last couple of years, taking care of her, running errands and things (just as if she deserved it, which she doesn't). So he comes up that back path when he feels like a visit with us. Or he did, before he went off away. That could be why I don't get startled when I look up to see Gerry walking toward me on that very path. Or why I don't pay attention to that smell of roses that's still rising up around me, growing stronger the nearer he gets. Instead I just leave the pail of water emptying at my feet and run toward him through the flowerbeds.

"Gerry!" I call out. "I can't believe it. Deirdre's just about to—" I stop short. "Hey, boy. You're wet as a hen."

We've both reached the gate at the same time, and Gerry's just standing there, dripping, with his hair—red like mine—matted down over his freckled forehead. He's wearing oilskins, the black pants fishermen wear aboard ship, and his green flannel shirt is spattered with blood and dirt. The queerest thing about it all is that he's carrying his fiddle, the one Uncle Angus left him when he died. Gerry's been using it to teach me lessons—or he was, anyway—every Saturday morning. (I'm aiming to be as good as Mrs. Thaddeus Mitchell, and she's the best around, man or woman.)

Gerry hasn't spoken yet. He just stares at me as he lifts the fiddle to his shoulder; draws the bow across it, slow as slow; and starts to play. At first it sounds like "Maiden's Prayer," sweet and lonely, but then the tune shifts to something older, with a strange rising and falling about it, coming from just beneath the melody. A shiver runs through me. The low, sad tune fills the air around me as two men appear on the bank behind Gerry. Like him, Joe Curley and Newmie Myers are soaking wet, ice-gray in the face, and solemn. There is a feeling growing in my chest, that cold, dark feeling I get on early winter mornings. I can't seem to move.

As Joe and Newmie reach the fence, Gerry lowers the fiddle, and all three men stand still on the other side, looking at me with great hollow eyes. The air smells rotten-sweet, like flowers left too long in a vase. Now I know for sure what I should have guessed when I first smelled the roses out of season, what my heart knew before my head did, the moment I saw Gerry walking over the bank.

We stand there for a while just looking at one another as a gust of salt air lets me know the tide is turning, coming in. The cold, dark feeling is spreading through my whole self now. I feel my lip trembling like a little kid's.

"Oh, Gerry," I whisper, as tears fill my eyes. "Oh, no."

He holds out his hand to me at the same time a new sound startles me—a cry higher pitched than Deirdre's birthing yells, but just as loud. I turn my head toward the house, where a light still shines faintly in the upstairs window. It's the baby I hear; the new baby is crying. When I turn back to the fence, Gerry and the other ghosts are gone.

CHAPTER TWO

April 25, 1949

Sarah Campbell

The Campbells' picture window looks out on the Strait, then farther, toward the orange-rimmed shadow of Nova Scotia. Sarah Campbell, as she's known, rocks back and forth slowly, calmly, in the big oak chair her late husband, Angus, carved for her when she was expecting their only child. Her eyes, green as kelp, take in tiny, spruce-covered Poxy Island, where the crew and passengers of a Scottish ship died in quarantine some 130 years ago. The graves of the victims are still out there on the island, but in all the time she's lived in this house, Sarah has never been out to visit them. She has no time for other people's sorrow.

Sarah's fine white hands—finer than could be believed of a soon-to-be grandmother—hold tightly to the pendant that hangs low on her dress of royal blue. The pendant is shaped like the shell of a sea snail, spiraling to a point, dipped in silver. The rocking chair keeps time as she hums a tune so quiet that it's hard to distinguish it from the sound of the waves that lap the sandstone rocks beneath her window. Sarah had that tune from an old, old woman, in another country, too long ago.

There is a knock at the heavy wooden door, but Sarah does not answer. The one knocking doesn't need an invitation. High tide on the Strait is calm on this April morning, the rising sun shining on water as smooth and iridescent pink as carnival glass. Red sky at morning, sailor take warning. A slow smile pulls at the edges of Sarah's lipsticked mouth. There is a storm coming; she feels it in the hairs of her smooth white arms. Far south, off the coast of Massachusetts, it has already begun. The song on her lips turns harder—like the edges of her beautiful pale face—but her green eyes remain soft and opaque as jellyfish.

The visitor enters the room, his face young and tanned, his hair a strange color like tarnished silver. The cuffs of his immaculately pressed trousers are spattered lightly with red beach clay.

"Your son is dead," the young man says in a voice like running water. He does not blink.

"Yes, Uist," Sarah Campbell says flatly. "And the child?"

"A boy. His birth wail is still ringing in my ears."

The earlier smile now spreads across Sarah's face and reaches her eyes, still green but lighter now, like the slippery moss that covers coastal rocks. As she turns away from the young man, Sarah catches sight of her reflection in the mirror that sits on the shelf beside her chair. There are many mirrors in this house; this one is small, silver framed, engraved with tiny dolphins. In it, Sarah observes the beginnings of a crease between her perfectly arched eyebrows. On her white hands, there is the slightest bulge of a blue vein starting. She will tolerate these things . . . for a year.

CHAPTER THREE

April 28, 1949

Beet MacNeill

The baby's name is Joseph. He's been in the world three days now, and it feels like we've always known him. He's a big one, too, Mom says as big as I was when I was two months old. Deirdre struggled so hard with him that Dad had to go for Dr. Roberts afterward. He's back for a house call today, just to see if she's healing. Mom gave Joseph to me to hold, and I can't stop staring at him, opening his chubby hands finger by finger, sniffing the top of his fuzzy baby head. He's wrapped in my baby quilt, and my white wicker bassinet is waiting for him beside the window. Mom says we don't use new things in this house if old will do. Still, I think it's strange she still has all my baby things, that she kept them for almost fourteen years. It's good she did, though, because I would give Joseph anything.

He's a little part of Gerry to care for and love, and I'm so glad of that now.

They brought home Gerry's body this morning, and Mom was the one who had to tell Deirdre. I wasn't allowed in the room, but I heard Deirdre afterward, crying so quietly and for so long it broke my heart all over again. I knew before anyone that Gerry was dead, but it still hurts like a raw, new wound every time I think of it. They say that Gerry, Joe, and Newmie decided not to sign on once the trawler was ready to set out for Georges Bank again. (Gerry was missing Deirdre too much, I imagine. The rest of us, too. I mean we sure missed him, especially me, not knowing that soon I'd be missing him forever.) Instead, the three of them hitchhiked all the way up through Maine and New Brunswick and got the ferry at Cape Tormentine. Dad got all this from Lee MacIsaac, who got it from the harbormaster at Borden, so it's hard to know what's real and what's made up. But according to the harbormaster, a fog rolled in during the crossing, so bad that the steamer had to wait it out in the middle of the Strait. It took hours for the fog to clear, and when it did, Joe and Newmie were missing. Overboard, Dad said. Most likely slipped on the wet deck.

A crewman found Gerry hanging by his leg from the port side chain. His head was underwater and his right hand was missing two fingers. I wasn't supposed to hear that last bit, and part of me sure wishes I hadn't, because now I'll have that picture in my head for the rest of my life. How scared he must have been, dying like that, all alone. If I think about it too much, I won't be able to bear it. Still, I guess I'm glad I know the real story, the truth of it. The strange and terrible thing is, the whole time the fog was in, nobody heard a call for help or even a splash. A couple of passengers said they heard music playing somewhere, but fog does strange things to sound. And what does that matter anyway, when Gerry's dead and gone forever? No more walks in the woods looking for foxes. No more fiddle lessons, trying out new tunes, copying the players we heard all those Saturday nights together by the bootlegger door, laughing to kill ourselves over the silliest things. Gerry will never see his baby boy.

My bedroom door is open, and I see Dr. Roberts come out of Gerry's room (Deirdre's now, I guess) and close the door behind him. He smiles and winks at me before covering his bald head with his cap.

"Don't worry, Beatrice. All will be well." His voice is kind.

When he heads downstairs, the room across the hall is quiet. I hope that means Deirdre is sleeping. Baby Joseph stirs in my arms and I hug him a little closer. I'm glad I didn't tell her what I saw that morning. I'm glad I didn't tell anyone. Some part of me still wanted to be wrong, to think that I was just seeing things, or dreaming. But I've heard all the stories people tell, about ghosts and apparitions, the scent of roses out of season, and that morning with Gerry was just too much like them to ignore. Gerry showed up near his own home when he was really dying far away (and *this* is his home, not Sarah Campbell's place); just like the phantom bell ringers at the Kirk of St. James in Charlottetown, so many years ago, or when Mary Boudreaux saw her sister Alice in the picture window when Alice was supposed to be working at a hotel in Moncton. Then the family got a letter that Alice had died of the flu on the same day Mary saw her.

I never believed those stories, and I still don't want to, but at least I don't need to tell anyone now. The real news of Gerry has come, real news from real people, and that's enough of a burden for Deirdre to carry. I don't ever need to let her know Gerry came to me before he died, to me and not to her. I can do that much for her.

Deirdre is going to need us now, even more than she already did. People will be talking and sneering, like they always do. Some people, anyway. Baby Joseph is going to need me, too, to look out for him, and always tell him the truth, maybe to teach him the fiddle someday. Just like I needed Gerry. I'm trembling again like the morning I saw him in the garden, and I've only just noticed the warm tears on my face.

It's midafternoon now, and the sky through the window is a bright blue, with the sun shining a little too hot through the glass, making the room feel like a church in July. Outside, gulls are calling to one another. I get up, carefully because I don't want to wake Joseph, and walk over to the window to open it. I lift it gently with my free hand, and the scent of the sea comes in clean and salty. It's high tide and the water on the Strait is green. Gentle waves are rolling in toward shore. There's a picture of Gerry and me on my bureau. Mom mostly keeps pictures in albums, but she let me have this one, us on Easter when I was five and Gerry was twelve. We're holding hands and Gerry's looking down at me, smiling in his Easter suit. I'm looking so hard at the picture I don't hear Mom come into the room.

"Little one has to have his supper," she says from behind me. I turn and she is already holding out her arms for him. Joseph stretches, raising his arms straight over his head and opening his mouth in a tiny yawn. I don't want to let him go. I bend toward him and kiss the top of his head. In my heart I say, "Don't worry, baby, I'll take care of you. I'll never let anything happen to you."

"Someone ought to let Sarah know about her son," Mom says as I hand her the baby. There is the tiniest sneer, at the corner of her upper lip. I only see it because I know Mom that well.

"Her son." I spit the words out. The baby lets out a little cry, then settles back in Mom's arms.

"Beatrice." Mom's quiet voice has a threat in it, but it passes quick. Then she just sighs and shakes her head. "I'll have your father drive over when he's done in the fields. Shouldn't be much longer now." Dad's been out since not long after they brought Gerry back home. The farm has to be worked, no matter what.

Mom's talking to herself now, a bit. "They brought Gerry to us, not her. It's best she hears from . . . family." She gives me a narrow, sharp-eyed look. "And you can save your bold comments, Beatrice Mary." She looks down at Joseph. "Time to see your Mama," she says to him in a singsong baby-talk voice. Then she rearranges the quilt and looks up again, rolling her eyes at me. "We are going to have to teach you how to wrap this boy up tight."

When Mom's gone, I go back to the window. In just that short time we were talking, clouds have started to dot the sky. A long-necked cormorant, black with a yellow beak, is drying its wings on the rocks beyond the bank.

A woman is making her way along the path at the back of the house. She's wearing a long, dark fur coat—like the ones in the ladies' magazines—even though the weather is much too warm for it. The coat is open so I can see how thin she is in her green floral dress. Her long blond hair has a silver streak that threads through her braid. Sarah Campbell's face is beautiful and hard. She has to be fifty, but she looks maybe thirty-five, though that streak in her hair is new since the last time I saw her. The thinness, too.

Mom must have seen her from the parlor window, because she goes out to meet her.

The wind has come up, so I only catch a few words of what they are saying—Gerry's name a few times, something about the ferry. The whole time Mom is talking, her face is grave, but Sarah's expression doesn't change at all. Stays just as hard and blank as marble.

Now Mom is nodding toward the house, pushing her hair out of her eyes as the wind gusts again. It carries some more words my way—"baby," "tea," "welcome," "sure?"

Sarah shakes her head, but her stony expression stays the same. The wind has stirred up some gulls. They fly low over

Mom and Sarah and land in the rose garden, a little flock of them. Mom says a few more things to Sarah that I can't hear, then turns away, shaking her head.

That's when Sarah's appearance finally changes, slowly, but even from this far away I can see it.

She's smiling.

CHAPTER FOUR

June 3, 1950

Beet MacNeill

Jeannine Gallant lights the yellow candle with a long wooden match. She's eyeing me like a mackerel. "Beet, how long since we had the cookies on Gerry?"

We're standing in my front parlor, in the little nook where the woodstove used to be, and where right now Sarah Campbell's body is laid out to be waked. It's the same place we waked Gerry after they brought him home.

"Well, he was brought in about thirteen months ago, a Wednesday," I say. "Funeral was a day or two later. Mind where you drop that wax, Jeannine. You don't want to ruin her makeup." I hold Sarah's mouth closed with two hands while Jeannine tilts the candle sideways, letting a few drops of yellow wax fall on the dead woman's pale, pinched lips. The house smells of tea and the cinnamon Mom has boiling on the stove to cover dead Sarah's ripening odor. Truth is, I've had too much time to think about Gerry dying, seeing him that morning in the garden, and again that last time when I was helping Mom get his body ready for visitors, putting makeup on his gray skin and covering his mangled hands with white gloves. But I can't think about that now or I know I'll start crying, and there's just too much to do, and too many people in the house, too many eyes to see.

Jeannine takes a pencil from behind her ear and spreads the hot wax between Sarah's lips with the eraser end, then takes over holding the lips together, with a look in her brown eyes like she's just stepped on a jellyfish. Jeannine's my best friend since we were five years old, and she's the only one I told about seeing Gerry's ghost that time, but she's right squirrely when it comes to touching anything dead. It's odd, too, since she loves—and I mean *loves*—reading books about ghosts and supernatural stuff. Lily Soloman at the library had to start special ordering them for her. "Old Sarah sure shriveled up in the last year," Jeannine tells me. "Since Gerry died, I mean."

I give Jeannine a speedy kick to the ankle and nod toward the kitchen door. Deirdre has just come in with a tray full of the fudge squares Mom only makes when someone dies or at Christmas. Baby Joseph is toddling along ahead of her. He has his mother's light brown hair and eyes, but the shape of him is pure Gerry, right down to the way he walks, like any minute he might start dancing a jig on the carpet. It makes me want to pick him up and hug him.

Deirdre gives me a quick smile (she doesn't talk much since Gerry died and the baby was born) and places the tray on the card table we put out near the hall entrance, covered in black crepe, to hold all the cookies and sweets for the wake. When she's done, she sits down in front of the open window in Dad's old red armchair, pulling Joseph onto her lap. The sheer white curtains behind them are floating a bit on the breeze from outside, and through the window the old garden fence looks as faded green as ever against the blue June sky. There's a big black-backed minister gull sitting on the fence, with a beak bent sideways like a wrong turn. Joseph spots the creature right off.

"Wook! Mama!" he cries, pointing over his mother's shoulder. "Wook . . . Boy."

Deirdre pats the baby's head and gives him that sad smile of hers. "Not 'boy,' sweetheart, 'bird.' It's a *birdie*."

The gull stays perched stock still on the fence post, looking almost as dour as Sarah lying nearby in her casket beneath Great-Granny Parker's pink lusterware tea set. Sarah's scrawny dead hand, with the red painted nails she wore until she died, is closed tight over her chest, her dark green church dress done up with pearl buttons all the way to her pointed chin. Mom's the one dressed the body, and she had a time finding a modest enough outfit. Sarah never wore anything but a sweetheart neckline her whole life—just as vain as a pet pig, even this past year since Gerry went over and she started losing her looks and her health so quick you'd almost think she mourned him. You'd *almost* think so, if you didn't see what I saw that day she came to the house.

Sarah was Baby Joseph's granny, but she never saw him once in the year since he was born and his poor dead daddy came to me out in the rose garden, playing that sad fiddle song that I still can't get out of my mind. Still, that smile of hers, after Mom told her about Gerry . . . well, it makes me glad Sarah stayed away. Mom says we have to give old Sarah a proper wake. "She's family," Mom says. "People would wonder." People around here are always "wondering" about something.

Mom comes out from the kitchen while I'm thinking all this, all five feet of her in a gray cotton dress, blue apron covered in flour. "You girls have Sarah's mouth stuck shut yet? The mourners will be here any minute."

"Mourners?" I say to Jeannine, who's holding Sarah's lips closed as daintily as possible. "More like beggars . . ."

Mom gives me a look would kill a spider. "Beatrice Mary, do not you be bold with me just because your father's not here."

"All right, Mom," I call after her as she heads back into the kitchen. "We're almost ready."

"Start counting, Beet," Jeannine says.

"One, two, three . . ." When I get to "ten," Jeannine lets go of Sarah's dead mouth. We get it closed firmly just as the front door knocker bangs. In the hallway that leads to the front door, the grandfather clock is striking two.

"Publicovers," Jeannine and I say at the same time. The Publicovers are always the first ones at a wake, mostly because they know there'll be food. They're twins, maiden ladies of seventy-three years, and live out at the edge of Skinner Harbour in a big house all made of red brick, with cut glass windows brought in from away.

"I'll get it," Jeannine says right quick, already crossing the room toward the hall door. "Freddy Soloman might be driving them today."

I give her a scowl behind her back, then take down the tube of pink lipstick—it's been sitting on the shelf next to Granny's teacups—and start painting up Sarah's stuck-together lips as quick and neat as I can. Outside the window where Deirdre's sitting, white clouds are starting to dot the sky. The old gull on the fence cocks his head as if he's listening for something.

The bird is still there a half hour later, when Joseph is asleep in his mother's lap, and the parlor's as filled up with "mourners" as it's ever going to get. Eddie MacIsaac is here (he's tending to the farm while Dad's in New Brunswick) and Les Martell's come out with his wife, Honey. Mom says Honey Martell never misses a chance to see the inside of other people's houses. Over by the sweets table, as far as she can get from Sarah's actual dead body, Nora Publicover has just polished off the last of the fudge squares and is eating her way through the shortbread diamonds.

"Poor Sarah aged so much near the end," Nora says, lifting a chocolate-stained hand to her iron gray marcel wave. "Must have been the death of her boy that did it."

"Lost her looks," Louise Publicover agrees between great mouthfuls of fruitcake. "Shame." I roll my eyes at Mom, but she just ignores me.

The Publicovers have brought some boy with them. He's the tallest thing in the room by six inches, and skinny with it, with black hair and skin as pale as a whitewashed barn. He's standing next to the shortbread, or what's left of it, with crumbs all down his shirt.

"Sheila . . . Beatrice." Nora waves Mom and me over with a hand full of cookie, her other hand holding the skinny boy by the elbow. "Come over here. Meet our grandnephew Sean, my niece Eleanor MacInnes's boy. Don't be shy, Sean." She yanks his elbow so hard he spills the cup of tea he's holding.

"Sean's from Boston," Louise puts in, only she says it like "Baw-stin." The sisters both worked in a hotel in Massachusetts for one summer, when they were maybe eighteen, but they try to put on the accent like they lived there all their lives. That is, when they remember. With their nephew here, I've got a feeling they'll remember a lot.

The boy is dabbing at his stained shirt with a napkin, and before he can say anything, Nora starts talking. "Beatrice is about your age, aren't you Beatrice?"

How would I know? I want to say, but Mom answers for me. "Beatrice turns fifteen this month."

"Well, how lovely!" Louise almost squeals. "Our Sean is six-teen!"

"Sean is staying with us for the summer," Nora adds, only of course it sounds like 'summah.' "It would be nice for him to make some friends."

Sean doesn't look as if he wants to make friends. I'd say he looks afraid someone in the room might touch him. Also, his ears stick out. I can't pretend his eyes aren't something to think about, though. They're true blue—not the steel gray that people call blue—with black eyelashes that I'm sure would make Jeannine just swoon away, if Freddy weren't in the room, of course. Me, I'm not one to swoon over anything, or anyone.

"I'm sure Beatrice would be happy to show him around," Mom says, in a voice that means she doesn't care if I am happy about it or not.

Meanwhile, Sean is staring across the room at dead Sarah. "Her . . . her eye." His voice has just the hint of gag to it.

Sure enough, dead Sarah's left eye has popped open, so she's giving me a wink. If you can be grateful to a corpse, I sure am. "Excuse me," I say, backing away from the Publicovers and their stuck-up stick figure of a nephew. "I have to attend to Sarah."

The candle and matches are on the shelf behind the teacups, so I light the wax quick and wait for it to melt. I hold dead Sarah's eyelids together, all crusted with the old wax, and drop more wax onto her lashes. By the time I have stopped counting to ten, Sean MacInnes is standing right next to me, staring like I'm some kind of bug.

"You have to touch her?"

I just want to push him, maybe because he startled me, but also because of that look on his face. "What's the matter?" I say. "Don't they have dead bodies in Boston?"

He opens his mouth like he's going to say something, but I don't want to hear it, and I don't want to be stared at like some creature in a zoo either. Instead, I walk off and grab the last piece of shortbread—just for spite—and head to the corner nearer the window, where Jeannine is hanging off Freddy Soloman's arm like a new purse.

The Publicovers bought a car but they can't drive, so Freddy drives them, when he's not out fishing, or *selling* fish, or helping his aunt Lily in the library, or traveling around King's County in his own disgrace of a pickup offering to do odd jobs for people. Jeannine's always saying she wishes she were just a few years older so she could go to the dances and dance with Freddy. All I can say is that I hope Freddy dresses better for dances—if he ever goes to any—than he dresses for wakes. He always looks like he's come from some chore or other, all wild black hair and dark eyes, in the too-big jeans his brother left behind when he joined the army. Still, Freddy's a nice fella—not the kind to stare down his nose at people—and he's sure being patient with Jeannine.

"Um, Freddy . . ." She's giggling away like a goose and playing with the ends of her black hair so as I want to kick her just for being a flirt. "My mom wants you to bring round some of them lovely Poxy Point quahogs . . . I mean, the next time you go diggin'."

"Sure, J'nine. Prob'ly be next Saturday." He smiles so that I can see the chipped tooth he got when he fell down fixing Mike Murphy's porch last spring, but the whole time Freddy's talking, his eyes are somewhere else—where they always are, on Deirdre and the baby. Freddy and Deirdre were neighbors over in town all their lives before Deirdre's parents chucked her out, and the Solomans are the only ones around besides Mom and Dad who treat Deirdre the same since Joseph was born.

"Hey, Beet," Jeannine whispers. She's let go of Freddy's arm and is gesturing across the room. "Who's the boyyy?"

I sigh; I knew she was going to ask, and it's exactly what I don't need. I'm ready to tell her anyway, if only to get it over with, but before I can, a feeling comes over me that stops me talking. I've had the feeling before, when I was six and got caught in a rip current up at Stanhope Beach. I was under the water all of thirty seconds, not even long enough to lose my breath, but I still remember how heavy everything seemed, with the salt water rushing over my face, pounding at my ears. I felt it as much as heard it, the sound of me dying. Now it's here in my own parlor. I turn around to where the feeling is coming from, and even as I do, there's a hand on my arm. Sean MacInnes.

"You looked like you were going to faint," he says.

"Well, I wasn't." I jerk my arm away from him.

But, to be honest, he could be right.

A woman is standing just inside the parlor, near the hall door, and she's so beautiful that the room has gone still. Even the

Publicovers are standing there in their matching green brocade dresses, holding tea sandwiches in limp hands.

"Goodness me," Nora Publicover says in a voice that's trying to be a whisper but failing. "What a striking young woman . . ."

"And so modern," Louise agrees, just as loudly.

I look at dead Sarah, hard and withered in her coffin, and then at the woman who has come into the room. Everything about this woman seems soft. Her hair is a warm honey color and frames her face in a pixie cut, with feathery movie star bangs. Her eyes are bright green as mermaid's hair, this kind of seaweed that grows on beach rocks. Even the skirt of her blue silk dress seems to float around her knees as she moves across the room toward Joseph, who's squirming himself awake in his mother's lap. The memory of that drowning feeling is still fresh in my mind, and I edge closer to Deirdre and the baby, just as a sudden gust sets the curtains flying.

When the woman speaks, it's only to Deirdre. "Is this Sarah Campbell's grandson?" The woman's voice is as flat as sand at low tide. There's a long silver chain hanging from her neck, with a pendant in the shape of a twisty seashell. It's beautiful and old, and also kind of familiar looking. She is staring at Joseph with narrowed eyes, a look that is almost angry, or maybe hungry, I can't tell. Either way, she's not smiling.

"Y-yes." Deirdre holds the baby closer as he rubs his eyes. "Who are . . ."

The woman holds out a smooth, white, long-fingered hand,

her nails painted an even darker red than dead Sarah's still lying in her casket. The seashell pendant swings back and forth as she steps forward, and I have the sudden urge to step between her and Joseph. "I'm Marina," she says. "Marina Shaw. I'm Sarah's niece."

CHAPTER FIVE

June 6, 1950

Beet MacNeill

"*Lorsh*, Beet! You call that a *tune*!" Jeannine is lying on my bedroom floor, hands covering her pointy Gallant ears. "Sounds more like you're drownin' rats in the wash basin!"

I draw the bow once more across the high strings of Gerry's old fiddle (mine now since they brought us his belongings), letting it squeal just enough to really set Jeannine's lips curling. Then I put the fiddle in its old black leather case and close it, eyeing Jeannine the whole time. "I had this tune from Gerry," I tell her. "In the rose garden." Somewhere outside my open window, gulls are mewing like stray kittens searching after milk.

"Oh, the *rose* garden," Jeannine sighs, and for a minute I think she gets why that matters to me.

But then she keeps on talking.

"You're so lucky, Beet, seeing Gerry's ghost like you did. I mean you're not lucky that he died. That was terrible." She says this last part quick and has the grace to blush a bit for being stupid. It doesn't last long, though. "But, really, truly experiencing the supernatural. I mean that's just . . ."

She goes all quiet and moony, the way she does when she's talking about Freddy Soloman or some other boy. All I can do is shake my head. Sometimes I regret telling Jeannine about seeing Gerry and those other ghosts. I'm regretting it *now*, for sure, especially with Jeannine reading every ghost story and fairy tale she can get her hands on, plus every "Ripley's Believe It or Not" they print in *The Guardian*. It's a miracle Jeannine hasn't told the world about my "paranormal experience" (that's what they'd probably call it in "Ripley's") except I made her promise not to say anything. I haven't gotten round to mentioning that drowning feeling I had the other day, when I saw Marina Shaw. No telling what Jeannine would make of that (or especially of Sean MacInnes being right there next to me when it happened). I'm not sure what *I* make of it for that matter, but I didn't like it. Didn't like how Marina Shaw zeroed in on Deirdre and Joseph either. I mean, I wouldn't trust anybody related to Sarah Campbell, but somehow I think there's more to it than that.

Jeannine must see my face as I'm thinking about all this, because all of a sudden her expression changes. "I really am sorry, you know, about Gerry." She even looks a little weepy.

"I know." I say, and I do, but I am still not ready to tell her about that undertow feeling. I'd like to forget all about it myself. I want to forget everything about that morning in the rose garden, too—the lost, sorrowful look on Gerry's face, the wet clothes, the blood and sand in his hair—everything but that tune Gerry played for me the moment I knew he and his friends were dead. Even with the pain of it, that's a gift I'd like to keep. If only I could learn to play the tune, *really* play it, like Gerry did, to honor him.

I've practiced almost every day since that one, and I've gotten fair at some tunes—"Saint Anne's Reel," "Flowers of Edinburgh," all the old ones—but not that one of Gerry's that I heard in the rose garden. I've tried everything, whether plucking each string separate, or gliding the bow from string to string in one motion. I've even tried left-handed, but that tune always ends up sounding like some poor dying creature. It's the undertone I'm missing, a kind of deep echo that softens the tune, makes it mournful. I just don't know how to call up that sound with a fiddle—maybe I never will—but somehow, I can't give up on it. That would be like saying goodbye to Gerry for good.

"So that Sean fella was nice," Jeannine says out of nowhere, only she says it like "niiiice." I actually can't believe it took her this long to mention him again, and I'm of two minds whether this subject is preferable to talking about Marina Shaw.

"I guess." I start up on the fiddle again, one I heard called "MacPherson's Lament," just to drown Jeannine out. No such luck.

"Oh, come on, Beet! Those blue eyes . . ."

"I didn't notice," I answer, even if it's not really true.

Besides, how could I miss them, the way he was staring at me?

"I mean, he's not as cute as Freddy," she goes on. "But he's American . . ."

I don't know why she thinks that will recommend him to me, blue eyes or no blue eyes. "Old Sarah was American, too, plus he's related to the Publicovers."

I try to keep concentrating on the slow, sad notes of the old air, but it's no use. Jeannine is off on a tear about how there are so few cute boys in Skinner Harbour school and how next year in Montague High School will be better *and* how any Skinner Harbour girl would kill to date a rich American boy.

"Not all Americans are rich, Jeannine." This is worse than the ghost stories. I have given up on the fiddle now, and I start to put it back in its case. I slide it under the bed just as Mom's voice comes roarin' up from the bottom of the stairs. She's got some lungs on her, little though she is. "Beatrice! Jeannine! Get down here and lend a hand, *please*!"

I roll my eyes at Jeannine, and the two of us head downstairs.

It's been a warm day, even for June, but downstairs on the front porch, the high-tide breeze off the Strait is starting to put a nip back in the air, bringing in the sweet, clean smell of bayberry and green grass. Our front lawn, dotted with buttercups and white clover, stretches down one hundred yards from the porch to the clay road that leads southeast to Skinner Harbour town. Past the road and another fifty yards of sloping green, white, and yellow, the red sandstone cliff stands over the mouth of the Cardigan River where it empties into Cardigan Bay and the Strait. The smooth water (smooth for now, anyway) flashes fire orange beneath a sky striped white and glowing rose. "Sky-blue pink," Dad calls it, the color of evening.

Mom eyeballs us the minute my hand touches the screen door.

"Well, you two, don't wait for an invitation." She's sitting stiff-backed in a metal folding chair beside the red-and-white porch railing, working a pair of knitting needles the way some people work a grudge. She casts a glance over toward Deirdre, who's busy making cherry thumbprints for next weekend's Skinner Harbour Day party at the Cozy Hall. There'll be a bazaar in the afternoon to raise money for the new playground, and later on a dance for the adults. That should go on until about one a.m., but Dad's letting me play the early set with him and Les Martell. It's kind of my debut.

With floured hands, Deirdre rolls balls of dough and arranges them on the cookie sheets spread across the long gray table. Baby Joseph holds on to a table leg, his fingers and round, tan little face covered with flour and the juice from the jar of maraschino cherries his mother has placed at her elbow. Jeannine and I pull up two more folding chairs and get started pressing the cherries into the dough. Deirdre gives us a little smile, but doesn't say anything, only guides Joseph out of my way with a free hand. Even when people are talking all around her, Deirdre usually stays just as quiet as churches.

Mom's knitting a pair of green-and-yellow mittens to add to the thirty she's already made for the bazaar, and she's talking nearly twenty words for every stitch. She's probably *been* talking since she shooed Jeannine and me upstairs after supper an hour ago. That's when Dad got back from his trip to New Brunswick. The minute he stepped out of Freddy Soloman's near-ancient Ford, Mom started in about Dad "insisting upon riding in a broken-down old truck with that Soloman boy." (Mom scolds Dad so hard, you'd think it was *her* who had eight years on *him*, instead of the other way round.) She didn't even give Dad a kiss when he got home—and probably hasn't yet—even though she's wearing her good dress, sky-blue pink like the sunset, *and* even though she made sure to keep a supper all warm and ready for him on the porch. Mom's still at it—needle, thread, lips, and tongue clicking along like one of those mechanical birds the scrap peddler brought round last October, trying to sell to us for Christmas, but she's moved on to a more interesting subject—Marina Shaw.

"She has her auntie's eyes from what I can see, and her clothes sense, too . . . if that's what you want to call it. Oh, the getup she was in, Donny! That dress was all blue silk, expensive no doubt . . . and with a *neckline*. . . . Dressed more for dancing than for mourning. That's all I'll say." Mom looks like she's going to spit, though I can't imagine her actually ever doing anything like that.

Dad slowly puts aside his empty dish and reaches into a shirt pocket for his old rosewood pipe. His blue travel suit and shock of gray hair are still dusted pink from road clay, but his hands are clean. "She wouldn't be the only one wanting to dance at our Sarah's wake," he says, filling the pipe.

I bite my lip to keep from giggling as a hint of music drifts toward me from somewhere on the water. Dad has more than enough reason not to like Sarah. Once, when I wasn't supposed to be listening, I heard him say how Uncle Angus would still be alive if he hadn't gone out on a crazy errand for her. Never knew what he meant by that, and he's not telling, but I've never forgotten hearing about it either.

Mom gives Dad a sour look. "It wasn't just that, Donny. She was wearing that necklace of Sarah's, the one with the seashell. I'd like to know where she got it from, that's all." So that's why the necklace looked familiar!

"Well," answers Dad. "It's not like Sarah can take it with her."

"That's not the . . . ," Mom starts to sputter, then just shakes her head. "Donald MacNeill, sometimes it's just not worth talking to you."

"They're family," Dad says. "Sarah probably left the necklace to her."

Mom does not look convinced, but she just gives a sniff and goes back to her knitting. Some fisherman must be playing a radio out there. It's a woman's voice, singing, just snatches of it here and there, depending on how the breeze blows. Little Joseph has stopped grabbing after cherries and is tilting his head in the direction of the sound. If Mom hears anything, you wouldn't know by looking at her.

"Really, Donny, you know how I feel about people calling attention to . . . well . . ." Mom looks quickly at Deirdre and then away again. "That Marina Shaw just announces herself to the room like some kind of royalty, gives Joseph the eyeball, then floats off without praying at the casket *or* tasting the cake." From the look on Mom's face, you'd never be sure which is worse.

Dad strikes a match on the sole of his black leather shoe, taps the side of the pipe's bowl, then lights it, the smell of apple tobacco floating through the air. "It's not all bad, Sheila," he says. "All the more cake for the Publicovers."

"Oh, so you think it's funny! Do you, Donny MacNeill? Bad enough you leave me by myself to greet all of Sarah's mourners while you're out runnin' the roads."

Dad just kind of laughs at that one. "Now, Sheila, you know I had to go to Moncton for that tractor part so I can harvest the new potatoes. It's almost time. Besides, how was I supposed to know the old witch would die with me not home?"

Mom gives him a glare that would turn cheese. I sneak a look at Jeannine, who has her face buried in her hands, pretending she's coughing. The thing is, though, I didn't like the way Marina Shaw looked at Joseph either, and I'm still remembering that undertow feeling, too. I probably would have fallen if Sean MacInnes hadn't been there (but he doesn't need to know that). I'm wondering if it isn't time I mention it all to Jeannine, even if she does "ooh" and "ah" about it like I'm the heroine of one of her ghost-story books.

A breeze blows, and I hear a snatch of that tune again. It has a wheedling kind of shrillness to it I don't like. Joseph has gone all still, too, and he stays that way until the sound fades, a fat ball of cookie dough halfway into his mouth. Deirdre grabs the dough before he can swallow any. Joseph's lower lip starts to quiver, and his eyes fill up. Poor little fella. She's right, but I hate to see him cry.

Dad stretches his long legs out on the step and takes a handful of soft yellow candies out of the paper bag that's sitting next to him on the porch—butter mints, Joseph's favorite.

"Your Marina Shaw must be living out at dead Sarah's place. Freddy was on his way to make a delivery there after he left me off." The baby reaches out his hand for the treat, all trace of tears gone.

"Freddy Soloman," Mom grumbles. "That boy'll go anywhere there's a dollar to be made. I'll bet he charged you the bank for that ride from Borden, and don't tell me he didn't, Donny."

"Aw, Mom," I say. "Freddy's nice. He just works hard." His great-aunt's an odd one, though. She came out from Charlottetown about two years ago to run the library, and she lives in the lot out near Jeannine's family, in a tiny little house painted candy colors like the witch's cottage in "Hansel and Gretel." Jeannine just loves Lily because she lets her take out as many books as she wants, and because she seems to know every supernatural story. Still, old Lily's got a way of looking right through people. Gives me the shivers.

Mom just goes on punishing those mittens with her needles. "That boy's always sniffin' around this house like a Newfoundland dog. I don't like it. What's he want, anyway?"

Dad looks over at Deirdre, now wiping the flour and cherry

juice from Joseph's face with the corner of her blue floral apron. "Sheila, if you don't know, I'm not gonna tell ya."

"I'm taking Joseph up for a bath," Deirdre says, with maybe the merest hint of pink in her face (although it's hard to tell, with her being so shy). She picks up Joseph and starts heading for the door, his little arms round her neck, one last butter mint clutched in his hand. The breeze has died down and those bits of music have fallen away, too.

"*Donny,*" Mom says sharp but quiet when Deirdre is gone. "You think it's all right, talking about such things when that girl's already got enough scandal. A baby out of wedlock, and now the likes of *Freddy Soloman* after her? Well, I just hope Deirdre learned her lesson the first time round. I hope she got herself some sense."

Dad takes another puff. "Sense has nothin' to do with it."

This time I can't stop myself from giggling; the sound escapes me loud and awkward, but it feels good, too. Until Mom has her say.

"Have you something to be laughing at, young lady?" Mom purses her lips. "It's only because your friend is here visiting that I don't—"

"Beet," Dad interrupts. "I see you're done with the cookies. Why don't you and Jeannine take a walk down to the beach and . . . well . . . find me a good piece of driftwood for that birdhouse I'm working on."

"Driftwood." Mom shakes her head. "Jesus, Mary, and Joseph! Sending two young girls down to the beach when it's almost night!"

"We'll be fine," I say quickly. I really do want to talk to Jeannine about Marina Shaw. "It's a nice night for a walk."

In a minute, we're off the porch and headed round the house.

"No farther than where you can see to Poxy Island," Mom calls after us, sharp as a pin, as we make our way through the just-budding rosebushes behind the house and toward the beach path. "Do you hear me, Beatrice Mary?"

Before I can answer, I catch Dad's whispered voice on the sudden sea breeze. "Let them be, Sheila. I'm still waiting for my welcome-home kiss."

The evening is quiet, like it always is out here—except in a storm—and aside from our voices, the only noise comes from those same few gulls I heard at the house. They are hanging on the breeze over two great beds of mussels, black shadows below the slow incoming tide. From farther away comes the low clanging bell of the Poxy Island channel marker, but we won't see the island itself until we reach the tip of Nelson's Point. On the beach, we take off our shoes and head south along the narrow shore, leaving tracks in the hard, pink sand as the sky turns from red to violet. There's not a boat on the Strait that I can see, so whoever was playing that radio must have made it to harbor. A minister gull lands on a heap of dried eelgrass and starts sauntering along beside us, pretending he's not looking for a meal. He's big as a young osprey or a small hawk, with a bent beak just so, the same gull that was sitting on our fence all through dead

Sarah's wake. His left wing is mottled, black and gray.

"My mom's not half wrong about that Marina Shaw," I tell Jeannine. "I mean, Mom's a right old critic, and she's too hard on some people, but . . . really . . . what's Marina so interested in Joseph for anyway?" And the necklace. How did she get the necklace?

Jeannine picks up a piece of driftwood, all gray and twisted. "Well, he *is* her cousin, Beet," she says, then goes on with a sigh. "Did you see that dress she was wearing, though? Probably bought in *Boston*." Jeannine gets all her clothes third- or fourth-hand from her older sisters. She chips a piece of sandstone off the bank with her free hand and tries to skim it across the low incoming waves. The stone falls without so much as a skip. I laugh, but Jeannine turns up her tiny, tanned nose like she's smelling a day-old clam.

The gull steps up right close to her, tilting its crooked face upward.

"G'way, you great winged rat!" Jeannine waves the driftwood stick at the creature. He stands still a minute, sizing her up with beady eyes. Then he slowly waddles away ahead of us, disappearing around the rocky headland.

"Listen Jeannine, I didn't want to say anything before but . . ." I tell her all about what happened when I first saw Marina Shaw, and exactly how it felt. Even as I tell it, I relive that feeling and I wonder what it is about that woman that worries me. When I'm done, Jeannine's brown eyes are wide as can be, and she's smiling.

"I knew it!" she says, pointing the driftwood stick at my face. "You've got the Second Sight, Beet. I'm telling you, first Gerry's ghost and now you've had a premonition, a forerunner about Marina Shaw. I wonder what Freddy's aunt would say about this. She says—"

"Oh, yes, please—please tell me what else old Lily has to say." I shake my head. "On second thought, don't." It's not Jeannine's fault, though, not really. For her these stories of ghosts and forerunners are exciting and fun (not to mention a chance to hang around the library waiting for Freddy Soloman to show up), but for me, they're real now.

We're at the edge of Nelson's Point—almost to where we can see Poxy Island and the Campbells' house. Although there are houses and shacks scattered inland, there's only one other home on the coast between our farm and the Publicover sisters' big stone mansion at the edge of Skinner Harbour town. That house belonged to Sarah and her husband, Mom's brother Angus, who died out lobstering some twenty years ago.

I never knew Uncle Angus, but I guess he was just like his son—always laughing, never getting above himself or acting grand, so Dad says. Uncle Angus was Dad's best friend. Dad was even there with Uncle Angus when he saw old Sarah for the first time, out on Morrison's Beach, back when she was young Sarah. They saved her from some kind of wreck, I guess. Angus built Sarah that house on Poxy Point—built it right out on the rocks, close enough for it to jump into the Strait if it felt like it. Dad says only fools and tourists build their houses so near the water, but whatever Sarah asked, that's what Angus did.

The wind picks up, and for a second I think I hear music again, that same wheedling woman's voice I heard up at our house, but it's soon drowned out by a chorus of angry gulls.

"Merciful mighty!" Jeannine sniffs. "What are they wailin' about?"

We round the point to where that same old black-backed gull is hovering above the grassy bank, along with a whole flock of other birds—ten or twelve ring-billed gulls, a few gannets even—all shrieking and hissing, their mouths open wide enough to swallow a frog. It's a horse they're hollering at, the prettiest little horse you can imagine, with long, slim legs and a coat so glossy it reflects the last traces of sunlight, making the horse itself look purplish and glowing. There's a bridle over its head, polished metal with something green twisting in and out of it—some kind of seaweed, I think. For all the racket the birds are making, the horse stands still and quiet, a slight breeze rippling its silvery mane. Behind the horse, a mile away, maybe less, Sarah Campbell's great dark castle of a house sits perched above the red rocks, staring out onto the waves.

Jeannine draws in a breath. "What a beauty, eh, Beet? Wonder how it got down the bank?" She runs at the birds, her arms waving. "Leave that poor creature alone." The gulls scatter, all except the crooked beaked minister, who stands close by on the bank, its beady eye staring. The horse hasn't moved an inch, and Jeannine steps in closer, close enough to touch its soft rippling mane, but as she reaches out her hand to do just that, the gull swoops right down from the bank and bites Jeannine on the thumb.

"Ow!" Jeannine hollers, bringing her hand to her mouth. "Wicked thing. What was that for?"

The gull gives Jeannine a proud turn of the head, at the same time the horse swings silently away and runs, almost gliding along the shore in the direction of Poxy Point. It's then that the singing fills my ears again, and I realize that it's been there all the time, hidden under the mewing and squawking of the gulls, which are now flying off in all directions. The singer's voice has a pull to it, drawing me to try to figure out where I've heard the tune before. It's a bit like Gerry's tune, but where that's high, sad, sweet, the sadness is all gone from this music. There's a mean, kind of gleeful squeal in its place, clinging to the notes, like someone laughing at another's sorrow. As the song gets louder, my legs get weak, the same way they did at Sarah's wake, just as if the music is trying to drag me off balance. The singer of it is close, too. As the horse runs the mile down the beach, I see her. About two hundred yards away, a woman is standing, barefoot, in a fitted blouse and a green circle skirt patterned with white flowers. She turns away as the horse gets near her, disappearing into the gathering shadows below the Campbells' place. I find my balance again and look toward Jeannine, who's sitting in the sand, the piece of driftwood in her lap.

"You okay, Jeannine?"

"Oh yeah, except for my thumb's killing me. Made me dizzy

for a second." She stands up as quick as if nothing had happened. "Wasn't that . . . ?"

The sky is purple now and the air has gone so still that my answer comes out louder than I expected. "That was Marina Shaw." And it's the second time I've been caught in that undertow.

CHAPTER SIX

August 2, 1930

Angus Campbell

"Well, Sarah, dear." Angus Campbell undoes the clasps on his dark gray mackintosh. His hands are still cold and stiff from a morning pulling fish out of Cardigan Bay.

Sarah stares down at the bucket of silver-scaled fish her husband has set on the rug beside her blue satin footstool. Her small white feet are bare beneath the folds of her shimmering blue straight-from-Boston dress, her pale hair hanging in a single waist-length braid over one shoulder. She has a hand on her round belly, the other fiddling with the silver shell pendant she was wearing the day Angus first set eyes on her. When she finally lifts her gaze toward him, the green of her eyes is as dull as sun-bleached kelp, her expression blank.

"This isn't what I wanted."

"But, sweetheart, that's as fine a catch of mackerel as you'll see." Angus turns to his brother-in-law Donny MacNeill. They've been out on the boats together since five this morning. "Isn't it fine, Donny?"

Standing in the vestibule in his flannel shirt and oilskins, Donny runs his fingers through his thick, wavy red MacNeill hair. "Grand catch, Angus. Just as—"

"I thought you were bringing lobster." Sarah's eyes stay on her husband, her words all stunned disappointment. Behind her, through the picture window, its lace curtains patterned with mermaids, strange fish, and swirling seas, the Northumberland Strait is as iron gray as the sky above it. If it were not for the ragged shadow of the spruce trees on Poxy Island, Angus would not be able to discern the place where the water ends and the sky begins.

Angus tries to reason with his wife. "Now, Sarah, you know the season's over by more than a month. Besides, who eats lobster but poor families? We can afford . . ."

"I wanted lobster." Sarah speaks slowly and evenly, like shore waves on a calm day, but her long sigh is the undertow beneath them. She looks away from her husband toward the window and the gray sky. "In Massachusetts we had lobster every Friday."

"There's a storm coming on, dear one," Angus says quietly, but he has already begun to refasten the clasps on his mack.

Donny MacNeill steps in from the vestibule where he has hung up his coat, his voice firmer and less patient than his friend's. "For Heaven's sake, Sarah, look at the sky."

Sarah smiles tightly at him, her eyes two hard green slits in her pale, perfect face. "Do keep your boots off my Persian carpet, won't you please?"

"Now, Sarah . . . ," Angus begins.

Before Angus can finish, Sarah gives a tiny gasp and presses the shell pendant against the top of her belly. Angus is by her side in a moment, his hands out toward her, trembling. She waves him away before he can touch her arm, then looks up. Fat droplets of rain have begun to fall against the window.

"All I ask for . . . not for me, mind you, but for the baby, your baby . . . is a bit of lobster for my poor supper. All the suffering I am going through . . . stuck here, not able even to go to town . . . and you . . ." She turns away as if to cry, but she makes no sound.

"Sarah, darlin', of course I'll go out again. You don't worry at all. Just . . . just take care of the baby."

Sarah says not a thing; she bends her head farther toward the window where the raindrops stretch themselves slowly across the glass. She begins to hum under her breath. Angus kisses the top of her blond head and turns to go.

"Have some sense, Angus!" Donny MacNeill paces the dark pink sand of the sheltered cove below Poxy Point and the Campbells' gabled and green-shingled house. Angus is dragging his dory toward the edge of the water. The boat is shallow, flat on the bottom, and white, with the words "Sarah Darlin'" painted in blue across the bow. On the cliff, the long green grass is shivering. Donny stammers from the wind, cold in August. "She'll live without the . . ."

"What's a bit of lobster for my own girl?" Angus grasps the dory by the gunwales, steps in quickly, and takes the oars. He smiles at his friend. "Go on, Donny, get yourself home to my baby sister. I know how young brides can be."

Donny takes a step toward the boat. "Angus, don't be a fool."

"See ya soon, boy!"

"Angus!" Donny is still calling as Angus rows away, past Poxy Point and the relative safety of the cove, then out into the open water just past Poxy Island itself. Angus has set his lobster traps there. He makes the sign of the cross as he rows past the island. He always does this, not just because he is leaving shelter and going into the bay, but also as a little prayer for the ghosts, the sorrows haunting that place.

Once clear of the last of the Poxy Island rocks, and still in sight of his house, Angus finds the first of the green and yellow buoys that mark his traps. The wind is loud and fierce out here, high pitched as an angry woman's voice, and the waves are white capped like the manes of gray horses. Angus manages to grab hold of the rope that attaches the buoy to the trap some thirty feet down. He's always been able to pull up the heavy traps without the help of a winch, using his own two arms like his father before him. It's a point of honor to him, and he plans to teach the skill to his own son, if God gives him one. After ten years of waiting, all Angus wants is a healthy child. He grabs on to the rope with a wet-gloved hand and begins to pull, his feet pressing against the bottom of the dory to keep it as steady as possible. As the wind sounds around him in a way that almost makes a tune, a sudden sea swell rises in front of the boat, blocking his view of the shore. The boat dips and he is forced to let go of his trap line to stay afloat. The swell passes, and through the rain Angus can once again see his house, where a light has come on in the picture window. The tune the wind was singing earlier has quieted, but now Angus can hear it in his head. It's that strange one Sarah is always humming, the one that was on her lips when he first met her. He begins crooning it to himself as he hauls on the trap line again, feeling the weight of the trap much more the second time around. The air around him seems to settle, become quieter, so that all Angus can hear is the rain on the water and his own voice. With one more pull, he brings up what he thinks is his trap, covered in fronds of kelp and what looks like eelgrass. A foul smell of rotted fish fills the salt air around him.

The dory is buffeted by another swell, higher than the last, and Angus sees what he has really pulled from the bottom. Something dead has gotten tangled in his trap line, a poor gray horse, floating on its side, eyes closed, seaweed knotted into its white mane. There is a jagged cut on its cheek from nostril to ear, and its eyes seem swollen under closed lids. The strange old tune still murmurs through Angus's head.

"Poor creature," he whispers angrily. His own words answer him. "Poor, poor creature. Who'd have done this to ya?"

Angus leans over the gunwale and, with both hands, reaches into the water to disentangle the horse from the rope. As he does this, he feels a sudden jerk. The horse's face is before him, its huge, bulbous eyes suddenly open and deep bloodred. It is only when the creature begins to dive that Angus realizes that his hand has become caught in the mane, gripped there as if by glue. It is only when he is being pulled from his boat into the sea that Angus sees the silhouette of his wife, lit from behind, in the picture window far on shore, and only as his lungs are filling up with water that he remembers he hasn't caught her any lobster.

CHAPTER SEVEN

June 10, 1950

Beet MacNeill

"Well, look who's out clammin'!" Jeannine's voice is sticky as molasses on toast. We're making our way along the shore toward Poxy Point, past the headland, the same stretch of beach where we saw that horse four days ago. Jeannine points out two specks of people on the sand just below the Campbells' house—a tall fella in hip boots and someone shorter and rounder with a head full of long silver hair scattering outward with every breeze. They're about a quarter mile from us over the flat red sand. "It's old Lily Soloman . . . and *Freddy*."

That's when I remember the wake, Freddy telling Jeannine he was going clamming this Saturday. I should've guessed it when Jeannine was so dead ready to come out to Poxy Point with me this morning. It was Jeannine's idea to get up just past dawn and head here after breakfast, with a couple of buckets for digging quahogs in the low-tide cove below the Campbells' place. She said it would be a good idea to get a look at what Marina Shaw's doing in that house, find out why she's so interested in Joseph. Jeannine calls it "reconnaissance," like they do in her ghost-hunting books. I should've known by the way she was dressed that she had something else on her mind, too. Who goes on reconnaissance in a pink skirt and her mother's tea rose perfume? Jeannine still has a dark pink mark at the base of her thumb where that crazy gull bit her. It matches the nail polish she nicked from her oldest sister, Joanne, along with those ridiculous sandals.

Now it's a bright and sunny eight a.m., and the sky looks clear blue as a robin's egg, minus the speckles. The waters of the Strait are blue, too, ink dark and shiny, with just a little ripple on the surface to show when a cool breeze blows. Ahead of us, below where Sarah Campbell's house stands blind and gloomy, over the sandstone cliffs of Poxy Point, the flat sand spreads almost to the clanging Skinner Harbour channel marker. The tide is still heading out. If you didn't mind getting a little wet, there are a couple of hours each day when you could cross the sandbar over to Poxy Island, with only a tiny swim at the drop-off. Not too many people do it, though, because of the ghosts, or the ghost stories anyway. (At least, I would have said they were just stories until last year. Now I don't know.)

The only person I ever knew to try was Gerry, back when he was my age. He was wild and brave even then, God love him. He went out there to see the graves of the smallpox victims, on a dare from Jeannine's cousin Hubie. Never did it again, though. Too creepy, Gerry told me. Said he saw the ghost of poor dead Captain Ferguson, peeking his pockmarked face out from behind a spruce tree. Of course, I didn't believe it (not then, anyway). Jeannine says that some people have seen the Devil's hoofprints out on Poxy Island, too, but then she believes the Devil walks free in Skinner Harbour every day but Sunday. On Sunday, it's Martians.

"I didn't know Freddy'd be here." Jeannine flips her black hair off her shoulders, then gives me those innocent cow's eyes.

I don't answer, just swing the metal pail I'm carrying back and forth as the wind sweeps the tall grasses on the bank above us. Then I glance at Jeannine's floral blouse. It's the one her second-oldest sister, Josephine, wore to the spring dance at St. Peter's Hall.

"Well, I *didn't*," Jeannine tries to give me her pursed-lipped schoolteacher look, but her mouth is twitching into a smile. "Okay, I did, but listen. . . . How do you think we're going to get inside old Sarah's house without Freddy?"

I give Jeannine the kind of look I'm used to getting from my mother when I try to get out of hanging the laundry. The wind sends another ripple across the water's surface.

"Don't make that expression, *Beatrice*." Jeannine flips her hair again. "Didn't your dad say Freddy does deliveries over to dead Sarah's house? He must see Marina Shaw all the time."

"Merciful Minerva, Jeannine. Dad said Freddy did *one* delivery there."

"Well, then." She looks at me like we've just settled a bet. "He's been in the house once more than we have."

I'm just about to admit that what she's said makes a tiny bit of sense when Jeannine looks toward Freddy and his aunt—who are bent over the sand, working—then arches her thin dark eyebrows like she's planning a crime. "And if we get around to talking about the Skinner Harbour Day dance while he's helping us, well then . . ."

"Jeannine," I tell her. "You are the worst flirt in God's creation." This is something she would probably be proud to hear, if she were listening. Instead, she just gives this little happy squeak and points toward the cove. "Ooo, look!"

Black hair, white T-shirt, and jeans, long legs like a spider, Sean MacInnes is making his way down the bank, with Lily Soloman waving at him like he was invited.

"Oh, for Heaven's sake," I say. "What's *he* doing there?"

"Well," Jeannine says, "the Publicovers are the closest house to Poxy Point, next to Sarah's . . . well, Marina Shaw's now . . . and anyway, it's a town beach. Anyone can use it."

"I guess." I shake my head. Just what I need: Jeannine all boy crazy, plus spooky Lily Soloman *and* Sean MacInnes all in the same place. And since when are he and Lily such old friends? How'd they even meet? She wasn't at the wake. Well, it's none of my business.

"Come on, Beet." Jeannine's using a singsongy voice that makes me want to wallop her. "Didn't your mother want you to be nice to him?" Not that nice, I want to say.

There's a squawking sound behind me. I look round just in time to duck as a familiar black-backed gull swoops over our heads. Then Deirdre comes struggling around the headland, holding Baby Joseph by one hand and a big, heavy iron spade in the other. Beside me, I spot Jeannine bringing her bit hand up close to her face.

Deirdre hands over the spade, all out of breath. "Your mom sent this along, said you only brought the one." Then she smiles, her eyes on Jeannine's rose-tipped fingers. "What was Jeannine going to dig with, her fingernails?" It's nice to see Deirdre joking.

"Thanks," I say. Joseph is wearing blue swim trunks and a red sweater and is already wet from splashing in tide pools. He runs toward me and lifts his arms for a hug. I pick him up, not even caring about my dry clothes, kiss him on both cheeks, then swing him around until he giggles. This makes Deirdre smile even more.

"That's just fine, Beet," she says as I set him back down. "Joseph was up early. Thought we'd go looking for hermit crabs. There's lots of them near Poxy Point." Gerry and I used to look for hermit crabs, sometimes. Thinking of it makes me miss him all over again.

"Mama!" Joseph is tugging hard at the hem of Deirdre's yellow cotton dress. "Mama come . . ."

"Okay, lover!" Deirdre scoops the little boy up in her arms and takes off again, running barefoot along the beach to Poxy Point. Joseph's giggles just about fill up the warm empty air between us and the Point—like tiny little brass bells. The three figures in the cove stop what they are doing and look in Deirdre and Joseph's direction.

Jeannine straightens her blouse. "I'll try talking to Freddy about the house, Beet."

"Why you?" As if I didn't know . . .

Jeannine just gives one of her high-nosed sniffs. "You're not experienced in these matters, Beet. You have no . . . no *finesse*."

"Whatever that means," I say, and we set off after Deirdre and Joseph—now running on his own, sending the flock of gulls hollering into the air.

"Well, I've seen some ghosts in my time." Old Lily Soloman gives a push to the spade with her black-and-red rubber boot—same as I'm wearing—and digs up another shovelful of red beach clay and clams. This stretch of hard, flat sand is all pinpricked with the clams' air holes. Once in a while, a tiny fountain of water squirts out through one of the holes, and the old woman attacks that spot with her spade. She's been doing this—quiet as a nun—ever since Jeannine and I showed up about a half hour ago, and probably for an hour before that. This is the first time Lily Soloman has spoken since I set my pail down next to her. With her long gray hair floating on the breeze around her dark, still, round face, she looks as if she could wait another hour for me to answer her. Trouble is, I don't know how to answer her. Never do with Lily Soloman. I've never met anybody who listens and watches as much as she does.

She's watching me now, so much so that I feel I have to look away. I glance over to where Freddy and Jeannine are digging side by side beneath the low sandstone cliff and Sarah Campbell's dark green and shadowy house. Well, Freddy's digging. Jeannine's just sort of sashaying around with the pail. She's supposed to be asking questions about Marina Shaw, but all she's done so far is giggle like a prize goose and bat her eyes. Deirdre is sitting on the sand about fifty feet away from Freddy and Jeannine, digging a little pond for the hermit crabs Baby Joseph keeps bringing her from the tide pools that are hidden all through the red rocks around the point. Every so often, Freddy stops his work and looks over at Deirdre and Joseph—at least until Jeannine taps him on the shoulder and asks for help pulling up her spade, or some such. Just beyond them, Sean MacInnes is all legs and arms, perched on a boulder, scribbling in a shiny black book. He looks up for a second and lifts his hand halfway, like he's going to wave, then goes back to scribbling.

"Lonely boy, that one," Lily remarks in a kind of quiet voice, then pushes a silver strand out of her left eye. Then comes another one of her long, long pauses, always like she's waiting for me to say something. When I don't, she goes on. "Knew his mother in Charlottetown. Came into my store a few times when she was working as a maid, before she went down to the Boston States. He looks like her, a bit."

She's still for a minute, like she's going to say more, so when she starts talking about ghosts again, I'm actually relieved that we're off the subject of Sean MacInnes. "Yes, indeed, and

Charlottetown's where I saw that ghost, too, right there in the street, when I was twenty-eight. Seen others besides."

"Oh," I say, trying to be polite. The air is just off flat calm, and a small flock of terns, black headed and gossipy, are gathered on the sandbar that leads to Poxy Island. Lily Soloman heaves up a spade full of clams and dumps them into the pail, all patience. Not like me.

"It was near the end of the Great War, March, right after St. Patrick's storm . . ." She stops and takes a deep breath, eyeing me the whole time. "Well . . . maybe it's a tale for another day. Anyway, Beatrice Mary, I just thought you should know, you're not alone, and if ever . . ."

And all at once my cheeks are burning.

"Jeannine," I mutter, half to myself, wanting to march over and wallop her with that pail she's not using. But Lily Soloman's dark down-turned eyes are looking at me, kind and serious.

"Now, don't be cross with your friend, dear. She told me about the rose garden on Thursday, when she visited the library. We share an interest in ghost stories and such. She's quite a reader is our Jeannine." And just like that old Lily goes back to digging, like she was never talking in the first place, which is fine with me. All I can say is, Jeannine and I are going to be having a conversation about keeping secrets, and the only one talking is going to be me.

Just as I think this, her voice comes whining toward me across the flat sand.

"Beet!" Jeannine's got that too-loud tone that says her

words are meant for someone else—say, Freddy. "Come over here and help me. I'm having such a hard time with this big, heavy spade." Her eyelashes are fluttering fast enough to raise a breeze.

"Freddy," Lily Soloman calls out, laugh wrinkles around her brown eyes. "Help Jeannine Gallant with those clams."

Deirdre has walked a little ways from the baby to get a pretty pink stone he's roarin' for. She's kneeling on the flat sand looking for it, her cocoa-colored hair draping her face. Beyond her, Sean MacInnes keeps scratching away in that book. He's pretty good at concentrating, I have to say. He has . . . I don't know . . . a seriousness, I guess, strange for a boy, not that I know all that many.

"Freddy Soloman." Old Lily chides him like she's talking to a little kid and not the twenty-year-old man Freddy is.

Freddy gives a little start. "Okay, Auntie. Yeah. Sure thing there."

Freddy walks over to help Jeannine, Lily's eyes on him the whole time. Then she gives a little nod toward Deirdre, who's picking up more stones in the skirt of her yellow dress. "It's good he's too shy," the old woman says out of nowhere. "That girl's not ready yet anyway, still not over the one she lost."

That's another reason I don't like being around Lily Soloman. She acts too calm about everything, too . . . knowing, like it's just altogether regular to guess people's thoughts and see dead folks walking in gardens. I wish she'd go back to being quiet and just watching things. Anyway, I don't want to talk about Deirdre or Gerry's ghost with Lily Soloman or anyone else. It's none of their business.

"Well, I'm done," I say, right quick. "I'd better get to Jeannine and start heading back home."

Lily Soloman eyes my pail—which holds only a few broken shells and some mud—and the laugh lines around her eyes go deeper. She points to her own bucketful of clams. "Help me lift this first, Beatrice."

The tide has gone out even farther since we started digging, and the flat sand reaches almost out to Poxy Island, where the flock of terns are sitting, still as stones. Lily Soloman and I carry the pail to the water line, about forty yards away, so she can rinse the mud off the clams she's gathered. She looks at every clam individually, holding it up to the light like she's inspecting the shells for cracks or something. The flock of gulls raise a chorus behind us, flying low over our heads, headed inland. A sharp gust of wind blows a few more strands of silver hair into the old woman's face. Out on the sandbar, the terns fly off as one. "Tide's changin'," Lily Soloman says.

Old Lily takes the pail and starts carrying it—without my help—back toward the cliffs, at the same time that Deirdre comes running toward me, with Sean MacInnes, Jeannine, and Freddy behind her. "He's run off, Beet! Joseph's run off. I just turned my . . . Beet . . . It's like he disappeared!" Deirdre's face is white as curdled cream, and she's shaking.

"I saw him wander off," Sean is saying. "I was just coming . . ."

"Then why didn't you stop him?" I snap, and even as I do

it I know it's not fair, but my whole body has gone cold now, thinking of what could happen, thinking of Gerry. I look toward the spot where Joseph was playing. No sign of him, except for hundreds of his little footprints in the sand—leading every which way from Sunday and mingling with the scattered footprints of the gulls that are filling up the beach, calling to one another. I focus on them and pull myself together. I need to help.

"Joseph! Joseph!" Deirdre cries, her voice cracking, over the mewing of the gulls. She starts to walk away from us, but Lily Soloman puts a hand on her arm.

"All right," Lily says, all business. "Beet will check south of the Point while I head northward. Deirdre, Sean, you stay put in case the boy wanders back this way. Jeannine, Freddy . . . you go . . ." Old Lily doesn't finish her sentence, just points toward the water.

Freddy and Jeannine head in that direction—not saying a word—as I turn toward the low cliffs, where Sarah Campbell's house stands watching us, its windows half-shuttered and sly. On the beach, the gulls are gathered in a crowd, their gray and white heads turning left and right. The creatures pace the sand, squawking and chattering to one another like some sort of search party. Then suddenly the birds stop their pacing and go silent and dead still. A wave of that undertow feeling washes through me again, just like it did at the wake. The feeling doesn't quite knock me over like it did last time, but it's still strong enough to set me a bit off balance. I take a second to steady myself and look up toward the cliff. As soon as it starts, the search is over.

"Joseph!" Just as Deirdre calls his name, I see him to the right of the Campbell house, surrounded by tall beach grass and slender lupine flowers, their pink and purple blossoms just starting to open. Baby Joseph is standing at the edge of the cliff, his small hand in the hand of Marina Shaw.

CHAPTER EIGHT

June 10, 1950

Beet MacNeill

Joseph!" Deirdre is already climbing the narrow path that leads up the bank to the Campbells' back garden. Damp red dirt stains her knees and the hem of her dress.

Joseph is giggling as Marina Shaw leads him along the bank toward the top of the path. Her foam green skirt lifts around her ankles in the breeze that's risen up with the changing tide, and the coiled shell pendant catches the sun as she walks. She reaches out her long, bare, white hand for Deirdre to take hold. Deirdre takes it as the rest of us follow her up.

"Hello," Marina says at the top of the bank. The word drifts from her mouth.

"Joseph!" Deirdre bends to place her hands on the baby's shoulders, and she kisses the top of his soft brown hair. "How did you get all the way up here?" Joseph blinks fast, like he's waking up from something. He squirms to get away from Marina, but she doesn't let go of his hand.

"I brought him," Marina Shaw says, in a voice so flat calm it doesn't seem possible she could sing a note of that strange music I heard the other night. It's an edgeless voice, the way her face and body seem to have no edges, only blurred lines like in old photographs. "I saw him from the window, toddling along all by himself, climbing up the bank. I was afraid he'd fall, what with no one watching him." As she says this last bit, she looks at Deirdre and parts those soft red lips in a smile. Even Marina Shaw's teeth are small and creamy white, almost baby's teeth.

"I *was* watching him . . . ," Deirdre insists, but she doesn't really seem sure of that, not from her voice anyway. Suddenly, I remember how hard it is for her taking care of Joseph alone.

Marina rests her red tipped fingernails on the edge of Deirdre's shoulder. "Of course, dear." For a moment, the wind dies down and none of us says a thing.

"Well, you can hand over the babe now." Lily Soloman breaks the silence, and *her* voice has edge to spare. Just as sharp as a razor, that voice. Her eyes are sharp, too, staring a long time at Marina Shaw the way she was looking at those clamshells earlier, checking for cracks. But there's something else in Lily's face, too, something like surprise, and maybe wariness.

"You have the look of someone I know," old Lily says, finally.

"Yes, certainly," Marina Shaw answers, just as placid as a

spring pool. "I have been said to resemble my departed aunt."

"No." Old Lily makes the word sound like an accusation. "Someone else." I didn't really notice at the wake, but I guess Marina does look something like dead Sarah, at least before she got all wrinkly. Lots of families are like that (I mean Jeannine and her sisters sure couldn't lose one another in a crowd). But Lily never met Sarah, so I don't know who else she could mean.

Marina Shaw's gaze stays on Lily Soloman's for a second, green eyes narrowing just slightly. Then she turns toward Deirdre, as if old Lily isn't even there, and puts a long-fingered hand in Joseph's hair, smoothing down his curls and making me want to grab him and run. "It's good you're here, Deirdre, I didn't have time to speak to you at our unfortunate Sarah's wake."

Jeannine interrupts, her voice all squeaky, like she's trying to please. "Well, sure. It must have been hard for you to stay there, seeing her dead body like that." She shivers.

"Our bodies are but shells," Marina Shaw says, never looking at Jeannine. Her hand moves to the silver chain around her neck, and she gives Deirdre one of those barely smiling smiles. "Why don't you come in and have some lemonade? Your friends, too, of course." She still hasn't asked our names.

"We've got to go back down the beach," says Lily Soloman coldly. "Got a full bucket of clams to retrieve." She gives Freddy a sharp look. "Come on, nephew."

Marina Shaw blinks, slowly, and for a second the pale of her skin looks a sickly gray. "The rest of you, then."

Deirdre shakes her head and starts to say something, but

Marina Shaw is already leading Joseph toward the house.

As old Lily turns, she puts a hand on my wrist. The edge is all gone from her voice, and her face is thoughtful. "Stop by the library sometime, Beatrice."

Then she looks at Sean MacInnes, who's been standing closer to me than I'd like, and talks quiet to him. "Sean, lad. Come with us. Freddy'll give you a lift to the library."

"But my aunts live . . ."

"I know, but I have some photos in the school files you might like to see. There's a lovely one of your mother."

At the sound of that, Sean gives a dimpled smile, and I realize I haven't seen him smile since I met him. Not that it's been that long, but still. He turns and follows Lily back along the path to the bank, where the silent crowd of gulls is still gathered.

Freddy stays a moment longer, casts one worried look at Deirdre, then gives me a quick nod and heads down the bank after his aunt. Jeannine starts to follow them, too (to follow Freddy, actually), but I grab her elbow and turn her toward dead Sarah's house.

"Come on, now, Miss Ghost Hunter. Here's our chance to do some reconnaissance."

Jeannine gives me a little thin-lipped smirk before following me to the big green house with black trim.

Marina Shaw takes us in by the back door. The front faces out to a long path heading down to Old Poxy Point Road and on through the spruce woods and birch trees to Skinner Harbour Road and the town itself. I'm first in after Marina Shaw, and I put my feet on the carpet as I step past the vestibule. She looks down at my muddy boots.

"I'm sorry," she almost whispers, like she's apologizing but not really. "In Massachusetts, we remove our boots before entering a home."

I kick off my boots and stare at Jeannine to do the same with her sandals. Deirdre looks down at her bare feet, red from the cliff dirt, and turns red herself. The merest smirk comes over Marina Shaw's smooth pretty face. She hasn't let go of Joseph yet.

"No matter," she says. "I'm sure we can find a basin."

Once we're finally inside, everything is just as I'd expect from a house that belonged to Sarah Campbell for thirty-odd years. Clean as a satin-lined coffin with almost no comfortable-looking furniture, except a soft chair and a blue embroidered footstool placed beside the picture window that looks out to the sheltered cove where we were digging and then past Poxy Island to the Strait and Nova Scotia. I think, so this is the house Gerry lived in for half his life. There's no sign of him anywhere, no pictures or knickknacks or anything to show that Gerry, or any boy, had ever called this place home. But then this wasn't really his home, was it? And thinking about that brings the ache of missing him back all at once.

Marina sits right down in that chair, gathering Joseph onto her lap as if he's her pet. The half-drawn lace curtains are patterned with mermaids and odd-looking sea creatures; the smell of salt and seaweed drifts in through the screen. On a wooden table is a tray already set with glasses of lemonade and a small stack of typed-up papers. The wind has died down, and the waters of the Strait are smooth, with only the slightest slow dips in their motion, just enough to scatter the noon light like jewels shining below the water's surface. The sandbar out by Poxy Island is already starting to disappear under the rising tide.

Marina flicks her hand in the direction of the lemonade and to three hard chairs by the door. "Please, do help yourselves." It sounds more like an order than an invitation, even as soft as her voice makes the words. Outside, the flock of gulls sets up a squawking to wake the Prophet's cat. Then all of a sudden, they stop.

There's a whooshing sound of a door opening, and in from the vestibule steps a man of about thirty in a dark gray Sunday suit, a bit out of fashion, sort of like the one my Granddad MacNeill is wearing in the picture on the mantel at home. The man has tan skin and high, sharp cheekbones, and deep-set eyes so black you'd think they were all pupil. He must have been out on the beach, too, because there are grains of red sand on the shoulders of his jacket and in the shiny brown-black hair that falls across his forehead. Jeannine stares at him, her mouth wide enough to shove a fist in, but Marina Shaw's expression doesn't change at all.

"Uist," she says, like she's calling a dog. "Come."

He doesn't look at any of us but walks slowly across the room to where Marina sits, watching him track sand on her fancy rug. She looks at his dirty shoes and breathes in ever so slightly, then gives him one of her half smiles.

"Glad you could join us, Mr. Uist." The afternoon sunlight through the lace curtains is casting shadows over Marina's face, strange creatures dancing. She turns to Deirdre. "Such a lovely coincidence that you should be here now, Deirdre. I have wanted to speak to you with Mr. Uist present. Mr. Uist is the Shaw family attorney, helping me to settle Sarah's estate. There are issues relating to yourself . . . well, more particularly to the young boy, to . . . Joseph, is that what he is called?"

At the sound of his name, Joseph gets that "just woke up" look again, like he had on the bank, and starts squirming in Marina Shaw's lap. "Mama. Mama . . . Want go . . ." His lower lip is quivering, and I'm this close to hauling him off of Marina's lap and out the door.

Deirdre makes to reach for him, but Marina Shaw whispers something in his ear and he sinks back into her lap without another word. Mr. Uist watches all this with a queer kind of gloomy expression in his dark eyes. Then he shakes out his hair, letting more sand fall onto the carpet. If Marina Shaw notices this, she makes no sign, just keeps talking to Deirdre in a lazy early morning voice.

"I was planning to visit you at your home . . . or should I say at the MacNeill's home. . . ." The corners of Marina Shaw's mouth go up ever so slightly. "But this is much more convenient."

Deirdre is going pink again, from her neck to the part in her hair. Convenient for what, I want to say, and what *estate*? Uncle Angus had a dory, a house, twenty lobster traps, and a fiddle—according to Dad, anyway—and the fiddle went to Gerry, and then to me, with his belongings, after he died. If he left Sarah any money, none of us ever knew about it.

Marina Shaw holds out her hand and makes a gesture almost like snapping her fingers. "Uist, the papers." He lifts the stack of typed-up papers from the table and hands them to her without a word. I don't know any attorneys, but I guess I thought they were supposed to talk more.

"My father was Sarah's half brother," Marina begins. "Our branch of the family has always lived north of Boston, in Newburyport. When Sarah married Angus Campbell, she left behind her Massachusetts family and a very comfortable life. Her desire to do so is understandable, certainly. Mr. Campbell's chivalry, taking her in after that terrible shipwreck . . . She would naturally be . . . grateful. . . ."

"How come we never heard about you before?" I say it before I can stop myself. Mom always says I'm too bold, and it's true, I guess. Marina Shaw turns to me right quick, her green eyes narrowed just enough to send that undertow feeling through me again. But this time I'm ready for it, so I set my jaw and stare straight back at her.

Her icy smile turns on Deirdre. "It is true that our family did not reach out to Sarah and . . . Mr. Campbell . . . as perhaps we should have. I would like to rectify that, if I can." She leans back in the chair with Joseph drowsing in her lap. The curtain shadows have stopped moving and a sunbeam falls across the top half of her face. For a second the green of her eyes looks less like sea moss and more like antifreeze leaking from a truck.

"Young Joseph here is the last of the Newburyport Shaws, aside from myself, of course, and I would like to do something for him, to make up for what was not done for his father, and for the years his grandmother spent on this . . . island. I am prepared to give him every comfort his grandmother denied herself, living here for so many years."

What did Sarah ever deny herself? I want to know. It was Gerry who was denied everything. Gerry whose mother didn't care a stitch for him. But this time I know better than to say what I am thinking out loud. I mean, Jeannine is the one who gets all weird about forerunners and premonitions and things, but even I have to trust how I am feeling right now. Marina Shaw is dangerous.

She holds out the papers to Deirdre. "I would like to take Joseph with me to Massachusetts."

Deirdre, who looks like she hasn't breathed since Marina Shaw started talking, says, "For . . . for a visit?"

Marina Shaw inhales, and gives what she seems to think is a gentle smile but which just looks phony. She speaks very slowly. "Why no, dear, to live there, to be raised there, to be sent to the best schools—Phillips Academy, perhaps Harvard. I'm sure it would have been his grandmother's wish. It's all here." Marina is still holding out the papers to Deirdre.

"But . . ." Deirdre's voice is small. "But I'm his mother."

Beside the picture window, Marina's words drift from her mouth like the tentacles of a jellyfish. "Yes, you are, dear, but you are also . . . alone. I'm sure you'd like to think about my offer."

"She's not alone," I say. I fight the undertow feeling that's come back again, and I keep my voice as steady and phony patient as Marina's, but what I really want to do is rip up those papers and pitch them at her face. "She has us, me and my mom and dad."

Deirdre puts her hand on my shoulder and squeezes gently. Marina Shaw's arm tightens around Joseph just enough to wake him up again.

"Owie! Mama!" He struggles in her lap again and Deirdre stands up. Mr. Uist tilts his head to the side, his dark eyes on Joseph, but the rest of him is perfectly still.

"No." Deirdre is holding her arms out to Joseph. "Miss Shaw . . . I . . . *no thank you.* Joseph, sweetheart, come to Mama." Marina holds on to Joseph for just a second more before he crawls off her lap and lets his mother swing him into her arms. His eyes are still half-closed like he's sleepwalking—but soon he is smiling, holding on tight to Deirdre's neck, and I let out a breath I didn't know I was holding.

Marina Shaw stands up slowly, handing the papers to Uist, who holds them limply by his side. She bends slightly to smooth out her skirt. "Well," she says in her flat calm way, "you think about it."

Deirdre turns away as if she's said as much as she's capable of saying, as if she's ready to run, and I wouldn't blame her if she did. Jeannine and I follow her out the door, but I turn back to see Marina Shaw sitting back down quietly in her chair, the folds of her foam green skirt spilling around her on the Persian rug. Her smile is soft as ever but her eyes flash that acid green color. I'm pretty sure I'm the only one to see it. Mr. Uist has disappeared into a far room.

As I leave the house, Deirdre is already headed down the bank with Joseph. Wherever those noisy gulls were, they're gone now, and the air is still as Sunday in a schoolroom. Jeannine stands waiting for me, staring down past her sandaled feet at the path that leads from Marina's door. There are hoofprints in the fine pink dust of the path, hoofprints leading from the top of the bank and stopping at the door to Marina Shaw's house.

CHAPTER NINE

March 18, 1918

Lily Soloman

Lily Soloman watches Prince Street from her storefront window. Yesterday, the storm kept everyone inside, though the snow didn't hit Charlottetown nearly as hard as it did the coast, especially out toward Montague and Skinner Harbour. Today the sun is already melting the snow, clumps of it falling from awnings onto brick sidewalks and sliding off roofs into a mess of pinkish slush and mud. The late-afternoon sun shines through the plate glass window of the shop, casting shadows of words across the table where Lily sits. YRECORG. SDOOG YRD. AET EEFFOC. She has spent the day arranging shelves, occasionally stopping for coffee and a chat with one of her customers. Lily is a small woman, maybe five foot four, and her black hair, shot with silver already at twenty-eight years, hangs down her back tied with a red scarf. She has a soft face and large, dark eyes turned down at the corners but with a twinkle that only partly masks the sadness in their depths.

After Lily lost her father, her Uncle Boutros—whom everyone called Pete—took her in and raised her alongside his four sons. She helped in the store for years before inheriting it when he died. Since then, she has added some shelves of magazines and books, as many as will fit. There are also a couple of tables covered in red-checked linen, where she serves coffee and Lebanese pastries, like the ones her late mother made—or as close as possible since it's hard to find the things to make them here on the Island.

People of all kinds come into Lily's store—students from the college, older ladies coming home from church meetings, farmers from Winsloe or Shamrock in town to buy feed or parts for machinery. They will come in for dry goods, paper, pencils, tins of beans, but stay for Lily's coffee and to talk. They pretend they are there for just one cup, but they always linger, telling her stories of the things that have happened to them—quarrels with their spouses, fears for their children—and things they wish would happen. Sometimes the stories are strange: John Rennie the druggist saw his cousin Owen standing at his mother's kitchen window in Charlottetown, even though he was away cutting timber in Maine. Later it came out that Owen had died in a Bangor boardinghouse that very night. And there are more like that, too—about strangers showing up at card games and leaving behind cloven hoofprints, about the woman in Georgetown who haunts the pond where she froze to death waiting for her son to come home from visiting a girl she hated. Lily lets the people talk as long as they want but doesn't say much herself; she has a reputation as a listener, and she loves stories. She has never married.

Across the street the steeple of the Presbyterian Kirk looks down on her from the corner of Prince and Grafton, its peaked red brick façade stern as judgment. A gull is perched above the entrance to the church, turning its head this way and that. Prince Street itself is full: some cars; some horses and carriages; women in long dresses, wool coats, and wide brimmed hats, lifting their hems amid the gray and pink slush; older men dressed for business at the Province House.

There are soldiers, too. Young soldiers are coming back from the Great War still raging on in Europe. The boys, because that's what most of them are, are rarely in one piece as she sees them walking by. Some are missing a leg, limping along on a wooden one; others are wrapped in bandages to hide their ruined faces. Their uniforms are clean, though. Lily notices this as she organizes the stock in the window, her hands working independent of the rest of her. The uniforms are always clean, the medals shine, and the olive-green britches are ironed to a sharp crease. The boys arrive by ship at the Hillsborough River, and many find their own way home. People are preparing for planting season and cannot be spared to pick them up. Many of the boys come from too far out in the country or their families don't own cars. Lily knows they will be welcomed with love, but she knows their journey is not over yet. There are many more still who never made it home and are buried, or still lie, in fields much like those in which the boys' fathers labor.

The sky is blue and cool and the trees are bare, the wind so still no one would ever know there'd been a storm—St. Patrick's storm some old people call it because of when it falls in the calendar. Lily goes to the door to take in the fresh air after being stuck inside for too long, either with snow or with work. She breathes slowly under the weight of the long and not yet finished winter. Right now, she wants to smell the spring that is still a month off but is hinted at here on this unseasonably mild day. The sun on the plate glass has made the store stiflingly warm. She opens the door wide and looks out onto the teeming street.

Lily thinks of her father, long dead. He didn't believe in ghosts or spirits, but like her he knew how to listen, and he knew how to work. She has been dreaming of him lately, dressed in his road clothes with his peddler's pack on the ground beside him, his hair the same black color it was twenty years ago and not a line in his face. Jack Soloman never talks in the dreams, but whistles some sort of tune, sad, like wind blowing through an empty house. He gives her a look, too, as sorrowful as the tune itself, and for a moment Lily's head is filled with that music and with the sense that there is something he desperately wants her to know.

Then she wakes up; it's the same each time.

On this March day, Lily hears the strains of organ music coming from the Kirk, the very tune her father has been whistling in those dreams. Her eye is drawn toward the spot where a couple stands, near the sign declaring the church's hours of worship and this week's Bible verse. The man is young, in the uniform of the Canadian navy: white-and-blue sailor's tam with a blue ribbon, dark blue wide-legged trousers, and a dark blue woolen peacoat. He does not appear wounded, though his face is as pale as pale, and he is looking up at the woman beside him with a mixture of longing and fear. She is perhaps an inch taller than the man, with an expression of disdain that Lily can see even from where she's standing, blond hair twisted elaborately beneath a tilted hat. The woman's face is turned away from her escort, toward Lily's shop. A sharp breeze blows through the open door, sending the papers on the shop counter flying, and Lily gets a feeling she hasn't had in a long time—a sense of losing her feet, of being swept up from below by a wild tide. She takes a step out onto the sidewalk, and another, weaving among the cars and carriages, the crowds of people, to get closer. Lily recalls a moment from her childhood and an old newspaper with this woman's picture. The woman knows her, too. Lily can see it in the steady stare of those upturned green eyes and the thin, cruel smile that greets her through the crowd. Even the glint of silver at the woman's neck is familiar.

A horse and wagon trot through the slush on the road between Lily and the pale blond woman, splashing pink mud on Lily's skirt.

"Get out of the street!" the driver yells, and by the time Lily recollects herself, the wagon has passed and the couple has disappeared into the crowd, or maybe into thin air. Lily will never be sure.

Lily retreats to her shop and sits heavily in the wooden chair by the window. It takes a while for her to acknowledge exactly what she has seen and, when she does, her eyes fill with tears. That woman in the street was as young and beautiful as the last time Lily saw her, so many years ago, but it can't be her. It can't be.

CHAPTER TEN

March 18, 1918

Donny MacNeill

"Look there, Angus. We've got company." Donny MacNeill points above his friend's head to the low snow-covered cliff overlooking Morrison's beach. A horse—pearl gray in color, like the March clouds reflected in the calm waters of the Strait—has been following them from above as they look for salvage along the shore. Angus Campbell and Donny are seventeen years old and best friends, too young to be called up for the Great War but waiting to sign up together when they both turn eighteen in November. Then their parents can't stop them.

For the past five years, they've come combing the beach after every storm. The wild tides of two days ago have left the beach littered with tangled skeins of kelp, beds of eelgrass already drying, and purple jellyfish by the hundreds, strewn in blackening patches along the beach, but also with things of use to the boys and to others: broken lobster traps that can be mended and used in the lobstering business they want to start together, shards of clay crockery to feed their mothers' gardens, driftwood for the sculptures Angus makes and sells during the Provincial Exhibition in Charlottetown, even bits of sea glass, smooth green and brown, blue or red if they're lucky.

As often happens after St. Patrick's storm, the day has dawned mild and quiet, warm as early spring, so that the only thing to be heard on the beach is the soft groaning of the great blue-white ice cakes breaking up along the Strait. Even the usually raucous gulls are standing motionless on the hard sand, waiting for the tide to lap at their feet. Nor is there a snort or nicker from the horse, standing perfectly still up on the bank.

"There's a quiet creature, eh, Donny?" Angus remarks. "Wouldn't've even known he were up there." Angus bends down to pick up a piece of sun-bleached driftwood in the shape of a twisted cross. He shows it to his friend. "How about this for the new altar at St. Peter's?"

Donny rolls his eyes. "The altar? Can you imagine Father Cole's face? And besides . . . Angus . . . ?"

Angus has stopped listening and is standing as still as the horse itself, his round, freckled face as calm as the smooth gray waters of the Strait behind him, his eyes closed like a sleeping child's. "What's that song?" he asks softly. On the bluff, the silent pearl-gray horse shakes its mane and paws the snowy ground.

Donny MacNeill stares at his friend. "I don't hear any song."

"There's no words to it. Just this voice, so beautiful." Angus's voice rises slightly, and his eyes, open now, get the clouded look of someone about to cry.

Donny shakes his head. "Angus, boy, you're pulling my leg." The horse starts to walk along the edge of the bank above them. Without looking at Donny, Angus heads in the same direction as the animal, toward Nelson's Point and the mouth of the Cardigan River.

"She's calling for help now," Angus shouts as he and the horse start running. "Something's wrong."

"She?" Donny follows clumsily. His gum rubber boots—filled with old newspaper for warmth—almost slip off his feet as he struggles over the storm-littered sand. "Who? Angus, what's going on?"

The pearl-gray horse stops just above a rocky headland that juts out into the Strait. "Here!" Angus shouts, disappearing past the jumble of rocks.

Donny's boots sink into the wet sand as he tries to follow his friend. Then the smell reaches Donny, a stench of rotting fish so strong that it sends a wave of nausea through his body, leaving his limbs weak and trembling. When he stops to steady himself, breathing as slowly and deeply as he can, Donny does suddenly hear the song that Angus has been following, though he doesn't hear it as beautiful. Instead, it's a querulous tune, pitched so high that it might be coming from a tin whistle, and mingled with what sounds like laughter—a woman's laughter, shallow and joyless. The music disappears and Donny, boots now ankle deep in the icy water, rounds the headland. Angus is there, standing near the gray-and-black wreckage of what looks like a lifeboat. Then Donny hears the tune again. This time not just in his head but in the air close by him. A woman is singing. He suddenly feels the dampness in his boots and mack, like that dampness is locked inside him. He shivers.

"Donny." Angus's voice. "C'mere."

A few feet away, a young woman sits against a red sandstone outcrop, amid beds of wet, black eelgrass and a pile of rags. Angus has draped his brown coat over her thin shoulders, but beneath it she is wearing a blue velvet dress spattered with red mud at the hem. She's looking up at Angus with large, half-closed eyes, green as limes, or as channel water when it gets deep. Her loose, wild hair is so blond it is almost white, and a silver chain hangs from her neck. She's gone as silent as the curious pearl-gray horse that has stopped just above where she sits.

"Miss," Angus says softly. Donny has only ever heard him speak this way to dark-haired Fiona Bourque the times he's asked her to dance. "Miss, what's your name?"

The girl's green eyes widen slightly as her hands move over the tangle of rags and eelgrass in her lap. "Sarah." The word drops from her mouth like a stone.

"Sarah," Angus repeats in almost a whisper as the wave of nausea, milder this time, washes over Donny again.

"Let us help you please . . . Sa-Sarah." Angus's voice is full of concern (and something else, a tremor of speech that worries Donny, though he's not sure why).

"My husband," Sarah says dully. "He's dead." A flock of gulls are mewing in the distance.

Donny steps forward now, his eyes finally focusing on those rags spread out beside Sarah. There's a body lying there, a young man's body, twisted and bent and bearing the dark blue and bloodied remains of a naval uniform. The man's head is cradled in Sarah's lap, his face cracked and blanched as an empty clamshell. She is combing her long smooth fingers through his hair.

CHAPTER ELEVEN

June 14, 1950

Beet MacNeill

"Would ya look at *that*, Beet." Jeannine's got her eye on the minister gull hopping along the wooden fence that surrounds the Publicovers' green-and-white painted gingerbread house at the end of Skinner Harbour Road. "Look at that crooked old beak. I'd swear it's the same damned creature as bit me the other day."

It's been four days since we went on reconnaissance down at Poxy Point, and we're heading home from Lavangier's store with a sack of flour and some comics, plus a bunch of books from the library, all Jeannine's that she got earlier in the day, new ones that Lily Soloman ordered just for her to try—*Folktales of the Scottish Highlands*, *Greek Mythology*, and *Ghosts and Legends of Prince Edward Island*. Jeannine goes to the library twice a week.

It's her favorite place, and not just because Freddy sometimes comes in to help deliver books to old folks or to the prisoners at the jail. I mean, he sure is one of the reasons, but Jeannine loved books before she ever thought of Freddy Soloman. Poor as the Gallants are with all those kids, when Jeannine's dad goes to Montague or Charlottetown, he'll sometimes even bring a book home for her to keep. She has them all on a little shelf in the room she shares with her sisters. Jeannine may be silly when it comes to boys, but she's sharp as a good knife, brains-wise, smartest in our class at school.

She's right this time, too. The gull is looking straight at us, like it's been hanging around waiting for us to show up. I've started to think it might be following me, too. Yesterday, it was hopping around the barnyard trying to get at the hens' feed. The morning before that, I met it on my way back from the outhouse. Jeannine picks up a stick and makes a play to toss it at the bird, then just drags the stick along the length of the fence as we head farther out of town toward her house, where we'll part ways. The gull hops along the top of the fence after us.

After the Publicovers' property, Skinner Harbour Road moves inland toward some of the poorer houses on the outskirts of town, before it meets Royalty Road heading out toward our farm. It's a bit of a cloudy day, with that thick feeling in the air that tells me it's going to rain any time now. Trucks roll past us on the way to the fish meal plant at the other end of town, and some of the Newfoundlanders that work in the plant wave and holler at us from the back of a pickup. They're thin and tan in open workshirts and jeans; I have to stop Jeannine from waving back.

"Well, this is just too strange," Jeannine says, wrinkling her dot of a nose. "First this gull bites me on the hand, for *no* reason at all, and now here it is following us all over Creation." She lowers her voice and looks around her. "And Saturday we see the Devil's footprints coming from Marina Shaw's house."

"Oh *Lord*, Jeannine. You'd see the Devil in a boiled egg." We've been arguing about this since we saw the hoofprints the other day. Jeannine thinks the Devil is after Baby Joseph and that somehow Marina Shaw is involved.

"Well, if it wasn't the Devil, then what was it?" Now we're walking along the edge of the ditch that separates us from Ted Clory's potato field, with its rows of bright red earth, and the green beginnings of potato plants. The field spreads out, like a chenille bed topper, right down to the black woods that separate Clory land from the Strait. The minister gull hovers above us for a minute, then flies off in the direction of the trees. Jeannine folds her arms and stares at me, hard. "Beet, you know when there's something bad going on in a house—some *sin* like card playin' or drinkin'—the Devil always shows up, joins in the goings on, and then leaves a trail of hoof marks by the door, and you know there've been hoofprints spotted out on Poxy Island, ever since that ship was quarantined, something like a hundred years ago or more. I'm telling you, that Marina Shaw is up to no good. I mean what's she want with Joseph anyway?"

"I don't trust her either," I say as we pass the Clorys' cow pasture, and it's true. I *don't* trust Marina Shaw, not the look of her, nor the greedy sound of her voice when she's singing. "But that doesn't mean she's getting visits from the Devil." Still, I'm glad Jeannine notices something, too, especially since Marina tried to take our Joseph. I mean he's Deirdre's Joseph, but he's Gerry's, too, and Mom's and Dad's, and mine. We're the ones that love him. Marina Shaw doesn't love him. She just wants to have him, and I sure wish I knew why.

Jeannine is still going on about the footprints. "All I know is what I saw. Those were the Devil's footprints. Satan himself."

I just shake my head as another truckload of plant workers passes by us, hooting. "They weren't even cloven hooves, Jeannine. Devil's supposed to have *cloven* hooves, isn't he?"

That shuts Jeannine up, for a while anyway. The minister gull lands out in front of us again, right in the middle of the road, and starts waddling along to our left.

"It was probably just that horse we saw," I say, after about five minutes of Jeannine wearing a schoolteacher's scowl on her freckled face. "Probably belongs to Marina."

"Sure." Jeannine gives me a satisfied expression. "A horse that canters up to the door of a house, then *disappears*. Where did it go, eh, Beet? That's all I'm saying. Where?"

She's made a good point, and I've been wondering the same thing, but I'm not in the mood to tell her so, and it turns out I don't have to because we've reached the track to her house. I can tell by the old faded sign: GALLANT AUTOWORKS. That's what Jeannine's dad does, fixes trucks and tractors. There are eight of them in the yard right now, crowded around a shed about a hundred yards from the family house, which is smaller than ours by half and painted a castoff Sears catalogue pink. The house is neat and clean, though, with all kinds of cunning little statues out front, and a small garden with marigolds and snapdragon starting. On the other side of the house, near the Gallants' back field, Jeannine's sister Jocelyn is hanging out sheets on the line while her younger brothers, Jim Jr. and Jack, chase a cat. All the Gallants have first names beginning with "J"; Mr. Gallant is Jim Sr. and Mrs. Gallant is Juliette. Jocelyn waves at me, clothespins in her mouth, as Jeannine heads down the track to the house.

"Bye, Beet," she calls, library books over her shoulder, swinging her sack of flour.

"Bye," I answer, then I can't resist. "Watch out for the Devil, now!"

I head off toward Royalty Road laughing, the crooked old minister gull following at my feet. "Well, come on, if you're coming," I tell it.

Royalty Road leads to the rutted clay track that runs to my house, through a wood of black spruce, with only a few houses on the way. May Curley's is first, with its miniature lighthouse out front by the mailbox, then Lou DeLorey's, and Les and Honey

Martell's, right next door to one another (Martells and DeLoreys are in-laws). Out past Jeannine's family is Lily Soloman's house, with its gingerbread edging, and pink and green front gate. Seems like a cheerful place for someone as quiet and watchful as old Lily to be living, but she's the one who painted it those colors, right after she moved in. Just another thing that makes her such a puzzle. Passing the house makes me think of Poxy Point, her talk of ghosts, and especially that look on her face when she first saw Marina Shaw. I wonder if it's worth visiting her at the library like she asked, maybe try to find out what it is about Marina that has both of us suspicious. Thing is, if I'm not ready to talk about it more with Jeannine, I sure don't want to share my business with someone I barely know, especially someone who looks at people the way Lily does.

As I turn onto our track, I put Lily Soloman out of my mind and let the clean smell of wet spruce fill me up. The gull hops along from tree to tree beside me for about a hundred yards before flying off into the woods. Our track runs parallel to the Cardigan River and there are a couple of footpaths leading out to the river's narrow beach. I can hear the faintest clang of a channel marker beyond the trees to my left. It's darker here than on Royalty Road, with only a strip of cloudy sky overhead, but in front of me I can just see where the woods open up onto our farmlands. With the rain coming, a crowd of birds has taken shelter in the trees. A murder of crows is cawing at one another on the ground, and from somewhere comes the bossy, drunken call of a blue jay. In the midst of all that noise, I don't notice the music at first, fiddle music, coming from the river off to my left. The song blends so well with the sound of the birds and the nearby river that it takes a moment to recognize it—Gerry's tune, the same as he played the morning I saw his ghost, the morning Baby Joseph was born.

High, sweet, and sorrowful, the notes pull me off the track, left and toward the water. Not looking for a footpath, I follow Gerry's tune through the stand of black spruce at the edge of the track right to where the trees lean over the bank that overlooks the river. When I reach the bank's rim, my bare legs and the hem of my skirt are wet and muddy. I look out onto the river, expecting to see Gerry playing the fiddle, just the way I saw him last year, and my heart hurts a little when he doesn't appear. Still, there *is* someone down below me at the edge of the river, but it's not Gerry. It's handsome Mr. Uist, the man we met at Marina Shaw's house. He's in his old-fashioned suit, his back to me, up to his knees in the greenish-gray water and wading out deeper and deeper into the river, almost to the drop-off.

"Mr. Uist!" I'm alarmed enough to call after him, but he keeps wading deeper, up to his waist first, then to his neck. I leave my comics on a rock and scramble down the bank as fast as I can, but before I reach the bottom, he has gone out over his head and disappeared beneath the rippling surface of the water.

"Mr. Uist!" I cry again. There's a fallen branch at my feet, long enough to reach out to a drowning man. I pick it up and head toward the water's edge. He hasn't come back up. I look to the far bank of the river to see if there's anyone who can help me, but I'm alone on the beach. The music that called me here has stopped, and it's begun to rain, drops piercing the surface of the river like needles. I go in up to my knees, the driftwood in my hands for him to grab on to if he should surface, but I'm afraid to go farther into the river. Mr. Uist might have gotten trapped in the muck of the riverbed. That happened to Robbie Jenkins in the fourth grade, and they didn't find him 'til the next spring.

"Mr. Uist, where are you?" This time I whisper it, shivering in the rain. About twenty feet in front of me, where the river bottom drops off deeper, the water's clouding over reddish brown, like something or someone's kicked up the sand. I wade in to my waist, stick at the ready and skirt ballooning around me, thinking—hoping—maybe Mr. Uist is trying to struggle up for air, and I can reach him. I don't see anything but sand at first; when I do see something, I wish I hadn't.

At first it just looks like seaweed floating at the surface of the murk, seaweed mixed with long gray-white hair that spreads outward like tentacles. I see the eyes next, bubbles of bright bloodred set in an oil slick–blue face that rises and sinks in the water just as a wave would, moving in toward shore, toward me. I feel my feet sinking into the bottom mud, and for a moment I don't even try to pull them out. I can't stop looking at that face, the red eyes glowing, the skin shimmering in patterns like rainbows. My feet are stuck now, and I can feel myself start to panic. A picture comes into my mind of what this thing might have done to Mr. Uist.

As it nears me, the creature raises its head farther out of the water, as if it's found its footing on the riverbed. It has a row of teeth sticking out beneath its blue-black upper lip, the way a horse's would, but these teeth are sharp and greenish yellow, seaweed hanging in between them. The creature is opening its mouth as it gets closer. A thick red tongue lolls along the jagged bottom teeth, and the smell of rotting fish almost makes me retch, but still, I'm not moving. I can't scream; I can barely breathe, but if I don't move . . .

It's coming closer, closer, no more than a few feet from me now, as I sink deeper and my heart races faster . . . when all of a sudden the creature stops, still as sticks, two gray-black ears raising themselves out of the water as if it's listening for something. I hear it, too—Gerry's sweet, sad fiddle tune echoing from the far bank of the river has stopped the monster in its tracks and started *me* moving. With that moment to breathe, I relax myself, then pull my feet out of the muck that's held them. I swim backward away from the still, skulking creature, tossing the stick of driftwood at it as I go. When I am knee deep, I turn and fight the water toward shore. From the splashing behind me, I can tell the creature has started moving again, but I don't stop to look. I make it to the river's edge at a run, and I don't *stop* running until my foot hits a stone and I fall forward, sprawled out on the hard, wet sand. Beside me, the river empties into the Strait, and our farm—the white house with its red trim, the faded red barn—looks down at me from the clover-dotted rise to my right.

That's when I see Sean MacInnes, standing on the beach with his mouth open like he'll never close it again. The music of Gerry's fiddle, which has followed me here, dies away in the thick splattering rush of the rain.

CHAPTER TWELVE

April 20, 1949

Sean MacInnes

Sean MacInnes has spent six months watching his mother die. He accompanies her to her doctor's appointments; he reads to her when she can't sleep; he prepares tea for her and cuts her toast into little strips so she can eat it slowly. They call it "hospital toast." She used to make it for Sean on days he was home sick from school. In the afternoons, when the weather is good, they go for walks. Lately he has been pushing her in a wheelchair through the Boston Public Garden, where they watch for the ducks in the lagoon, as they did when he was little. And just as when he was little, it is always only the two of them. His father is too busy with work and travel.

On what will be their last visit to the Public Garden, it is mid-April, the day after the Boston Marathon. It has been raining and the ground is still muddy, but the sky is bright blue and the Swan Boats—filled with schoolchildren—float slowly past the weeping willows on the banks of the lagoon. There are hints of tender green at the tips of the ancient tree branches. Sean pushes the wheelchair past the daffodil beds, toward the small suspension bridge that crosses the lagoon. In the middle of the bridge, a busker is playing. He's probably a few years older than Sean, red haired and tall and dressed in a fisherman's raincoat over a plaid shirt and jeans. He smiles at the people as they pass on the bridge, and even winks at Sean and his mother, but never seems to lose his place in the tune. The busker's fiddle case is open at his feet, filling quickly with coins and dollar bills. Pinned to the inside of the lid is a black-and-white photo of a girl with long hair and dark eyes, standing beside the sea.

"Sounds like an Island tune," Mama says, her voice raspy. "Let's stay and listen." More than anything, Mama wants to go back to her Island, to see it once more, but Dad says travel will weaken her. Even before she got sick, Dad has never allowed time for Sean's mother to go home to see her family and friends. When the two of them are alone, Mama tells Sean stories of her small harbor village, the adventures she had there as a girl, and how she followed her friends down to Cape Cod to work in hotels the summer after her parents died. There she met Sean's father, while he was vacationing at a small hotel on Nantucket Island. The family has been back there many times, but when Mama tries to tell the story of their meeting, Dad changes the subject. Sean and Mama stay on the bridge for a long time, listening to the redheaded fiddler. Mama closes her eyes and taps her feet on the metal footrest of her wheelchair.

Less than a week later, in the silence of early morning, Sean sits by his mother's bedside, holding her hand as her breathing comes slower and slower. There's a sound outside, and from nowhere, Mama's eyes open and she smiles. It takes a moment for Sean to realize that the sound is music—a slow, sad song like weeping—coming from somewhere out on the street.

"Ever so lovely," Mama whispers. "Sean, go to the window. See where it's coming from."

He doesn't want to let go of her hand, but he obeys.

Out the open window, the sky is changing from dark blue to purple, and the breeze that moves the curtains brings the smell of salt with it. Under the fading streetlight stands the red-haired fiddler from the Public Garden. He is bent over his instrument playing a tune so soft that it is no wonder Sean did not hear him right away. The music rises and falls with the breeze, slower and slower, like the rhythm of his mother's breathing, but sweet too, and full of feeling.

Sean is already crying when he turns from the window to find that Mama has gone still and silent.

CHAPTER THIRTEEN

June 14, 1950

Sean MacInnes

Sean's father sends him away to school not long after his mother's death. At fifteen, he is just that tiny bit too young to be on his own, says Dad, though Sean has done just that for the last six months. After a lonely year in a New Hampshire boarding school, Sean receives a letter from his mother's aunts, Nora and Louise Publicover, asking him to come for the summer. Sean expects his father to say no, but he doesn't.

Sean has never met his great-aunts until the day he arrives in Skinner Harbour. The journey from Boston includes a fourteen-hour bus ride through Maine and New Brunswick, a ferry crossing on the choppy waters of the Northumberland Strait, and then a car trip to Skinner Harbour mostly on clay roads, raising clouds of pink dust all the way. Just past Charlottetown, Freddy

Soloman has to stop the Publicovers' car so Sean can throw up in a ditch.

When he arrives, his great-aunts are kind to him, if gossipy, and they make a great show of not talking about his mother. The people in the town are friendly, too—most of them, anyway—but they all seem to have had long conversations about him behind their closed doors. He spends most of his time looking out of the Publicovers' front window or walking the bank or lower beach down behind their house. They have a back lawn that Freddy Soloman mows once a week. Freddy's not much for conversation. Maybe that's why Sean likes him. He likes Lily Soloman, too. She's kind and a good listener, and though she sometimes has a hard edge to her, it's usually saved for people who deserve it, at least from what Sean has seen. Lily found him that photo of his mother, just as she promised. It's a class portrait from Skinner Harbour School, taken two years before Mama left the Island for work. Mama is sitting in the front row. She is about fourteen, smiling, in a plaid skirt and sweater. Sean sees his own face in hers, and it fills him with gratitude.

Today, the Publicovers' newly mown lawn ends in a patch of marsh grass with a path through it—swarming with mosquitoes most days—leading to a creek and a red-sand beach. The creek empties out not far from Poxy Point, and Sean has already walked the beach three miles in each direction: southward past the fishing pier and the fish meal plant that stinks up the town each Thursday night and is always loud with the shouts of workers, and farther up the river to some private cottages partly hidden by birch trees;

or northward past Poxy Point with its tiny island offshore, then past some farms and stands of spruce to Nelson's Point and inland along the Cardigan River.

Sean takes notes and draws pictures in the little black leather-bound sketchbook his mother gave him—the last one she bought before she got too sick to go out shopping in Harvard Square or Filene's downtown. Each day he watches seabirds—like the gulls, terns, and long-necked black cormorants that flock around Poxy Island. Then he draws them—on the sand, in flight, floating in the waves. He has picked his way around dead jellyfish all up and down the beach, and he's seen beds of mussels and crabs scuttling under piles of driftwood. He has carried fairy shrimp in a bucket, to see them close-up. The water is cold and clean, the red sand dotted with deposits of pink clay that he plans to take home and turn into sculptures. Sean has filled the pages of his black book, front and back, until they are crowded with notes and sketches. He owns several other sketchbooks as well, all from Mama—filled with pictures and notes on buildings and trees and all the sights from home and his travels. He brought them all with him from Boston, in his suitcase. It will be time to buy another book soon, and he has the money for it, but he can't bring himself to put this one away, not yet.

Today Sean is sitting on the grassy bank, looking out on the Strait where it meets the Cardigan River. He's still thinking about that wake, meeting all those people, seeing the old woman's dead body, her tight face and thin red lips, as if she'd died angry.

When he saw the girl, Beatrice, touching the dead woman's face with such calm, all he could think about was Mama, that early morning when he'd turned from the window to find her dead, the hand he had just been holding hanging open, waiting for him to take it up again. He'd called the ambulance, and his father, who was away at a conference. He'd closed his mother's empty eyes and felt the cold skin of her cheek; he never wants to feel anything like that again.

But Beatrice . . . she didn't seem to mind at all, touching the old woman's cold skin, dripping wax onto her eyelids. He's never met a girl like her, so flinty and unafraid. Then again, he hasn't had a chance to meet any girls at all lately.

On the bank, Sean decides to draw from memory the sights he has seen so far: the small peak-roofed houses of the village, some faded gray, others painted pink or bright turquoise, or white with red or green trim; the rocky beach littered with shells and stones and dead jellyfish; the pretty redheaded girl with the dripping wax candle.

The air is salty and the dark green water moves in slow swells. In his mind he hears the sound of the busker's fiddle, its song rising and falling like the green water, like his mother's dying breaths. His pencil moves across the page, drawing the waves on the Strait. Above them the clouds shimmer with the rain that is surely coming. The fiddle tune continues to echo, and he looks up from the notebook with a jerk. He is not just remembering the busker's music; it is not in his mind after all. It's filling the air around him.

Sean turns his head, looking for where the sound is coming from. There are no houses on this stretch of beach. The last one he passed was the MacNeill's farm, with the old whitewashed house he remembers from the wake. He stands up, puts his book in his jacket pocket, and scrambles down the bank as raindrops begin falling. He follows the music inland along the river, stopping where a wall of red rocks cuts the shoreline. The tune is fading slightly, but the sound is coming from beyond those rocks. He climbs over them carefully as the rain falls in fat, cold drops. Lowering himself to the other side, he encounters Beatrice MacNeill, looking as if she has fallen on the sand.

The music Sean was following has stopped, and for a moment he doesn't say anything. The girl is soaking wet. Her red hair curls around her face, which is tan, without freckles. It's such a striking look, a redhead without freckles, that he can't help but stare. She struggles onto one knee, wincing. Her dress is covered in mud.

"What are you doing here?" She snaps at him, her face wild, but pretty, too. "Were you watching me or something?"

Sean blinks back the raindrops that are hitting his face. "I wasn't . . . I was just out walking, and I heard this music."

Beatrice's bright eyes widen, just slightly.

"What are you talking about?" She seems to think for a moment, then shakes her head as if she's angry. "Look, I just saw someone drown . . . I think . . . We have to get help . . . Ow!" She's trying to get herself into a standing position, but ends up sitting on the hard sand.

"You're hurt," Sean says, as if he just noticed, and isn't surprised when she scowls at him.

"No kidding." She slowly stretches out her right leg, favoring it, and winces again. But what she says next doesn't sound pained, just bossy. "Now go up to our place and get my dad. . . . Not my mom, my dad *only*."

He stands still another minute, wondering what he's supposed to do if her dad's not home. He could help her, bring her to the house, but he's pretty sure she'd bite his head off rather than accept that. He's pretty sure he knows what she thinks of him.

"Do you want to help or not?" She sounds like a grumpy schoolteacher. "Dad'll be in the backfield right now, always is. No need to go to the house." She winces again, then looks ready to growl at him, and Sean is off.

Twenty minutes later, he's back with Mr. MacNeill.

"Mr. Uist . . . ," Beatrice tells her father. "I saw his head go under and . . ." She trails off, and Sean thinks she is going to say something more, but she doesn't. For a second her practical, hard-headed expression shows a hint of worry, or maybe fear.

Mr. MacNeill bends down beside his daughter and checks her ankle. Mr. MacNeill is calm and kind, so unlike Sean's father.

"Don't worry, Beet," Mr. MacNeill says. "Ben Clory was near shore in his dad's boat. Once Sean mentioned drowning, I sent Ben out to look. He's got Ted and Marty on the radio as well." He smiles. "Not too much swelling. Just stay off it today."

"Dad, Mr. Uist . . ."

He shakes his head. "You've done what you could for him, Miss Beet. The current is strong, but we'll try."

Beet (is that what they call her?) has tears in her eyes. Sean can see them, just for a second, before she looks up at him, and he wants to reach out to her. Then her face turns hard, like she's never shed a tear in her life. It's raining with force now, and the red dirt of the bank looks slippery.

"Sean, boy," Mr. MacNeill says. "Could you get her back up to the house?"

Beet shakes her head, that hard look still there. "I don't need any help!"

Mr. MacNeill's kind voice becomes firm. "If you want to play this weekend, you'd best do as I say."

But he smiles at her as soon as he says it. As he turns to go, Beet grabs his arm. "Dad, be careful, there's something . . . Just be careful, okay?"

"Okay, Beet," Mr. MacNeill assures her, but he looks puzzled, and he hesitates a second or two, his eyes on his daughter. Then he is off to meet a fishing boat just making its way around the point. The boat is white and bright turquoise with the words "Clory's Glory" painted across the bow.

Sean puts his hand out to Beet, but she waves it away. She won't let Sean touch her, except at the elbow and only when they are climbing the bank. The whole way to the house, she doesn't say a word. When they get there, the door is already open and Mrs. MacNeill is standing inside. She is blond but looks otherwise just like her daughter, including the expression on her face, a look that says, “Mind your own business.”

Mrs. MacNeill stares her daughter up and down, thanks Sean (which is more than Beet does), then closes the door, leaving him on the porch. Sean sighs, shakes his head, and starts back for his great-aunts’ house in the rain.

CHAPTER FOURTEEN

June 17, 1950

Beet MacNeill

Three days after what happened at the river, I come down to breakfast to find a shock: Mr. Uist's gray suit jacket, damp and muddy, stretched over a wooden clothes rack by the kitchen window, next to a card table laden with fruit-shaped crocheted potholders, plus tins of cookies stacked and ready for the Skinner Harbour Day bazaar and dance. There are still a half dozen trays of molasses cookies waiting to be packed. But the jacket . . . is he alive?

"Brought that jacket in last night," Dad says before I can ask. "Freddy Soloman found it right before they were going to call off the search . . . washed up on the rocks by Cardigan Ferry Wharf." It's early Saturday and Dad is sitting at the yellow kitchen table with a cup of coffee and a copy of yesterday's *Guardian*. He's just back from seeing to his traps, still in his oilskins. His coat is hanging up on a hook near the stove, where Mom's bent over the bacon and eggs, making a project of not looking at me. She's been on a tear ever since Wednesday, when I got home soaking wet, escorted by Sean MacInnes. I'm still not sure what she's most angry about, me "chasin' into the river after some strange man and maybe getting killed" or the fact that I ruined my dress. All I know is that every time she sees me, she starts mumbling curses, while Dad just looks at her with a twinkling eye as if to say, "Isn't she entertainin'?"

I didn't tell Dad about the monster, of course, only that Mr. Uist went under the river. I'd have said something about it, right there in front of stupid Sean MacInnes, but I couldn't face Dad not believing me, and I thought maybe they wouldn't go looking if they thought I was making things up, or believing fantasies like Jeannine does. So, the last few days, Dad and the other men have been taking turns dragging the riverbed with grappling hooks, all on my say so, and every day I've been thinking the same thing: What if that creature came back, and I never warned them? They were still out searching last night while I was in bed having nightmares about red-eyed horse-faced creatures rising up from the riverbed to drag my dad under, along with Les Martell, Freddy Soloman, and three or four of the fellas from the fish meal plant. Either that, or I lay awake listening for Joseph to start shouting for his mother. He's been waking up wailing every night around midnight, ever since the day we met Marina Shaw at Poxy Point. The more Deirdre tries to comfort him, the worse he gets.

"Did they find Mr. Uist's body?" I can hear my voice shaking when I ask. The breeze through the open window is spring sweet, and the sky outside glimmers bright above the shadowy Strait, flashes of sunlight sparkling like jewels just below its dark surface. You wouldn't know it today, but the radio says there's a storm coming. It's a few days off from us still (down south in the States, Georgia or something). Time enough to move out to sea, but there'll be rain by the full moon at least, and waters too rough to keep up a search.

"Nope . . . no body," Dad answers between sips of coffee. Mom comes over from the stove and drops a plate in front of me with a bad-tempered sigh. "Happens like that sometimes," he goes on. "Current knocks 'em right outta their clothes. Uist will've been taken into the Gulf by now, probably was before we even started lookin'." Dad puts a sunburned hand on the sleeve of my blue checked blouse. "But we'll keep lookin' for him a few days more anyway. The Clorys are out there now. You're a good girl trying to help him, Beet."

I'm grateful to him for that, especially once Mom puts in her two cents.

"Good girl," Mom repeats, kind of like she's going to spit, but I don't care if she thinks I'm good or not. I'm just glad Dad won't be out searching on that river anymore, not while that creature's out there.

Mom gives a sniff at the jacket and curls her lip into a frown. "All I want to know is when is that smelly pile of wool going to be leaving my kitchen? Didn't this Uist fella have any family?"

"Marina Shaw's his only known connection," Dad says. "Not many people in town had even met him before this happened. Our Beet here was one of the few . . ."

Upstairs, Joseph wakes up hollering like someone just slapped him awake with a fly swatter. "Yep," I say, between bites of fried egg. "When Marina Shaw offered to buy Joseph from his own mother." Just the mention of it makes me want to throw something at the wall. Joseph yells out again, and I can hear poor Deirdre trying to hush him with a song.

"I wouldn't mind selling the child at this moment," Mom says, right snippy. She takes my dish away before I've finished eating. "Haven't had a full night's sleep in days, what with him up roarin' half the night."

Dad just lets out a slow breath. "At any rate, Lou and I were out to Poxy Point to tell Marina Shaw what happened to her friend . . . you know, find out if he had family or the like, but she didn't seem too concerned. Pretty much shut the door in our faces." Dad's mouth gets hard for a tiny moment, before he goes on talking. "Cold fish, that one, just like old Sarah. Got those same cold green eyes, too." He pushes himself away from the table. "Well, I'd better get those seed potatoes squared away if we're going to be ready for our Beet's big debut tonight."

Mom looks at Dad like he's just suggested taking Joseph out for beers at the Legion. "You don't really think Beet can play tonight, Donny? Not after seeing that man drown. . . . What about her nerves?"

While I guess it's nice to know Mom cares about my nerves,

right now I just want to holler at her. The one thing keeping me from going crazy these last three days was knowing I was going to play tonight. "Dad . . . ," I start to say, but he just winks at me.

"Miss Beet'll be fine," he says, giving my red ponytail a tug. "She's tough as any old-time fiddler, only ten times as pretty."

Mom opens her mouth to say something, but before she can Dad adds, "Just like her dear mother."

He kisses Mom's cheek and heads out the door toward the barn.

"Well, Beatrice Mary," Mom barks at me as the door slams behind Dad. "These cookies won't wrap themselves. And as for the dance, you'd better be done playin' before they bring out the liquor."

"I *told* you, Beet!" Jeannine's burst rubber ball of a voice squeals and bounces up and down the Cozy Hall, from the ceiling beams to the polished wooden dance floor. The Publicover sisters, in twin flamingo pink A-line dresses, stare at us from under the red-and-white banner that reads "Skinner Harbour Day Bazaar and Country Dance." Jeannine gives them a queenly wave, and turns to me, whispering. "I *told* you it was the Devil."

The hall—all whitewashed wood paneling, lined with pictures of summer cottages and breaking waves—is about quarter full, and still smells of cinnamon and molasses from a day's worth of cookie selling. It's eight p.m. and most of the bazaar-goers have gone home, except for some few who are waiting for the dance to start. Dad and his band are tuning their instruments. Mom and

Honey Martell are counting the money made at the craft tables. Sean MacInnes is in the corner near the door, writing in that black book of his. He's been doing that since we got here, his dark hair hanging in his face the whole time. It's almost sweet, the way he's concentrating.

Jeannine and I are supposed to be setting out treats for the dancers. Jeannine lines up the cherry thumbprints on a doily-covered tray. She's in her Sunday dress, the purple one with ribbon edging, because she heard Freddy Soloman might be showing up with a "delivery" from Norm Gotell's still. "I'm tellin' you, Beet . . . those bloodred eyes coming right out of the water like that? Devil's got bloodred eyes, you know."

"I thought the Devil had horns and a long tail," I say, breaking off the corner of a molasses cookie while Mom's busy across the room.

Jeannine rolls her eyes like she's asking for help from Heaven, then goes on, slowly. "Sometimes the Devil has horns and a long tail, sometimes he has bloodred eyes, sometimes—"

"Sometimes he looks like your Aunt Marie's Newfoundland dog," I break in, before she can go through the whole list of King's County Devil sightings.

"Well," Jeannine sniffs. "Sometimes he does." She places the last cherry thumbprint on the tray and fixes me with her brown eyes. "Beet, you're going to have to start taking this seriously. And by the way, I can't believe Sean MacInnes was there and you didn't mention that he saved you."

I can just feel my face turning red.

"I *am* taking it seriously!" Now my voice is bouncing off the beams, too, shutting down the conversations all around us. Over near the cash box, Mom shoots me a distrustful look. I lower my voice. Jeannine has no idea how seriously I'm taking it, how many nightmares I've had. "And Sean MacInnes didn't save me from anything," I add, just as he comes into earshot, still holding his black book. Right now I'd thank the floor for swallowing me up.

For a second, he stands there almost smiling, like he's going to say something important, but all he ends up saying is, "Have you seen my aunts?"

I want to ask him if he has eyes, since his aunts are about ten feet away, examining the nearly filled cookie trays. Instead, Jeannine jumps in, all eager. "They're over there!"

"Okay, thanks," he says, slinking away like a scared rabbit.

Jeannine opens her mouth to say something else, but I give her a hard look before she can make one more peep about Sean MacInnes.

"Look, Jeannine Gallant," I whisper. "Nobody saved anybody, and this isn't something out of your library books. Just because I don't think it was the Devil doesn't mean—"

"Okay, okay. You're right," Jeannine says. She hands me a shaker of icing sugar. "You finish up here. I'm going to ask my mother if I can stay over at your house tonight." She turns away and heads across the room.

The Cozy Hall is in the middle of town, on the third floor above Lavangier's store. To get to it, you have to climb an outside staircase to a pair of double doors at the back end of the building. Jeannine's mother and sisters have put two small tables right next to the doors and are setting up a bowl of strawberry punch on one. The other is stacked with box suppers, ready to auction off to the dancers. With their black hair, pointy noses and ears, not to mention their love of the loudest and frilliest hand-me-downs this side of Montreal, Mrs. Gallant and her daughters look like copies of Jeannine, all at different ages. Even the baby, Justine, is wearing a bright pink romper with three rows of lace fringe on the behind, clean and ironed like dirt wouldn't dare touch it, despite the fact I *know* that outfit's been through at least four owners already.

Jeannine says something to her mother, and Mrs. Gallant gives me a little wave from across the room. Jeannine's got her permission to sleep over. Not that Jeannine asked *my* permission or anything. Still, I'm glad she's coming. Mom and Dad will be staying at the dance until late, and I like as many people in the house as I can get since . . . since the monster. Jeannine may be talking out her ear about the Devil, but that doesn't make what I saw in the Cardigan River any less real. That monster lured Mr. Uist in over his head and got him—ate him for sure—and if it weren't for Gerry's fiddling, the same would have happened to me. My blood goes ice cold just thinking about it.

Sean has drifted over next to me, close enough to stage whisper. "So, my aunts say the men found his coat." He's only a little less loud than Jeannine, and way too close, giving me a flustered feeling, which I wish would go away. I take a step back.

"How did they know that?" Not that I'm surprised. It's not like anything in this town is a secret. I take a deep breath to calm myself.

"The aunts know all," Sean says in a spooky voice. Trying to be funny, I guess. It's not working. Across the hall, Jeannine is watching us. I do not like her expression at all. "Um." Sean's face is turning kind of pink. "How's your ankle?"

"Fine." I suppose I should thank him for helping me to the house. He sure looks like he expects me to, and to be honest, it's mean of me not to. I know it. (If Jeannine keeps making those faces at me, I'm going to walk over there and strangle her.) "So th—" I start to say.

"All finished laying out those cookies, Beet?" Mom comes up beside me, holding a small manila envelope in her left hand, looking pleased enough to forget about ruined dresses and me almost drowning. Mom's crocheted potholders and mittens made more money for the new playground than anyone else's at the bazaar, even despite the fact that Honey Martell and her sister-in-law set up a table selling bright-colored flowers made from beads and copper wire from a kit. (Mom hates kits. She calls it cheating.)

"Your father needs you to tune your fiddle for the first set," Mom says. She favors Sean with an almost friendly looking smile. "First set *only*, Beet. Then Lou DeLorey's going to drive you home. Well, *go on*, then. Break a leg." I head off without another look at Sean.

The stage is at the back of the hall, beside the first of a row of tall, narrow windows that line the room, facing out toward the

Old Harbour Road. A dented brass curtain rod stretches from wall to wall above the lip of the stage, but I don't know when there's ever been an actual curtain hanging there. Up onstage, Dad is sitting on a high stool tuning his six-string guitar. He's in a dark blue, fringed shirt, like the cover of a country record album. Les Martell, his salt-and-pepper hair slicked into a curl at the center of his forehead, plunks out a few notes on the shiny brown bass fiddle resting between his knees. Gerry's old fiddle is in its case on top of the upright piano, where bald-headed Lou DeLorey's sitting, tapping out scales with one freckled hand. He looks up as I reach for the case.

"Hey, Beet." He smiles at me and lines crinkle up around his blue eyes. "We'll have a jig for the lead up. How 'bout "The Dusty Miller"?

I give Lou a nod as I open the case. Outside the tall windows, the cloudless sky is salmon pink above the rooftops of Skinner Harbour. Dancers are starting to crowd in through the double doors, bringing with them a cool, salty-smelling breeze. Someone has turned on the electric lights that Glen Lavangier got installed last year—one of the first places in town to get them. The lights give the hall a dim yellow glow, forcing darkness into the corners of the room as the sky outside the windows turns a deeper red. As Dad steps up to the microphone to call the first tune, some dancers are already paired up and waiting, hand in hand, around the shadowy edges of the hall. I place the fiddle under the left side of my chin, tightening the strings with the ivory frog. My heart's beating hard as it was two days ago when I ran from that monster in the river, even though, this time, nothing's going to eat me. I'm not scared at all. In fact, I can't wait to step to the front of the stage.

When I'm ready and tuned, I take a deep breath and draw my bow through the first high note of "The Dusty Miller." It's a tune I learned from Gerry when I first started to get good at my lessons, and it makes me happy to be playing it on his fiddle now. Lou DeLorey joins right in on the piano. Dad plunks away at his guitar just like he's Hank Williams, without the drinking, and Les taps his feet on the floor in time to the low notes of his big old bass.

The dancers enter in two rows down the center, moving their feet, right left, right left, like they're going to march away wherever the music takes them—Honey Martell and her brother Joe; Mom and Cousin Nelson Hansen, his straight black hair combed over his bald spot; round old Alice Mack, the barber, and her skinny husband, Jack Mack; plus six other pairs, mostly people from out near Montague.

Jeannine has stepped out from behind the sweets table (where the Publicovers have set up a right little camp for themselves) and is watching the dancers, swinging her purple skirt back and forth as she claps. Sean MacInnes is sitting near her in one of the folding chairs, writing in that book again. He keeps it so close, you'd think it held his darkest secrets. Someone tall is standing perfectly still in the half darkness a few feet behind Sean and Jeannine, but I can't tell who it is. Across the hall, Jeannine's sisters are taking turns dancing with their baby sister, while Mrs. Gallant joins the line with Jeannine's dad, whose clothes are as plain gray as his wife's are bright and flowery.

Then it's "Ladies In the Center," and time for me to start in on "Herring Reel." Dad taps out its rhythm, toe heel, toe heel, hard on the stage's polished floor, then joins in with his guitar. Les follows, counting time, as the notes of the reel turn round and round on themselves, like the couples circling one another on the floor. I'm playing so fast, it feels like the music is spinning out of me, as if it could lift me up right into the air. The music is pulling the corners of my mouth in a smile big enough to block out any thoughts of horse monsters hiding in riverbeds, and leaving only thoughts of Gerry and me at the bootlegger door, tapping our feet and singing. The cloudless sky outside the windows has gone from red to bruise-purple, and the electric light has filled the room, pushing the shadows even farther into the corners.

Then the man who's been standing behind Jeannine steps forward, out onto the dance floor in one long stride, his upper body as still as if he hadn't moved at all. I swallow hard. It's Mr. Uist! He's just *standing* there, in the middle of the dance floor, as the dancers twist past and then round about him in the grand chain. Mr. Uist's hair is wet and slicked back from his high forehead, and he's wearing gray pants, a vest, and an old-fashioned high-neck shirt—the same suit I saw him in when he disappeared into the river, all except for the jacket, which is hanging up in my kitchen. He's still as still, body bent slightly forward like something wants to pull him toward the stage, like a crooked stone in the middle of the snaking river of people. His eyes are closed, and he has a dreamy smile on his face. Sean MacInnes has stopped scribbling, and this time I don't blame him for staring. I don't know what to think, whether I should be relieved or scared to see Mr. Uist alive, but I keep on playing, uneasy as I feel.

It's good that I know "Herring Reel" so well (it's always been one of my favorites). My hands know where to put the bow, even if my eyes are on something else. So, instead of stopping, I find myself playing even faster, hitting each string so quick that Dad and the others almost don't catch me when I move on to another tune. Lou DeLorey's the first one to notice the change, letting out a whoop at the sound of the wild opening notes of "Whisky in the Jar," an old Irish tune that Gerry taught me to do up as a reel. The whole time, nobody really notices Mr. Uist. If it weren't for the fact that people are dancing round him, instead of through him, I'd think I was seeing another ghost, the way I saw Gerry in the rose garden. Mr. Uist is no ghost, though; he's right there, alive in the middle of the dance floor. If nobody pays him any attention, it's because nobody in the room has seen him before, except me and Jeannine, who's looking away out in the direction of the double doors.

Old Lily has her eyes on Uist from clear across the room, and though I'm fairly sure she hasn't met him, she seems to know him anyway. When she's not squinting at him like he's some sort of specimen, she's staring up at the stage, watching me. I mean she's always watching, but this feels different, like she's expecting something to happen. On the floor, the dancers whirl each other round and round. I turn away from Lily Soloman and fill my head with the words to the song, my dad's low voice singing it while I play.

"Whack fol the daddy-o, whack fol the daddy-o/There's whiskey in the jar." When we get to those last four words, the crowd, swinging left and right through the hall, sings—more like shouts—along. Mr. Uist still doesn't move from where he's standing, even when Josephine Gallant walks up to him in her pink ruffled shirt and holds out her hand for a dance, bold as ever. At just that second, Jeannine turns her head away from the doors, toward her sister and Mr. Uist. Then a look crosses Jeannine's face like she's seen . . . well . . . the Devil. And this time, I don't blame her. She steps forward, grabs her sister by the left arm, and pulls her away in a dance. Sean has set aside his book and looks like he is heading toward the stage. Mr. Uist just stays where he is, his face turned upward toward the music, even as Josephine and Jeannine tussle right next to him. He's opened his eyes and is looking up at the stage, looking at me, smiling.

"I counted out his money and it made a pretty penny,
I put it in my pocket and I took it home to Jenny."

The dancers are snaking through the room, calling out "There's whiskey in the jar" each time the tune comes to it. Without my noticing it, Mr. Uist has moved in closer, almost to the rounded edge of the stage. He must have inched there slowly, the way the monster came up on me in the river. His eyes are closed again, and that smile hasn't left his face. He looks so peaceful, you'd never know he was ever near the water, let alone been pulled under it by some kind of sea beast. I play faster, stepping back a bit from the edge of the stage, away from him.

The tune moves on to "Saint Anne's Reel," the dancers going as if they can't stop, partners arm in arm, swinging, spinning, and changing direction like gears in a machine. Dad's sweating out the notes on the guitar, his feet stomping on the echoing floorboards of the stage, Lou DeLorey banging the piano keys hard enough to bust 'em. For a second, I just let myself feel the pure thrilling gladness of all this. I'm up onstage with my dad, playing my fiddle, making people dance, and the man I thought I'd seen die . . . isn't dead. He's right there, listening to the music like everyone else. That's a good thing. No need to get worked up. As long as I don't look out into the hall, I can believe this and not wonder *why* he's alive when I thought I saw him die, not wonder what it was I *really* saw. But I do look out.

I'm partway through "Moonlight Bay" when I see the change in Mr. Uist's face. The smile disappears and his eyes widen like he's been pinched or something. He takes a step backward from the stage, almost bumping into Mom and Cousin Nelson, both still dancing up a storm. It takes me another half second to hear the sound that's woken Mr. Uist from his trance. Across the hall, just past the main doors on the outside stair landing, someone is standing, singing. It's not your usual tiddle-tar-tum along with the music either. This person is singing full throat, a tune clear enough for me to hear across the crowded hall, with a rhythm and quality that's just the contrary of what we're playing onstage.

Where we're fast and spinning and joyful, this contrary tune is slow and sharp and keening. The undertow feeling sweeps through me.

There's a familiar melody to the song, a bit like the tune that Gerry's ghost played. The notes are true and high, sung slowly, but without the sweet sadness of Gerry's tune—more like the music I kept hearing out on the Strait last week, what I thought was the radio. There's that hollowness to the tune as well, like sound carrying over water. I almost lose my balance as that familiar undertow feeling passes through me again, quick as a puff of air, and is gone. It's Marina Shaw I'm hearing.

The figure outside the doors slips away as I recognize Marina's voice, but the singing goes on. Her voice reaches higher than I've ever heard a human voice go, high as a flute, as a bird's song, as the whistling of an October wind. The difference is, those sounds make a person *feel* something. Marina Shaw's voice is empty at the center, no emotion at all, except for, maybe, greed. She seems to want to call things to her with that voice—not only Mr. Uist, but anyone who can hear her.

I try to keep playing my own happy music, but the sound is all wrong, and I know Dad and the others are struggling, too. Marina Shaw's voice is changing the music we're playing, dragging it in her direction, pulling the music under—not just drowning it *out*, but drowning it, killing it, the way a man might disappear in a rip current. And it's emptying me out, too, bringing back the loss of Gerry even worse than before. A minute ago, we were playing a reel, now it's more like a song for the dead.

The hall goes still as a funeral, the dancers stopped, staring as Mr. Uist backs away from the stage and turns toward the open double doors. I can see the looks on some of the faces, startled and scared but at the same time longing for the high-pitched, empty music to draw them away as well. It's what I saw on Baby Joseph's face, not even two weeks ago, on the porch, and later again when he stood holding Marina Shaw's hand at Poxy Point. Les and I stop playing at the same time, while Dad trails off with a few sour notes on his guitar, and Lou lets the piano cover fall over the keys with a bang. The voice outside goes quiet, and Mr. Uist strides out through the main doors, passing by Jeannine, whose mouth has just about *dropped* open.

Sean MacInnes catches my eye as the music trails away completely. He looks as if he's seen a ghost, or maybe heard one. But why?

The hall stays silent until Dad takes the microphone, making it squeal like a mouse in a trap.

"Well, folks, anybody else feel like singin'?" Dad says, his voice loud and a little shaky, but people laugh anyway, sounding almost grateful. Dad's got a way about him, even at the worst of times, and even I feel like I could laugh a bit. "Band's gonna take a tea break now. Back in ten minutes." Slowly, everybody starts moving and talking again. Mom and Nelson head toward the back table for a sandwich, and Nora Publicover finishes the molasses cookie that's been hanging from her mouth for the last five minutes. Behind her, Lily Soloman—eyes narrow—is the only one in the room still standing as quiet as she was while Marina Shaw was singing. Lily's face has that same look of wariness I saw the other day, but if I'm not mistaken, there are tears in her eyes, too. The sight of her makes me realize that I've started trembling. I take a deep breath to calm myself down.

"Best get ready to go home, Beet." Dad's voice breaks into my thoughts, and I turn and try to smile. He's still holding his guitar, still looking like he's not sure what just happened. Then he smiles and puts a hand on my shoulder. "Grand set, sweetheart. Gerry would be proud." A sharp, cold gust blows in through the doors, and someone closes them. Outside, the three-quarter moon winks in the purple sky.

"What *was* that?" Jeannine whispers to me when I meet her at the snack table.

We're waiting for Lou DeLorey, who's still up onstage, packing up his gear. Dad and Les warm up with Cousin Nelson and John Duncan Phillips, who are getting ready to take Lou's and my places up there. "It's like she had everyone hypnotized or something. That *was* Marina's voice, wasn't it?"

"Yes." The remains of Deirdre's cherry thumbprints are laid out on the table beside me. I pick one up and take a bite. I don't even like cherry thumbprints all that much, but my hands need to move. "Yes, it sure was." Jeannine's giving me one of those wild-eyed "supernatural phenomena" looks of hers. Around us, everyone is talking and eating, waiting for the next set. No one seems to be talking about what just happened, though, except Jeannine.

I've got my eye on Sean MacInnes with his aunts. They are packing up more leftover food to take home (of course). He looks at me like he wants to say something, before Nora Publicover hands him a bag of sandwiches and pulls him away by the sleeve.

"And what about Mr. Uist?" Jeannine goes on. "I thought you said he got . . ."

Before she can finish, Lou DeLorey comes up behind us. "Pickup's parked just outside, girls. It'll be a tight squeeze in the cab, 'less you want to ride in the back, get some air."

"The back sounds fine, Lou," I say, leading the way out through the main door. I step into the cool evening air and almost walk right into Freddy Soloman, who's heading up the rickety wooden stairs two at a time. There are still no clouds in the sky, but I smell rain anyway.

"Sorry, Beet." Freddy looks as troubled as I feel. His face is white as a fish belly under the outdoor lamps, and he's breathing hard.

"Hi, Freddy, what's the—"

"Is my auntie in there?" he says, not harsh exactly, but not the usual mild old Freddy either.

"She's just inside," I say slowly as Lou and Jeannine step out behind me.

"Thanks," Freddy says, edging his way past Jeannine and Lou with nothing but a nod.

"What's gotten *into* him?" Jeannine whispers in my ear when we reach the bottom of the stairs. Lou is ahead of us now and already starting the truck.

I don't answer, but I'll add that to the list of my worries. About twenty feet away, just within the pool of light from the open door of Lou's pickup, the crooked beaked minister gull is sitting on the churchyard fence, watching us. I take a step toward the gull, and it flies away.

CHAPTER FIFTEEN

June 19, 1950

Beet MacNeill

The Skinner Harbour Post Office is in a two-story brick building nearby the old fieldstone courthouse with its tiny jail and exercise yard. Upstairs from the post office is the library. There's a community rose garden between the courthouse and post office, and a playground not fifty yards from where the prisoners—mostly just drunks and bootleggers—are playing ball behind the tall chain link fence. That same old black-backed gull, the one with the mottled wing, is hopping along the top of the fence, looking down at the ball players with its beady eyes. The creature is barely away from my side these days. Bit strange, I know, but I don't really mind it.

I've been to pick up the mail. Usually Dad does, but I said I would. I was planning to see Lily Soloman at the library—

maybe to find out what she knows about Marina Shaw. The way she looked at the dance, and the other day at Poxy Point . . . well, it's sure I'm not the only one suspicious of Marina Shaw. It was more than suspicion with Lily Soloman, though. She acted like she'd met Marina before, and not a happy meeting at that. But when I went upstairs to the library, it was all locked up, no sign or anything.

On the bright side, it's my birthday and there's a card at the post office from my uncle Stewart in Saint John. He works for an oil company there, and always sends ten dollars in a beautiful card with roses on it, just for me.

I sit on one of the playground swings to open it—a lovely card with yellow roses for my scrapbook and five pink two-dollar bills. I place the card and bills back in the envelope and tuck them safely into my jacket pocket. Then I lean back and take a swing just for the fun of it. I close my eyes and keep them closed as I glide back and forth. In my head is all the music we played at the dance, me onstage with Dad and the others, like a real musician, before Marina showed up to ruin things. I hum the tune to "Moonlight Bay" and let the swing lift me up in the air. The chain squeaks and the swing set shakes just a little, but for the first time in a while I'm really smiling, swinging up and down, my hair hanging behind me, like a little kid.

"H-happy birthday."

I open my eyes right quick, and the soles of my feet hurt as I stop the swing. Sean MacInnes is standing there, close enough for me to kick out my legs and knock him over.

I can't help but gasp at the sight of him. "Mother of mercy! Do you just like sneaking up on people?"

He starts to stutter, "N-no . . . I . . ."

But I don't let him finish. "How did you know it was my birthday?" I know I sound mean when I say it, and I guess I feel kind of bad about that.

He just smiles, and I notice again what a nice smile it is for the few times he's used it. "I told you before, the aunts know all."

Not too far away, Jeannine walks past us on the dirt road. She stares in our direction, like she might come over, just as a ball comes flying over the chain link fence, setting the old black-backed gull to squawking. The ball lands at Jeannine's feet and she stoops to pick it up. Then we watch one of the prisoners—Jeannine's cousin Hubie in blue jeans and a white undershirt—as he climbs over the fence to get the ball. Jeannine hands it to him, then he gives her a kiss on the cheek and climbs back over the fence into the exercise yard.

All I can do is laugh. Sean's laughing, too.

Jeannine gives us another considering look, then wiggles her fingers at me and makes a big show of not coming over, before heading off in the direction of Lavangier's store. I know what she's about, and I'll have words for her later.

Sean sits down on the swing next to me. The air is as still as it's been in a while, and the sun is warm enough to almost make me forget all the strange and scary happenings of the last week.

"Hey," I say. "Thanks for helping me out the other day, getting my dad and everything."

He nods, but he looks like he's working himself up to say

something else. Jeannine has disappeared, and a bell rings from inside the courthouse. The yard door opens, and the prisoners head inside for dinner. It's the middle of the day and the sky is blue as forget-me-not flowers, but the town seems empty. It's just me, Sean, and that curious gull perched alone again on the tall fence.

Sean pushes his hair out of his pale face, like he does all the time, before finally speaking. "I'm sorry I startled you just now, really, but I wanted to ask you something. The other night at the dance . . . The woman's voice, did you hear it?"

"I'm pretty sure everyone heard it," I say, but I know what he's trying to tell me.

"Yes, but did you *recognize* it?" He's not looking at me, but his voice sounds a bit like he's pleading.

I stare up at the blue sky for a whole minute, not a cloud to be seen. "Yes," I say at last. "I recognized it." And I think Lily Soloman did, too, I want to add.

He lets out a breath like he's been holding it in for days. "Okay, okay good, because . . . It wasn't the first time I've heard her, or seen her." He has a small knapsack with him, old and faded (Dad would say it looks like it's seen the wars). He unlaces it and pulls out his black book. It's actually a sketchbook, I see now, filled with pictures, real lovely ones of flowers and birds and the sea, but also of city streets and people. He flips through until he comes to the page he wants: a woman in a long dress, standing by the water, her short hair blown back from her face. The picture is filled with all kinds of perfect little details, so much that I recognize the woman right away. Even from the side, I can tell she's beautiful. She is smiling, but the smile is hard, like a sneer.

"Marina Shaw!" My own voice shocks me. Out of the corner of my eye. I see the minister gull standing a few feet from us and realize with a start that I never even noticed it fly off the fence.

Sean keeps going, talking so fast that I remember he's American. "I can just see her house from my aunts' guest room window. At night, her parlor light is on for hours. A lot of times I can't sleep because . . . well . . . I just can't sleep. So I look out that window onto the Strait. And I'll draw sometimes. The water looks different every day, what with the moon and the tides, the wind blowing or not . . ."

He pauses again. I just wait. He's right about the Strait, how it's never the same, and it makes me think well of him that he notices. Not everybody does. Must be because he's an artist. Also, listening to him, I really start to notice how he drops his r's on "pahlah" and "wahtah," and how his a's sound broad like "cahn't." It irritates me to high Heaven when his Publicover aunts do it. The difference is, they're putting on a show and he's not. It's an okay accent when it's real. Got some charm to it.

"Anyway, a few nights ago I was looking out the window, and I had my sketchbook. It was just turned dark, and the moon was shining on the water so that it looked like glass, so still, you know, just not moving at all. Then I heard this woman, singing. The song came from that house, Marina's house. It was quiet, and kind of beautiful, really . . . and sweet sounding, like a strange bird, maybe. But it also had this tone to it that I didn't like, a dullness, underneath. The voice got louder, and I started to feel . . ."

"Dizzy?"

His blue eyes get wide. "Yes, and kind of scared, too. The water on the Strait started moving, just a bit, you know? Just small waves, and it seemed like they were moving *with* the music. Aunt Louise came up to look in on me, and I asked if she heard anything, but she just shook her head and checked me for fever."

While he's been talking, he has blown his hair out of his eyes about five times. He does it again, and I can't help but smile. "The next day, I heard the singing again, so I went down to the bank, and there she was, standing at the edge of the water. I was afraid to get closer to her. I didn't like the way the music made me feel. So, I drew this . . . afterward."

"From memory?" I don't know what's more amazing, that or the story he has just told me. I hold out my hand to take a closer look at the sketchbook. He hangs on to it a second too long before handing it over. A truck rolls past us on the clay road. The gull has wandered off somewhere, but I can hear it calling.

I look at the sketch of Marina again before I say anything. It doesn't just look like her, it feels like her, enough to make me shiver. "Be careful of Marina," I tell Sean. "I don't know why . . . just . . . don't let her know you're watching." She came here to steal Joseph, I want to say, because now I'm even more sure of it. And I have a feeling she's not going to give up so easy.

Sean nods like he's really listening, like he agrees. "That's what Lily Soloman says, too."

"You've been talking to old Lily?" I ask, a bit too sharp.

Sean nods. "Since the day on the beach when the little guy . . . Joseph . . . when he went missing. She found me this really nice photo of my mother, and I've been helping her in the library since then . . . looking through old newspapers and things, for any stories about Skinner Harbour. Haven't found much yet, but she's paying me a bit, and it's kind of interesting. I've got this box of old documents in my room to go through." He's been talking fast again, as if I might not let him finish, but when he says this last part he slows right down and looks me in the eye. "I think she's trying to find out about Marina Shaw."

And as he says it, I know he's right. The breeze has lifted, bringing a salt smell with it, and some few cars pass us on the road, raising dust behind them. I tell him about the day we were all at Poxy Point, the way Lily looked at Marina like she was surprised to see her, or like . . .

"It was like she recognized her." He's getting excited now. "She even kind of said she did."

And then at the dance, I think to myself, with that look in her eyes . . .

"I was going to go see Lily today," I tell him. "But the library's closed."

"Really?" Sean says. "That's so strange, because Freddy never showed up to do the lawn today. The old aunts were not happy about it either." He gives a quick laugh, and I notice his dimples. They make him look like a little boy.

"What do you think . . . ?"

It takes me a second to realize he's talking.

"Where do you think Lily is? Beet?"

"I don't know," I finally answer. "But I sure would have liked to talk to her."

We sit there looking at each other for a minute as Dad's truck is coming over the top of the hill by St. Peter's Church. He'll be here soon to pick me up. "Gotta go," I say, and hand Sean back his sketchbook.

He opens it, flips through, then seems to think a minute before tearing out a page and handing it to me.

"I . . ." He blows the hair out of his eyes again. "I thought you'd like to have this . . . because it's your birthday."

I kind of gasp when I see what he's drawn. It's a picture of the stage at the Cozy Hall, and a girl, or actually seven girls, or the same girl in seven attitudes—still, head down, head up, moving, serious, smiling, spinning around—and they're all me, playing the fiddle at the dance. I want to be mad because he didn't ask my permission, but the pictures are so good, and I'm so pleased with the way he sees me in them. I look like myself; I look like I'm happy. I can feel the same smile spreading across my face right now.

I put the piece of paper in my jacket next to the card from Uncle Stewart.

"Thanks," I say, just as Dad pulls the truck up not far from the courthouse.

"Hey, Birthday Girl! Want a lift home?"

I look at Sean for just a second more, then turn and say, "Sure, Dad."

"H-happy birthday again, Beet," Sean stutters as I head to the truck.

"Thanks." I smile. "Thanks for the picture."

Dad leans forward to open the passenger door for me, and there's a strange look in his eyes, like they're sad, but with a twinkle all the same. As I'm climbing in, he asks, "Was that Sean MacInnes?"

"Yup" is all I say.

He puts the truck in gear.

"All right, then, let's head home. Mom baked you a chocolate cake."

CHAPTER SIXTEEN

November 10, 1883

Jack Soloman

Mrs. Gray! Mrs. Gray!" The house's side window is open, despite the November chill, and the edge of a sheer white curtain floats upward through the front window. The oak door is carved with sea horses and mermaids, its brass knocker shaped like a horse's head and no doubt costing more than anything Jack Soloman's family has ever owned. Jack has already knocked on the door twice, with no answer. Inside, a woman is humming a tune, low and olden sounding, like something he should recognize, or that he once knew but can't remember.

This is the first time Jack has ever been to the home of Thomas Gray, the shipbuilder. There's no other house like it in Port Christine or any of the towns along this stretch of the North Shore toward Rustico, maybe no other like it on all of the Island, set as it is on a hill overlooking the harbor with the Gulf of Saint Lawrence beyond, glimmering reddish gold in the early evening sun. The house can only be reached two ways: by boat or, from town, by a steep and narrow path overgrown with bayberry and wild rose, the way Jack has come. He takes another breath from the climb. Through the window, the tune increases in pitch, like the wind that is rising around Jack, ruffling the feathers of the silent gulls that crowd the wider path in front of the Grays' home. There must be about twenty of them—black-backed gulls, gray ring-billed gulls, laughing gulls, with their black heads, red eyes, and wings the dull slate color of the sky before a storm. Each bird stands motionless, its head turned toward the many-roomed house. Probably food the birds want, Jack thinks, but the sound of the woman's voice stills him as well, and for a moment he finds it hard to remember why he has come. As the tune dies away, he tries the knocker a third time.

"Mrs. Gray! Are you in there?" The wind, rising quickly just a moment ago, begins to die down.

Jack is still wearing the green smock from his work gutting fish at the wharf. He has always been proud to be able to add to the family income, and that he has learned to speak English so well in only two years since arriving on the Island from Lebanon (even though he still cannot get used to the new way of pronouncing his name, "So-lo-man" instead of "Aboussleman," and even though only his parents and brothers call him Jakub now). He even plans to use part of what he earns to help buy a horse and cart, and join his father on the road selling pots and pans, trinkets and books to the farm families who cannot make the trip into town. His father was a bookseller in the old country, a million years ago now.

But any sense of pride in his accomplishments disappears before the woman who opens the carved oak door. Instead, Jack is suddenly conscious of the smell that must be on him. Jack's mother, Maryam, with her kind brown eyes and golden complexion, has remained his image of beauty, even on this Island of red-haired women and freckled, sunburned men, far away from his family's village, with its sunny skies and olive trees. The woman who stands before him now will challenge that image forever. She is tall—taller than Jack, who is seventeen—and thin, in a green silk gown edged with lace below her collarbone. Her eyes are as bright green as the soft moss that floats above sea rocks, her long hair the pinkish gold of the dunes. At her throat is a silver shell pendant on a slender, threadlike chain.

"Yes." The word drops from her lips. Jack is not even sure he saw them move.

"I am sorry to disturb you, Miss. They've sent me for Mrs. Thomas Gray."

"I am Mrs. Gray." The breeze has stopped completely, and Mrs. Gray's voice is as flat and dull as the air has become. She does not move at all.

"But you're . . ." Jack does not finish. The woman standing in front of him cannot be older than twenty-eight, and the Grays have lived in this house for twenty years. There's no more than a line on Mrs. Gray's face, only one, just starting, on the pale skin between her eyebrows. People in town talk about Catherine

Gray's beauty, at least those few who have glimpsed her riding in her carriage to Charlottetown or leading her pearl-gray horse along the cliff's edge. To see her close up makes Jack's legs feel weak, as if they are being dragged out from under him by the tide. He has to steady himself before he speaks again. When he does, the words come out in one breath.

"Well, Mrs. Gray. Frank MacEachern was out on his boat just this morning, about ten miles out, near the channel, and who do you think he saw? Your husband, Ma'am. I mean, not just your husband . . . your husband's ship, the *Catherine*. They hit some choppy seas off New Brunswick and are offshore making repairs. Frank and the boys are running out some more timber to them and all should be well by tomorrow. You'll see your husband by tomorrow night."

Catherine Gray only stares at Jack and briefly touches the spot between her blond brows. The gulls around the house have not moved since she opened the door. Neither has the wind. The late-autumn sun has dropped behind the spruce trees that line the westward side of the path, edging them with orange light.

Jack takes his gaze away from Catherine Gray's pale, beautiful face; pulls a brown parcel from the front pocket of his smock; and hands it to her. "Oh, and there's something else. Your husband sent a gift ahead. Told Frank it was something you've been waiting for, and to bring it right up to you. Frank gave the job to me, and here I am."

Mrs. Gray's smile is thin, a fishhook's edge, and her green eyes narrow briefly. She takes the package from Jack without thanking him and opens it in one tearing motion, letting the brown paper fall to her feet. She holds the gift out in front of her, arms spread wide. It is a green silk shawl patterned with starfish. Jack does not know much about clothes or ladies' things, but even he can see the shawl is finely made, its delicate fringe beaded with crystal and each starfish different from the others. He imagines it to be from a Boston shop, maybe even made in France or Italy. It is the kind of thing that Jack's mother would save for only the most special days (if she ever were to own such a thing) but Catherine Gray merely lets out a breath and throws the shawl over her shoulders like an old wool blanket. Behind her, a man steps into view, tall with short dark hair, in a suit of clothes Jack might see in pictures from old books. The suit's trousers are wet and coated with red river mud at the cuffs.

"Mrs. Gray . . ."

She looks at Jack as if she's surprised he's still there. "Yes?" Mrs. Gray says finally, flatly, her fishhook smile all but disappeared.

The wave of unsteadiness comes over Jack again. He holds his hands out slightly, to straighten himself. Behind Mrs. Gray, the man bows his head, and kicks once at the floor. She turns toward him slowly, her green eyes narrowing again.

"Mrs. Gray," Jack says. "They are asking if you have anything to tell your husband, before they set out with the timber. What should . . . ?"

"Nothing." The word barely disturbs the stillness in the air.

"Mrs. Gray?" Jack is finding it hard to keep standing up,

and the air seems to weigh on his chest. Without another word, Catherine Gray closes the carved oak door, leaving Jack in the evening glow, surrounded by the still, silent gulls. He stoops to pick up the brown paper she has left on the ground and balls it up in his fist. As he turns to head back down the hill, he hears the humming start again, perfectly melodic and clear, but empty, too, the sound of a wind-up box. He shivers, and with the tune, a gust of wind rises, following him on the path toward town. Under the slowly darkening sky, the gulls part to let him through.

Two hours later, Jack Soloman will be standing on the Skinner Harbour wharf when the *Catherine* limps into port carrying the broken body of Thomas Gray, the last of the shipbuilders. His eyes will be open, a grin on his ashen face. In his one remaining hand is clutched a tattered piece of fabric, velvet as from a lady's gown, mixed with a slick black seaweed, long and thin as horse-hair. This time, when Jack Soloman is sent out to the grim stone mansion to carry the news to Mrs. Gray, he will knock in vain at the carved oak door. Only the gulls will speak to him.

CHAPTER SEVENTEEN

June 20, 1950

Beet MacNeill

Boy! Boy!" That old mottled-winged gull has just landed on the rose garden gate, and Joseph is bouncing up and down like he's seen his best friend. He's such a beauty, our Joseph, and watching him like that makes me long even more to keep him safe. I haven't seen Marina since the dance, but I know it's not the last of her. The bird tucks its wings against its sides and cocks its head in Joseph's direction, then turns a considering eye on Deirdre and me. It's been three days since what happened at the dance, quiet days, with no evil horse monsters or magical singing or drowned strangers coming back from the dead. The only curious thing—besides Lily Soloman not opening the library yesterday—is that the gull shows up everywhere I go, ever since I saw it perched on the chain link fence outside the courthouse. Even when I go inside, I can see it through the windows, still as a sentry. The sight of it gives me a shiver, though it's not the oddest thing I've seen in the last while.

"Boy! Boy!" Joseph calls out again. "'ook, Mama! Boy!"

Deirdre is standing beside me in her yellow dress, a basket of cut roses by her feet. Her face is ashen pale, except for the shadows under her eyes. She puts a gloved hand on Joseph's shoulder. "Not *boy*, sweetheart. *Bird*. It's a bird."

He just keeps saying "boy, boy, boy," making me laugh.

The three of us have been out here in the back garden for half an hour. Under the clear sky, Dad's roses are starting to bloom—rows and rows of pink, white, red, and pale yellow. Their smell is cool green and candy sweet at the same time, nothing like that perfume Jeannine sometimes nicks from her mom's bureau. As pretty as Dad's roses smell and look, I'll never come near them again without thinking about Gerry—his ghost in the bare April garden, that sad, sad music and that scent of rotting flowers all around me. I almost never come back here anymore, and I wouldn't be here at all if Mom didn't need all these roses for the MacLeans' ruby wedding anniversary. It's too bad, because I used to love this garden. Maybe I will again someday, but I can't see that day yet.

Deirdre adds another deep-pink American Beauty to the bouquet she's been gathering. They're having the party up in Rollo Bay tonight, and Mom wants three dozen roses to place on the tables in the hall. Dad, Lou, and Les are playing, but I'm not allowed to go this time—too late an evening, Mom says, too far a ride home. Beyond the fence and the low cliff path down to the beach, the Strait rises and falls in swells that say a storm is somewhere out in the Gulf, somewhere not far. The high tide rolls into shore with the low rumble of crowds talking, and the breeze blows in cool from the water, sending a shudder through the back field and into the spruce wood beyond. Joseph lifts his face to the breeze and closes his eyes, smiling. He's given up on the gull now and is plunked down in the dirt beside his mother's feet, humming some sort of low-pitched tune to himself (I think it's "Happy Birthday") and crumbling bits of red earth in his fingers. Pretty soon it will be time to start teaching him to play fiddle, like Gerry taught me.

Deirdre brings the whole bouquet up to her face before setting the flowers in the basket. Her tired eyes seem to mist over a little, but she's smiling. "It's funny, you know. The morning Joseph was born, I could smell them . . . roses. Can you imagine? Roses, even though it was April." From not far away comes the hum of a car's engine, the drag of tires on the clay road.

I don't say anything, but my hands close tighter around the bouquet I've been gathering—so tight, a thorn goes through the glove I'm wearing.

Deirdre's looking out past the Strait now. "It was as the pain was getting to its worst, before I saw Joseph for the first time. The scent of roses came in through the window . . . faint as faint. . . ." She stops for a second, like she's deciding whether or not to tell me the rest. That black-backed gull has hopped closer to us, along the fence. I can just see him out of the corner of my eye, so still now, you'd never know he'd moved. Deirdre goes on. "And there was something else, too. Music, really just a whisper, but it was music. I'd never heard anything like it before, so sweet sounding, but sad, too, the way the sound sort of swelled, then shrank away again, like someone trying to catch his breath . . . like . . . someone working himself up to . . ."

". . . to cry," I say, mostly to myself.

"Yes, yes, that's right. How'd you know?"

I just shake my head, but inside I'm trembling, sad for Deirdre but something else, too. I'm starting to figure something out, something about Gerry's song when I play it.

From across the field, the ticking of that car's engine comes nearer, though I can't see anything of it from where we are, not even a cloud of road dust. Joseph is still humming low—too low for a baby, I would have said—like the rumble of the waves below us. Deirdre goes on telling her story; her eyes are wide now, the mist in them gathering into tears. "The tune was gone even before the baby gave his first little cry, but something about that music helped me to . . . to . . . keep going, to bring Joseph into the world safe and . . . hey!"

There's a rustle past my face as that mottle-winged gull raises its fat self off the fence and lands right on the edge of Deirdre's basket of roses.

"Boy!" Joseph stops humming, looks up, and reaches out his hand to the silent staring creature, which is standing dead still again, and close enough to touch. I never realized how big that bird was until I saw it standing next to the baby. It looks as if it could carry him off if its beak were big enough. But Joseph doesn't look afraid, just curious. That's his daddy in him.

"Shoo. G'way, creature!" I wave my hand at it, but it stays put, staring at Joseph.

"'ook, Mama! Mama! Boy!" Joseph puts a hand right on the creature's wing, and it flinches not at all, even when Deirdre raises her voice.

"*Joseph!* . . . Don't touch that bird. It'll *bite* you!" Deirdre waves her arm at the gull, which lifts itself off the basket and back onto the fence, just as casually as can be.

Joseph is bawlin' to break my heart, "Boy!"

Deirdre sits down, puts her arms around the baby. "I'm sorry, sweetheart. I'm sorry." She buries her face in Joseph's curly hair, and that's when her tears, the ones that have been filling her eyes since she started talking about Gerry, finally start falling. As she sobs, shoulders heaving, up and down in a rhythm like the swells on the Strait, the idea comes clearer to me, the thing I've been trying to figure out. It's what Deirdre's been telling me about the tune she heard the morning Joseph was born, the same one I heard, the same one I saw Gerry's ghost playing right in front of me in this very garden. I know what's missing when I try to play Gerry's tune now. It's sorrow, like the fiddle itself is crying. . . . No . . . more like the fiddler's tears themselves are part of the tune, vibrating through the fiddle's strings like waves that ripple, then rumble, then crash on shore—Gerry's tears at not being with Deirdre, not ever being able to hold his son. Sorrow was what filled Gerry's tune and made it so beautiful. Without that real feeling, a song is empty, or worse, it's like the other night with Marina Shaw hidden in the shadows, singing her snare of a tune and sucking all the joy out of a room full of dancers. No one wants to dance to empty music. I'm close to tears myself, but I can't show them. I brush one away when Deirdre's back is turned.

On the fence, that gull isn't moving. The wind has died down, and Deirdre's sobs have, too. There's just that car now, coming closer along the swamp road.

Deirdre looks up at me, her tired, pretty face just as pale as a plaster angel's. Her voice is steady now, and her arms have loosened around Joseph, who is lying still with his head in her lap. "I'm just so tired, Beet. The way Joseph's been crying at night . . ."

I try to make like I haven't heard anything, but Joseph has been roarin' to scare the Devil every night this week. Deirdre just shakes her head.

"Don't tell me you haven't heard him, Beet. Everybody in the house has, and . . . and . . . last night it got worse. Last night he wouldn't let me put him to bed. He paced up and down in front of the bedroom window until he was so tired, he just lay on the floor and went to sleep. It was like he was searching for a way to climb out."

Deirdre looks down as she speaks to me, her hands smoothing the baby's sandy hair. The scent of all these roses is making me sleepy. "Your parents have been so good to me, letting us stay all these months, but I can't be here forever. Joseph and I are going to have to make our own way . . . soon . . . and what will that mean for him? That woman . . . that Marina Shaw . . . wants to take him with her. Maybe I'm being selfish, saying no. Think of the life he could have in Boston. . . . But, Beet, he's *my* baby. Mine and Gerry's. And besides, I don't trust her. Not just because she's rich and vain either. The first time I saw that woman, I felt . . . like I was losing my balance or something. . . . It's a good thing I was sitting, or . . . There's something *wrong* with her, Beet. She's . . ." Deirdre trails off here and bends down to kiss the side of Joseph's head. The breeze is starting up again, setting the rosebushes dancing.

This is the most I've heard Deirdre talk ever, and all I can think is, *I'm* not the only one. She didn't see Gerry that night, but she *heard*—and she knows there's something wrong about Marina Shaw. This isn't Jeannine, reading books and wanting to believe. I wonder, should I tell Deirdre that I recognize it, too, that off-balance drowning-in-an-undertow feeling? Should I tell her about the dance and Mr. Uist and the monster? About Gerry in the garden? At least I've had Jeannine to confide in all this time (nosy as she can be sometimes), but Deirdre's the one who's been raising this baby without his father, and who does she have to talk to? But if I tell Deirdre about Gerry, about all of it . . . I mean, won't she wonder why he didn't come to her? Why all she got for a goodbye was the smell of roses and the whisper of a tune? I take Joseph up in my arms a minute and breathe in his baby sweetness, like I did that first day after they found Gerry. When I put him down again, he gives me a big smile.

Deirdre and I look at each other for a moment, and it's on the tip of my tongue to tell her. Then, from across the garden comes a bellowing like a sick seal, the car's horn sounding from the end of our path. Joseph turns toward the house at the sound, then back, looking for that nuisance of a gull. "Boy? Wheya boy, Mama?"

Deirdre, wiping her tears on her apron, doesn't answer.

"I expect that's Jeannine," I say finally, leaning down to smell one last sweet yellow rose. Jeannine's staying over tonight while Mom and Dad are at the party. (She says I'll want the company, not that she asked.) I take one rose-filled basket by the handle, then the other. "Better go in. I'd say we've enough roses for ten ruby weddings."

Deirdre just nods and takes Joseph's other hand, as he waves over his shoulder at the gull resting still as a stuffed toy beneath a tangle of American Beauties. "Bye, boy!" Joseph calls. "Bye, boy. Bye!"

On the kitchen table, there's a tray of diamond-shaped scotch cakes and a set of green glass vases all ready for us to sort the roses in. A pot of tea is steeping on the table by the closed parlor door. Voices, slightly muffled, are coming from the other side. Through the window I can see the car we heard coming up the swamp road, and it's not one of Mr. Gallant's pieced-together rattletraps either, but that fancy black car that Freddy chauffeurs the Publicovers around in. No sign of Freddy, which makes another day he's been missing. I'm starting to worry about him, and Lily. Sean—pale, lanky, and dear as can be—is leaning on the car's hood and looking down at his shoes like they are a puzzle to be solved. Behind him the deep-blue Northumberland Strait is rising and falling in great swells.

There's a little flutter in my heart looking at Sean, I won't deny. I haven't shown anyone the picture, which is sitting in my top drawer right now, next to my socks. Today he's dressed in blue trousers and a clean white shirt with a tie, but his hair still looks like it never saw a comb or brush. I laugh about that to myself, and it's like he hears me because he looks up from his shoes right quick and squints into the window, then looks away when he sees me.

"Be back in a minute, Deirdre," I say. I leave her to the roses and step outside to say hello.

"Hey, Sean." I don't think I've ever said his name out loud before. It surprises me, the whispery sound of it. "Where's Freddy, anyway? No one's seen him since the dance."

Sean shakes his head. He looks about as happy as a wet cat. I guess I would, too, if I had to work for the Publicovers. Behind him, gulls are hovering above the Strait. Farther in the distance, a gannet soars and dives, bright white against the sky.

"What's wrong?" I ask. A gust of wind cuts through me. I should have kept on my sweater. "What are your aunts doing here? And why'd they put you in that getup?"

"Beet, I'm sorry . . ." His face is getting pink now, and I notice that his voice is shaking.

"For what?" Another gust of wind, and I hug myself to get warm.

"Marina . . . she . . ."

Before he can answer, there's a squeal of the screen door. "Beet." Deirdre is standing in the doorway, holding Joseph. "Your mom wants you. Bring Sean, too."

Inside, Mom's "I'm just being polite" voice is getting louder as her footsteps come nearer the kitchen. They are followed by a high-pitched little girl squeak, and another quite the same—the Publicovers—and a fourth voice, too, dull and flat.

Mom steps into the room and lifts the steeping teapot off its trivet. "Deirdre . . . Beet . . . Sean . . . quick, you three. Someone pick up that tray of cookies and bring them to the parlor." The stiff lines round Mom's mouth say not to argue. I grab the tray and follow her into the parlor, with Deirdre and Sean behind me carrying the scotch cakes. In the corner of the room, where just a few weeks ago dead Sarah's coffin sat beneath the shelf of pink lusterware teacups, Marina Shaw half reclines in our best green brocade chair. She's wearing a gray blouse of layered chiffon, beaded at the neckline in dark blue, and loose blue trousers. The look on her face is as smooth and serene as the Strait after a storm, her green eyes glittering like the water's surface. The smell of the Publicovers today is cookie crumbs and lavender perfume. They sit at the very edge of the couch in green-striped shift dresses, their legs wrapped tightly in tan-colored stockings. Each sister holds a teacup in her right hand, a fistful of Mom's Queen Elizabeth cake in the left. Marina Shaw's hands are empty, though, folded over each other in her lap. The undertow feeling is gone for once; the anger I'm feeling, just looking at her, doesn't leave much room for anything else.

"Hello." She looks up, her smile a thin curve. "I'm pleased to see you girls again." The Publicovers just keep nibbling, dropping crumbs and raisins for Mom to clean up later.

Tight-faced, Mom pours tea into the Publicovers' cups while Marina Shaw waves her away with the flick of a hand, like a servant. Whatever Mom feels about that, she doesn't show it. I hand her the plate of cookies, and she places them next to the Queen Elizabeth cake, already half gone. "Beatrice, I wish you'd told me about your visit to Miss Shaw's home." I look at Deirdre, standing in the doorway, pale and shaky, holding tightly to Joseph's hand. He's struggling to make her let go, his eyes on Marina Shaw the whole time. Sean finds a spot by the window but not before tripping over a footstool. I try to catch his eye, to smile, but he's looking down at his shoes again.

"We certainly would have reciprocated before now, Miss Shaw," Mom goes on, all smiles and apologies. "I mean had I—"

"Oh, we had a lovely visit," Marina Shaw cuts her off, then looks straight at me for the first time since I met her. The glittering eyes harden just slightly, for me alone to see, and for a second I do feel the undertow again, only a second, though. "Beatrice, I hear you're quite a violinist. Mr. Uist says he enjoyed his time at the party the other night."

"Ah, Mr. Uist." Mom offers Nora Publicover a scotch cake, just as she grabs for it, then gives me a hard look. "We were so glad to see that Beet was mistaken about his disappearance."

"You're quite a singer yourself," I say, ignoring Mom. Joseph has squirmed out of his mother's grip and is tiptoeing toward Marina, sneaking up on her almost.

"Really." Marina Shaw's flat voice doesn't alter, but the edges of her mouth twitch upward. "When would you have heard me sing?" Not waiting for my answer, she turns to Deirdre. "My dear, you must not have told Mrs. MacNeill about my offer." Marina puts a long, white, red-tipped hand in Joseph's curls, drawing him toward her. A little gasp escapes me, but I cough to cover it up.

Deirdre answers "No" as if she's gasping the word.

"That's all right." Marina Shaw's fishhook smile twitches again slightly. "We've just been discussing it." A gust of wind lifts the parlor curtains, filling the room with the smell of salt and roses.

"Now, Sheila." Nora Publicover opens her mouth, a currant stuck to her teeth from the Queen Elizabeth cake. "Surely you can convince Deirdre. It's such a grand opportunity, living in Boston."

"You know, Sister and I lived in Boston." Suddenly Louise Publicover is pronouncing the word "*Baw*-stin," and dropping her r's like she's the Queen of Beacon Hill. "We spent a season at the *Pah-kah* House with *ow-ah* Uncle *Mahk* Publicov*ah*, and . . ."

"Sean loves it there," Nora Publicover adds. "Don't you, Sean?"

Sean doesn't look up, let alone look at me, but he says "yes." I spare a thought to wonder what's gotten into him, but what's going on in front of me is much more important.

Nora goes on through a mouthful of cookie, "And Sean's *fahthah* owns a house on Nantucket . . ."

"Where the best people *summah*," Louise puts in, and I'm about to find her r's for her with my fingernails.

"Yes, the very best people. Sean can't wait to go back, can you, Sean?" She stares at him until he answers.

"It's nice here, too, though." His voice is weak, but he finally looks at me, like he's begging for help or something. This is what he was trying to tell me before, that they were going to do this. Now it's me who can't look at him.

"I have to check the car," he says quietly, then he's gone like a ghost from the room.

Deirdre has been quiet all this time, and when she speaks, her voice lifts and flutters like the white curtains a moment ago, but there's strength in it still. "I don't want to give up Joseph." For a second or two, the room around her is quiet. Even the Publicovers have stopped chewing.

"Why of course not, dear," Marina Shaw says slowly, her hook of a smile widening until it almost seems real (almost, except for the eyes). "I'm sorry if you didn't understand me the other day. My plan is to take both of you with me to Massachusetts, you . . . and the boy."

"That's not what you . . ." Deirdre's voice trails off to a whisper.

"Well, now." Mom pours Louise Publicover a third cup of tea, slow and careful. "That's quite the offer." The parlor curtains start dancing again in the rising wind.

I look at Marina Shaw's beautiful, stony face, and I just boil over.

"Deirdre doesn't want to go to Massachusetts with you." I take a step toward Joseph, reaching for him. "Joseph, baby, come away from Miss Shaw."

Deirdre's brown eyes cast me a grateful look, but Mom's voice is careful, quiet, sharp as a lady's hatpin. "Beatrice . . . don't be bold."

I take another step and lift Joseph away from Marina Shaw, her hands still tangled in his hair like seaweed. "Ow! Hurt head!" Joseph cries out before she lets go, and the fact that I caused him pain only makes me madder.

"Beatrice Mary!" Mom gasps.

I glare right at Marina Shaw, her slippery smile, her cruel green eyes.

"Deirdre doesn't want to go to Massachusetts with you, and she doesn't . . ." I can feel my voice rising and I hate it.

"Beet!" There's a warning in Mom's voice, but I don't care. I hug Joseph to me while he struggles. Louise and Nora Publicover look scandalized enough to maybe stop stuffing their tiny round faces, at least for a second.

"Well, she doesn't," I say angrily to Mom, then turn back to Marina. "And she doesn't want to give up Joseph either. She told you that already. So leave us alone."

Mom goes quiet and calm again, but underneath she's as hard and snarly as a caged mink. If possible, her eyes are colder than Marina's. "Beatrice, please bring the baby upstairs so the adults can talk."

"You mean talk about sending Deirdre away!" I'm almost yelling now. "I won't . . . I won't . . . You just . . ." But what can I say about Marina Shaw that anyone would believe?

"Go to your room, Beet." Mom's voice is only slightly raised, but it has something in it that you can't say no to. Even the Publicovers are so nervous that they bend down and start picking up the crumbs they dropped. Marina Shaw looks satisfied. I stare at Mom with all the anger I have, but she just says one word. "Now."

I don't know what else to say, and I don't want them to see me cry. So I pick up Joseph and stomp out of the room, catching Deirdre's scared, grateful eye as I go. Behind me, Mom is apologizing for my rudeness.

In the kitchen, Sean is standing by the screen door, like he's been waiting.

I wrap my arms around Joseph. (They'll have to pry him away from me.) "I thought you had to see to the car." I say it slow and mean. I know it's mean because I can feel it in my face, which is getting tighter by the minute, like Mom's face in the parlor just now. Sean doesn't back away as I get close enough to him to whisper.

"You knew she was going to be here. You let us walk in there, you let Deirdre walk in there."

"I tried to tell you . . ." And he's right, but I don't care.

"Your family wants to help her take Joseph away. To Boston! And you agreed with them. How could I have trusted you?" It's hard to keep my voice quiet when all I want to do is yell, but I manage it. "And I thought . . ." I just trail off. What did I think? I'm not sure. It's not like I know Sean really, not like we're friends, even though . . . But it doesn't matter now. Only Joseph matters.

Sean looks as if I just slapped him, and believe me, I sure would like to.

"Beet, my aunts are only trying to help. . . ." He backs out the screen door and I follow him outside. The door slams behind me, which Mom will hate, but I'm glad because I hate everything right now. It's gotten even cooler outside. The sky is slate and there isn't a bird in sight.

"Help what? Help steal my baby cousin?" I hold Joseph even closer and he grabs my hair, tangling it in his little fists. I kiss his head, breathe him in for calm.

"No! Just . . . help give him a better life. . . . Him and Deirdre . . ." He looks as if he knows he shouldn't have said that. "I mean . . ."

"What's wrong with life here?" Now it's my throat that's getting tight. I can hear the angry squeak in my voice.

"Nothing . . . I . . ." He stops still and takes a long breath.

My mouth is so hard now, I'm surprised I can get words out at all. But I do, slow and sharp as cutting paper. "Look, I'm sorry we're not good enough for your prissy Boston ways. But I'd take living here with my family over living with Marina Shaw . . . or anywhere near you!"

I turn to go inside, and Sean puts a hand out like he's going to try to stop me. I slap him back with a look.

"I just mean . . ."

"You just mean you're better than us!" And I can feel the tears starting again, but I fight them. I turn myself to stone.

"Listen, Beet, please. I need to tell you what I saw. . . . I have something for you. . . ."

"I don't care what you saw." I say it slow, so he can hear me. "And I don't want anything from you." I push past him and swing open the kitchen door, then let it slam behind me again.

Heading upstairs with Joseph, I catch a glimpse of the minister gull, peering in through the open window on the landing.

CHAPTER EIGHTEEN

June 20, 1950

Beet MacNeill

Mama!" Joseph is yelling. "Want go Mama!"

My window looks out over the back garden, then east toward the Strait. Outside, clouds are starting to throw shadows over the bright red and green of the potato fields, the rolling gray water. The Poxy Island channel marker is clanging in the distance, slow as church bells, in time with the movement of the waves. I've got the fiddle out, trying a few tunes to soothe Joseph, and to get my mind off what's going on downstairs (what with Mom getting ready to hand Deirdre and Joseph over to that Marina Shaw, either that or to put them out in the road). Joseph doesn't care for "Maiden's Prayer" or "My Blue Heaven" either. All he does is pull at my leg and holler for Deirdre.

"Oh, for God's sake, Joseph. Could you sit still?" I'm sorry right away for being sharp with him, but we've been up in my room for about a half hour, and I've had to sit in a chair against the bedroom door to keep him from opening it and going head-first downstairs.

"Want go *Mama*!" Joseph tries to dig his little nails into my bare knee, but they don't do much damage. Now he wraps his arms around my leg, squeezing tight as a noose. I draw the bow across the high strings in a long squeal and start my version of Gerry's tune from the rose garden. Joseph loosens his grip, then lets go and covers his ears.

I just wince. On my bureau, next to the picture of me and Gerry, is the drawing Sean did of me. I took it out meaning to tear it up, but I just couldn't do it. I look at the image of myself playing and try the tune again, keeping an eye on Joseph.

It's supposed to have a sound like someone weeping. Deirdre talked about it that way, and I heard it, too. But this sounds more like those poor drowning rodents that Jeannine mentioned. So, how do I copy what I really heard? How to learn a melody played by a ghost? I let the bow quiver a bit along the strings to see if the note rings closer to true. Joseph is crying again now, and I'm starting to wonder. Maybe the sound didn't come from Gerry's fiddle at all. Maybe it was something his fiddle called up, out of the air, or . . . out of wherever it is that dead people go. Heaven? Hell? Gerry's tune didn't sound like it came from either place, not from what I've heard at Mass anyway.

I try to think about weeping. What does it sound like? Then I look down at Joseph, my sweet baby cousin who I love so much. Tears are running down his face, and his shoulders are shaking up and down like waves. "Mama!" he cries, gasping, like he can't catch his breath, like he's drowning. "Mama, Mama, mama-a-a-a-a!" The sound of his sobs comes in waves, too. Waves. I try to imitate it with the fiddle. Up and down the scale slowly, letting each note drop lower and come back up loud as I play the tune. Outside, the air is still calm but the swells on the Strait are getting higher, the sign of a storm on its way. Gulls ride the water as it rolls slowly toward shore. I try to fit my tune to that rhythm, billows rising and falling like sobs, or deep gasping breaths. Tears, the sea, all rolling movement and salt water. It's what we are made of—water, I mean. At least partly. I learned that in school. That part matters somehow. Somehow it all goes together; I'm starting to hear it, the way the tune sounded. Joseph takes his hands off his ears and looks up at me. His face is still, fixed on the music. The tears keep coming but he's not hollering for Deirdre anymore.

"We've almost got it," I say to him, but I don't stop playing. The notes are lower than I thought they'd be. This is as close to Gerry's tune as I've gotten yet. The rightness of it tingles in my hands, and then . . .

"Beet." It is Mom's voice from behind the door. I let the tune fade away; for a moment everything is quiet, and I feel the tears on my own face like a surprise.

"Beet," she says again, "please come downstairs." She doesn't sound angry at all. I thought she would, after the way I talked to her before.

"Coming." I hear her footsteps walking away, and I put the fiddle to rest in its case on the bed. Joseph is still sitting on the braided rug, his grave little face streaked with tears. "Come on, darlin'." I reach out my hand; he takes it and stands up to follow me.

When I come downstairs, Deirdre is sitting forward on the yellow chair dragged in from the kitchen, a cup of tea beside her on the end table. There aren't any tears in her eyes. She pushes the cup away from her as Joseph climbs into her lap and rests his head on her shoulder. From the kitchen, the strong, sweet smell of the baskets full of roses warms up the room like a greenhouse. Marina Shaw is still there, seated beneath the shelf of teacups. She has the same haughty expression on her face, but she looks different, too, paler (if that's possible) and for some reason she is sitting on the very edge of the brocade chair, like she's ready to get up and run. I look around for Sean, despite myself. He's nowhere to be seen.

"Beet," Mom says. She's pouring the Publicovers more tea as they gobble up a plateful of molasses cookies. "Beet, are you ready to apologize?"

I speak to the Publicovers first, as sincerely as I can. "I'm sorry for losing my temper."

They nod, just barely, and go back to the cookies.

Mom gives me a look. "And to Miss Shaw . . ." My heart hardens inside me, but I do what I'm told.

"Sorry . . . *Miss* Shaw." Her name tastes like poison in my mouth. I can feel my upper lip pulling back from my teeth, stiff with a fake smile. A funny little gust of wind rattles the window out of nowhere.

Marina Shaw just nods her head, not even looking at me, looking anywhere *but* at me, in fact. When she stands, the Publicover sisters pop up like jack-in-the-boxes, jostling the table and Mom's blue-and-white cups. "Mrs. MacNeill," she says, her narrowed green eyes still avoiding me, "thank you for the tea." Even though it doesn't look as if she drank any. Marina Shaw nods to Deirdre, who's still holding Joseph in her arms, then floats toward the parlor door without a second look at her. The Publicovers scurry behind like little gray mice.

Just before leaving, Marina Shaw turns toward me and gives me a long, long stare. I will myself not to feel the undertow. Then Mom sees them to the front door. She always walks people out, to be polite.

Now I'm angry as a bear in a trap—because I've lost the tune again. I was so close, and I've lost it. And because of Mom, too. She's just going to let Deirdre and Joseph go away . . . with *Marina Shaw*. Mom doesn't want them here; she never did, and now's her chance to get rid of them. I'm shivering I'm so mad. Outside the kitchen window, the wind is moving through the stand of poplars that shades the house, without sound, making the leaves shiver, too. The Publicovers' car starts up and purrs away down our track. When the sound of its engine is no more than a sigh, Mom comes back into the parlor, her face stiff as a new hat.

"Beatrice Mary, don't you ever talk to me like that in front of company. Is that clear?" I give her the look I'm used to seeing from her, but I don't say a word. Then, out of nowhere, Mom walks up to Deirdre, throws her arms around her, and hugs her to break her in half. Caught between them, Joseph lets out a little struggling squeal. He'd suffocate if Mom weren't so small, but she lets go, and I'd swear there are tears in her eyes.

"Good for you, Deirdre," Mom cries. "Good for you, you brave girl!"

Through the door to the kitchen, I can see the roses standing tall in their baskets. The channel marker clangs in the distance. Mom is beaming at Deirdre, shedding tears I haven't seen since Gerry died. I shake my head. "What just happened?"

"Marina Shaw and her greedy little hangers-on spent the last half hour trying to convince our Deirdre to take Joseph and move to Boston. Deirdre said no, of course." Mom beams at Deirdre again, prouder than if she just won the rose show. "And don't you worry. That whitewashed Bostonian isn't taking Joseph anywhere. This is his home." She looks into Deirdre's face, which has started to tear up. "And yours, too, Deirdre. You can stay as long as you want."

Mom sure can surprise a person. I can't help but smile from the relief. She's got something else to say, too. I can tell by looking at her.

"Sit down, Beet," Mom says. She hands me a plate with two of the ginger snaps she was making for the ruby wedding party, pours a cup of milk, and sits down in the chair closest to the window. Joseph's head rests on his mother's shoulder. Mom looks at him, an almost-smile on her face. Behind her, through the window, the rosebushes are moving in the breeze.

"We asked Sarah to come stay with us," Mom began. "After my poor brother was drowned, your father and I invited her to stay here while she waited for Gerry to be born—so she wouldn't have to be alone. She said no to us, though, and stayed out alone at Poxy Point until it was her time. Then she sent for a doctor from over in Charlottetown to come all the way out here, and she paid a night nurse to take care of her and the baby after the delivery. None of us saw Gerry for the first few weeks of his life, not even the priest to have him baptized.

"Then one day Sarah walked here from Poxy Point and just left him. I saw his carriage sitting at the end of our track when I was out hanging laundry. Who knows how long he'd been there. There was no note. She just left him in his diaper, covered in a flannel blanket. Gerry cried and cried the first few weeks we had him, but I didn't mind, not for my sake anyway. Your father and I had just gotten married and we wanted a baby so badly. I held Gerry every night and sang to him. Your father did, too, in the mornings before he went out to the fields and last thing before he went to bed at night. He told Gerry stories, even though he was too little to understand them. I made him formula from corn syrup and canned milk, like I had learned in my nursing course before marrying your father. After a few weeks, Gerry stopped crying so much. He'd smile when your father sang to him, or when I carried him over to the garden window to look at the goldfinches in the feeder or at the gulls and gannets diving into the Strait. His first word was 'bird.' We watched him learn to pull himself up in his crib, to walk and talk. His second word was 'Mama.' He called *me* 'Mama.'"

Mom chokes back a sob here, but she keeps going.

"When Gerry was just under a year old, your father and I had him baptized at St. Peter's. We wouldn't have waited so long, but we kept expecting Sarah to come back. Then she *did* come back, about six months after the baptism. She'd been off in Boston, never explained why. She just rode up in the Publicovers' car looking trim and pretty. More than pretty, she was radiant—her skin bright and fresh as a sixteen-year-old girl's—in her new Boston clothes, and wanting Gerry back, like she deserved him. Your father flat out refused her, but I differed with him. I'd been helping at births since I was your age; I saw how hard it is to carry a baby, wonderful but hard, too. It gives some women the melancholies, and Sarah had lost her husband, after all, *my* brother. More important, she was Gerry's real mother. A child should be with his real mother.

"That's what I told your father anyway; that's what I told myself, to make it easier to give Gerry back. Fool that I was, I wish I hadn't. I wish I'd fought for him. Maybe he'd be alive today."

The whole time Mom's been talking, the tears have been running down her face. She hasn't brushed them away; she just lets them fall. Now she takes her rose-embroidered handkerchief from the pocket of her apron, dabs the tears away, and looks at me hard. In the Strait, the clanging of the channel marker has gotten faster and louder. Joseph is fast asleep on his mother's lap, snoring like a little old man.

"It didn't take us long to realize the mistake we'd made—since that baby got no more love from his mother than she'd show a codfish—but we tried to soften things for him as best we could. Gerry was over here practically every day once he was old enough to find his way alone. Your dad's the one who taught Gerry how to play that fiddle, Beatrice, just like he taught you. You know that. Still, if we'd kept him with us . . ." Mom strokes Joseph's curls. "So don't you worry, Deirdre. Don't you worry at all."

None of us say anything for a long moment. The outside air is filled with the sound of gulls now, on top of the clanging of the channel marker.

Deirdre gets up, taking sleeping Joseph in her arms. "Well, this little fella needs a bed," she says, and carries him from the room as gentle as can be.

I'm about to follow, back up to my fiddle, when Mom puts a hand on my arm. There's a thick brown envelope on the table and she hands it to me. "Sean MacInnes left this for you."

When I try to say I don't want it, she looks me in the eye with her regular hard stare, like she never said all those kind things: "Beatrice Mary, the Publicovers are foolish but they are not evil, and that boy hasn't done anything but be helpful to you. He needs a friend." She pushes the envelope into my hand just as a car door slams outside.

Before I can say anything else, Mom gets up, straightens her apron, and starts to clear the tea things, and you'd think she didn't just tell us her most important secret. Then comes the creak of the screen door and Dad appears carrying a stack of library books. He's grinning.

"Look what I picked up on the road."

I can hear Jeannine's voice before I see her. "Lord, it's half windy out! Dust flying everywhere. I almost had to walk all the way from town but your dad . . ." She steps into the kitchen and stops, looking about the room like a deer looks around an empty field. "What's going on? What did I miss?"

CHAPTER NINETEEN

October 5, 1851

Father Ray Parent

Bodies litter the beach at Emil Cove, twenty of them at least, with more floating facedown in the water, clothes sodden and torn, some missing fingers from where the fish have started to nip at them, others with parts of their faces gone, the tips of their noses, their eyes. The surf is high, bringing in more wreckage as it rolls in wave by wave. As the bells ring from the Church of Our Lady Star of the Sea, five times for five o'clock in afternoon, the sun is already almost down. Two miles across narrow St. Emil Bay, a lighthouse flashes beneath a sky of blood-tinted cream.

Father Ray Parent, the young pastor of Star of the Sea, picks his way through the wreckage that lines the beach. The mast and torn sail stick out of the flat sand like Christ's cross, and lying in that same sand is the gold-painted figurehead of an eagle that identifies the ship as the *Robert Burns*, out of Dennis, Massachusetts. The vessel was brought in a wreck last night, all hands lost, along with three members of a New Brunswick ship called the *Loyalist*, now swamped on a sandbar, its hold full of rotting fish. The storm came out of a clear night sky, say the survivors of the *Loyalist*, occurring mostly out in the gulf, battering the *Robert Burns* to pieces. There is almost no sign of the storm here at Emil Cove, only the leftover wind, finally dying down, the broken bodies of the dead, and the *Loyalist* foundering offshore. Emil Cove, an Acadian community, remains largely isolated by language and faith from the far-flung surrounding villages on this part of the Island, but Father Ray has lived in Halifax and his English is good. He walks around translating for the dazed and bruised survivors of the *Loyalist* as the villagers of Emil Cove take them ashore in rowboats. He also stops to minister to the dead of the *Robert Burns*.

Father Ray covers his mouth to hide a yawn. He has had little sleep. Last night, before the storm that never reached shore, he thought he heard someone singing from far across the harbor, near Port Christine. The sound traveled across the bay in ghostly bursts as the wind rose, then fell and changed direction with the tide. It was a sound he still cannot get out of his mind, not because it was beautiful, though it did have a sort of cold beauty to it, pitch-perfect and as falsely intimate as some of the confessions he has heard. Father Ray could hear beneath the song the sound of someone who wanted something from him, and would whine and wheedle to get it—like the voice the

Devil was supposed to use when he whispered temptations into your ears.

For a brief moment, with the wind in just the right direction, the emptiness of the world was made clear to Father Ray by that music, so clear that he had almost followed its echo into sea. Only the distance to the water had stopped him, and the fact that the song was not directed at him—somehow he knew that. The feeling dissipated as the bells of Star of the Sea rang three in the morning, and Father Ray felt he had passed some sort of test; he was relieved, though he did not get back to sleep that night. Later the bells rang again, this time clanging in alarm, as the wreckage of the *Loyalist* and *Robert Burns* began to be sighted by fishermen up early to get out to the grounds.

On the hard sand beside the broken mast lies the body of George Bixby. One of the survivors of the *Loyalist* has recognized him from the newspaper. He is an Islander who has been living in America, in Boston, working for the shipping company, traveling back and forth between Boston and the Island on business. George Bixby was lashed to the mast with a young woman of about twenty-five, but now both are cut loose and sprawled on the sand. Bixby has lost his shoes and the flesh is mostly gone from his feet below the ragged cuffs of his pant legs. Father Ray stares down at the corpse, nearly cut in half by the rope, its fists clenched and full of seaweed, along with strands of something long and coarse and silver white. Even in death it is clear that George Bixby was a handsome man. His gray hair, now matted to his only slightly swollen face, had been full and longish. His eyes, still open, may have been blue. The lines in his face show him to be in his late fifties.

The woman next to him is much younger and, unlike Bixby, looks as though the fish have barely touched her. Only her pallor and the fact that she is not moving, not breathing, would give the impression that she is anything but asleep. She is wearing a green dress, soaking wet and heavy. Her long blond hair is tangled with seaweed, her eyes closed. Around her neck, a silver chain glints in the late afternoon sunlight and long shadows. There is some kind of pendant hanging from it. Father Ray kneels beside her and briefly imagines he sees the pendant rise and fall slightly as the pale skin of her chest rises and falls. It is a seashell, curled and spiked. The song comes back to him now, as he looks at George Bixby, and with it a bewildering loss of balance, a dizziness that passes as quickly as it comes.

Father Ray also serves the nearby Mi'kmaw village, and many of those parishioners have come out to help clear the beach and tend to the bodies. One of them, Mickey Bernard, is calling to him now.

"Father!" Mickey's face is half hope, half agitation as he picks his way through bodies and broken barrels of fish and other cargo. "Quick, Father, we need your help!" When Father Ray turns back to the woman, he realizes that what he thought he saw was an illusion. She is not breathing.

Father Ray spies a dark-haired young man wandering nearby, looking pale and perhaps confused. His clothes are wet and covered in red sand, but otherwise he appears unharmed. Mickey gestures to Father Ray to follow him.

"Attendez," Father Ray says to the pale young man, then realizing his mistake, repeats in English, "Wait."

The young man slowly raises his head, and Father Ray can't help noticing how black his eyes are, almost all pupil. The priest speaks slowly. "Stay here, sit, and someone will get you a blanket and some food."

The young man nods, and Father Ray whispers a prayer over the unknown woman and the body of George Bixby, then follows Mickey around a rocky outcrop. In the shelter of an overhanging cliff, pocked with holes for swallows' nests, are more bodies than the priest had thought possible. He helps to separate bodies from cargo from wreckage, to make an accounting, and it is a while before he again thinks of George Bixby or his companion. Only when the doctor from Cavendish comes to relieve Father Ray does he remember the poor confused young man, but when the priest returns to where he left the bodies, the man is gone, as is the body of Bixby's companion. Only the battered corpse of George Bixby remains, and beside it a woman's small narrow footprints, leading away from the body and into the sea. There is another set of prints as well, not footprints but hoofprints. Father Ray looks out into the becalmed sea, past the wreckage of the *Robert Burns*, as a feeling of vertigo washes through him.

CHAPTER TWENTY

October 5, 1851

Tam Gray

The North Shore of Prince Edward Island is filled with high, pink dunes, covered in sharp-edged ribbons of broad grass that can cut the soles of bare feet. When the sun sets over the Gulf of Saint Lawrence, the whole world seems lit by distant fire. Pink dunes, red sky, water sparkling orange gold beyond. Tam Gray is walking in such a world the evening after what will soon be known as the Yankee Gale. Two ships cast up at Emil Cove alone, with others wrecked on beaches all along the North Shore. Tam got in with a rescue party at Emil Cove, where the gnawed and twisted bodies of the dead drifted amid salvage of every kind. Plenty of salvage, plenty for Tam to steal.

The largest ship, called the *Robert Burns*, had a full hold, with stores from down in Jamaica—rum, molasses, and strange, colorful fruit. Tam had no use for any of that, except maybe the rum, but there was money, too, good gold and silver coin, and he could always use money. The cache was in the captain's quarters, where such things were always kept. Tam went there directly while the others, would-be rescuers, took down the bodies and searched the lower decks in futile hope of finding someone alive. Tam placed the ship's two strongboxes in a sack he had brought for the purpose, and then he slipped off the ship in the early morning confusion, past the bodies laid out on the hard sand. He'd seen the young priest from the French church walking head-down among the dead. The father had raised his head for a moment as the church's bells had rung but was called away before fixing his eyes on Tam. That had been close. The priest probably would have taken the money for the church, or more likely for himself.

Now Tam carries the heavy sack slowly along the dune trail, a hollow of pink sand that leads back to his shack in the dark wood that separates the dunes from the farmlands. It is all spruce along the edges, but farther in grow the old trees, hemlock and beech and sugar maple. The forest is too dark to wander through unless you are up to no good—the perfect place for a family like the Grays. Tam has a still in the woods that Papa set up, and some other kinds of operations running, too. Tam comes from a family that has made their living on thievery and illegal doings. He has been on his own since he was sixteen, when Papa went to jail for the second time. Mama ran off not long after, and Tam's three sisters have all made their way to Toronto to work (if that's what you want to call what they do). He knows what he could do with this money, however much it turns out to be. He can start again, fresh, buy a farm or start a store in some village where they do not know him. A nice farm set back from the water, and if there happens to be a view of incoming ships and a cellar for a still, all the better.

Walking barefoot, Tam passes the edge of the pond, what the French call a barachois. The dune rises on his right, its high reeds cutting at his ankles. Mosquitoes are everywhere in little clouds around his head and rising along the edge of the barachois to his left. He is tired, and the sack is starting to feel too heavy. He rigs up a way to drag the sack behind him in the sand. The sky above him is going from red to violet as the sun sinks behind the dunes. From where he is, he cannot see the ocean but he can smell it, especially when the breeze blows, as it does only occasionally—salt and seaweed and a hint of the cabbage-y organic smell of rotting bodies—the bodies he left at the wreck. Behind him, the distant evening chorus of crows and gulls surrounds the unseen wrecked ships, like an endless quarrel. For a moment, underneath it, he thinks he hears a woman singing, but the wind shifts and the sound goes away.

Ahead of him is only the violet sky above the bending dune trail. Tam trudges it with increasing difficulty. A fox crosses his path but does not stop. With the wind, the sound of singing comes again briefly. Tam starts to plan what to do with the money. It keeps his mind off the weight of the sack, and the sudden uneasiness in his stomach. He looks down to yank up his trousers. When he looks up there is a horse standing in front of him.

Not just any horse—this beautiful, shadowy creature is a purplish gray, like the sky itself, with black eyes that seem to flash with the sun's last rays. The horse does not move at all, and Tam wonders how it could have stepped into the path without him hearing it. That thought does not last long, because what he sees next makes him forget everything else, even his dreams of gold.

To call her a woman would be like calling an angel a bird. She steps out from the reeds and stands as still as the horse, the only movement her hand reaching for the gleaming silver bridle. Her hair is soft blond and falls to her waist unpinned, something Tam has never seen. Her feet are shoeless and white. Her green silk dress is shot with silver thread, and a silver seashell pendant hangs from a chain at her throat. Tam can tell her shoulders are bare beneath her blue shawl.

She does not speak. The sky is turning darker and the breeze has ceased. Looking at her makes Tam dizzy, as if he has stood up quickly after sitting on his heels for a long time. It also makes him think, If I could have this woman, I would never steal again. What he does not think is, What is she doing on the dunes at evening? Her appearance just seems meant for him, like the storm and the two strongboxes in the captain's quarters of the *Robert Burns*.

"M-Miss, may I help you?" he asks haltingly.

She does not answer. Perhaps she has no English.

"B-Bonsoir, Mademoiselle?" He gets the words out but then

has to gasp for breath as if he is sinking underwater. He does not stop looking at her.

"I'm . . . Catherine." She says this slowly in a voice as flat as the air, and unsmiling, but the way Tam's stomach dances on hearing her, she might as well have kissed him on the lips.

"Catherine," he repeats. She turns, and the horse follows, toward Tam's shack. Tam follows, too. If there is something in his mind, telling him to stop, to wait, he does not listen.

The sky is indigo now. A gull flies above him. The smell of cabbage is slightly stronger. The woman starts to sing, the wind rises briefly, and Tam walks faster.

CHAPTER TWENTY-ONE

June 20, 1950

Beet MacNeill

Hey, Beet . . ."

Somewhere out beyond the shadow of Nova Scotia, music is playing. Just on the edge of my hearing, beneath the sound of gentle surf and faraway gulls. It's Gerry's tune. I'm listening hard for it, tapping my foot slowly, as out my window, the pearly evening sky melts into the slow-moving Strait. Then Jeannine's voice breaks through again, imitating my mother.

"Be-a-trice. Can you hear me?"

Jeannine has a book open in front of her and is grinning at me like she just got the right answer in school. Mom and Dad left for Rollo Bay not two hours ago, and Jeannine's been sprawled out on the bed ever since, looking at library books and muttering to herself about monsters. Now she shows me a book with a ripped tartan cover, with *Folktales of the Highlands and Islands* printed in gold lettering. It's open to a picture of a horse with blue-white teeth like frost. The horse stands on its hind legs, a man's legs, with its front hooves pointing upward. Underneath the picture is a caption: "The kelpie in transformation."

"This is what you saw in the river, isn't it?" she asks.

I shake my head. "Not that." But then my eye flicks to the picture on the opposite page, a monster with red bulging eyes, raising its long scaly head just above the surface of the water. The creature has a mane like a tangle of dirty seaweed. My heart almost stops. "But this one, yes." Outside, Gerry's tune is still playing, but getting fainter all the time.

Jeannine rolls her eyes like she's talking to a four-year-old. "They're the same thing, Beet, just different forms. Listen."

She reads the text to the left of the picture: "'The kelpie is a beast that haunts the streams and rivers of Scotland, mostly in the guise of an elegant horse, sometimes as a handsome young man. Legend says that should anyone try to mount the horse, that person will become immediately stuck to its wet mane and be dragged under the water. There, the creature transforms again into a vicious monster that devours . . .'" Jeannine trails off for a moment, her eyes still on the page. "Oh, yuck! There's a story in here about a kid who escaped by cutting off his own fingers!"

The music outside fades in and out while's she's talking. "That's all well and good," I say. "But first of all, this isn't Scotland. And second, it's not like I actually saw Mr. Uist turn into a monster. There was just Mr. Uist, and then there was this . . . thing." Still, as I'm looking at the picture, I'm wondering.

Jeannine pushes the book aside and sits up, swinging her legs over the side of the bed. "Come on, Beet, just because you didn't see it actually happen . . . Plus, we know the monster didn't drag him underwater or anything, because he was at the dance, and Marina was controlling him. She called to him, just like she . . ."

". . . called to that horse on the beach . . ."

Before I can finish my thought, Deirdre opens the door. Joseph is snuggling on her hip with his head nestled against her shoulder, his eyes half open, smiling. A bit of Gerry's tune reaches me from the open window, then dies away to almost nothing again.

"You left this downstairs." She hands me Sean's envelope, then holds out Joseph so I can give him a kiss.

"Good night, Beet," Deirdre says, stroking the baby's hair. "Good night, Jeannine."

"Good night," Jeannine says, all sprightly, but she closes the book in front of her with a snap. (As if anyone would think it was weird for Jeannine to be reading a book with a monster in it.)

Deirdre smiles. "This is the quietest he's been in weeks. Maybe he was picking up my worries all along. Knowing your mother wants us to stay means so much."

"Maybe." I smile as she turns and closes the door. I wish I could say she's right, or take comfort as well, but Mr. Uist is still out there, and Marina Shaw has some kind of power over him, over *it*, if I believe Jeannine and her library books—which I'm starting to. I take Sean's envelope and put it in my fiddle case.

"What's that?" Jeannine wants to know.

"Nothing," I say, probably too quick. What I don't need right now is Jeannine pestering me about Sean MacInnes. I know I was mean to him, but I'm mad, too, and I don't want to talk about why. Whatever's in the envelope, I'll look at it later. "A letter from my aunt."

Jeannine narrows her eyes, all nosy and suspicious, but for once she lets it go.

Out the window, the water and sky have turned the color of copper, and the sound of gulls has gotten closer. I listen for Gerry's tune again, but it's gone.

Later, I'm lying on my bedroom floor, dreaming of a whirlpool—blue, almost black water spinning and spinning inward, in time to the sound of a woman's voice. It's Marina Shaw, singing that same odd melody that pulled Mr. Uist to her in the Cozy Hall, only this time the tempo is more like some crazy kind of a reel, sung faster and faster as the water spirals with it. Above the whirlpool, gulls are hovering, beating their wings to keep from being sucked into the water. Some are not strong enough and get pulled in, mewing like kittens drowning in a sack. Then I recognize the crooked-beaked minister gull. He's squawking loud as a brass band, beating his wings high above the water. The whirlpool disappears, and all I see is black, but the gull is still crying and Marina's Shaw's strange music, though fainter, keeps going, too. It takes me a few seconds to realize I'm awake, but when I do open my eyes, the first thing I see is that gull outside my window, its crooked beak knocking against the glass before it flies off into the deep night sky.

I unzip the sleeping bag I'm in and take my blue robe from the bedpost, pulling it on over my nightgown as I make for the window.

"What's that racket?" Jeannine mumbles from the bed. Her new library books are still scattered on the bedspread with *Ghosts and Legends of Prince Edward Island* open, facedown, next to her.

Mom and Dad are staying overnight in Rollo Bay until late tomorrow or I'd be hearing them stirring by now. Outside, the moon is a day off full, lighting a silvery trail along the edge of the Strait, and the sky is crowded with stars just starting to fade in the tiniest stirrings of far-away morning. I'd put the time at three a.m., but I can't see the clock. There is just enough light to make out the moving shadow of something small out on the path between the rosebushes. It's Joseph, running, following the faint, eager sound of Marina Shaw's undertow voice, which is coming from some place out on the beach. I race downstairs to the kitchen door, Jeannine following in her pink flannel pajamas and cardigan. I grab a flashlight. As the screen door slams behind us, Deirdre's voice cries from the top of the stairs.

"Joseph! Joseph! Where are you?"

By the time I get outside, the baby is already through Gerry's gate and toddling along the path toward the edge of the bank. The music of Marina Shaw's voice is farther away, and above my head, a flock of gulls have joined the minister, all calling and hovering, sometimes even swooping in, right close to my face.

"Joseph!" Jeannine calls to the back of his head as a hard wind comes up, pushing me back almost onto my bottom. In that moment, Joseph is over the bank and gone.

There's the sound of a slamming door and Deirdre screaming again, "Joseph!" Jeannine and I run down the path between the blooming rosebushes as the music grows fainter still. We scramble down the bank to the beach, but Joseph is nowhere to be found.

"It's her!" Deirdre cries, following us down the bank. "Marina Shaw. She's taken Joseph. I heard her . . . *singing* to him."

The stars and almost-full moon reflect enough light for us to see the hardpacked low-tide sand marked over and over with Joseph's small footprints, first crowded together, then joined by what look like two more sets of feet, and then something else . . . hoofprints.

A chill goes through me. I look at Jeannine, but she shakes her head. "See, Beet." She points at the prints. "They lead along the beach. Not into the water."

Deirdre is already running, following the trail, and we go after her. The gulls fly over us, swooping and hollering. The wind has risen during the night and cuts through me like it's March instead of June. By the time we've rounded Nelson's Point, the horse is nowhere in sight, but its hoofprints continue south with the sound of Marina Shaw's slippery voice, just above the lapping waves. The night is clear, with the merest violet hint of the dawn that's coming, as Deirdre, Jeannine, and I reach the place where the hoofprints end. They've gone the length of the beach, to disappear up the rise just below the Campbell house. As we reach the cove there is still no sign of the horse, and Deirdre is already on her way up the cliff.

Jeannine turns to me, panting like a sick dog. "We're just not fast enough . . . to catch them. . . . I don't know why we thought we could run after . . ." An old blanket lies crumpled in the sand at her feet. When she stoops to lift it up, the underside sticks to her hand so she has to shake it off. She looks up at me. "It's sticky, the way the book says the kelpie is supposed to be. Maybe the horse was covered with this . . . to . . . to protect Joseph."

It makes sense, if anything about this can. Whatever Uist took Joseph for, it wasn't to drag him into the sea, at least not yet. There's something else going on here. But what? And where did they take him? I have to stop myself from imagining the worst. Beyond the high bank, the house is dark; the gulls have left us. I don't even remember them going, or when the sound of their cries faded away.

"We should check the house," I say. "And find Deirdre."

The rocky path up the bank to the Campbell house is even more dangerous at night. Jeannine and I take it slowly, trying not to put our feet wrong. Not only are there no gulls anymore, but the wind has died down, too. The only sound is the slap of the waves on the shore, quick and regular. The air is thick with salt and the smell of rotting seaweed. Deirdre is standing by the house. She tries the door just as we reach her, and it opens.

"Someone's inside," Jeannine whispers, holding me back, but Deirdre speaks out to the darkness in a voice stronger than I've ever heard her use. "Marina Shaw! Where's Joseph? Where's my baby?"

The parlor is empty, in shadow, and the fading moonlight through the picture-window curtains makes patterns on the floor. There is a rustling from the direction of the dining room. Jeannine gasps as a man steps into the pool of shadows and moonlight. At first I think it's Uist, so I pull Jeannine back in a panic. But then Jeannine lets out a squeak of joy and surprise.

"Oh, hi, Sean." She turns to me grinning. "Look, Beet! It's Sean!" I suddenly remember that I am still wearing my pajamas.

The sky has started pinking up to dawn now, the wind is down, and there's still not a gull in the sky. Sean is driving the Publicovers' car, with Deirdre up front next to him so she can scan the road for Joseph. From the glimpses of her face in the rearview mirror, it looks as if she's ready to jump out at any second. A cloud of clay dust rises from the road behind us, and Sean turns the car onto our track.

"What were you doing in Marina's house?" I want to know. Since I'm in the back seat I have to raise my voice so he can hear me, and I probably sound angrier than I mean to.

Sean takes a deep breath, and I start to think he isn't going to answer. His voice is steady. "I heard that music again."

"What music?" Jeannine cuts in, but that's all Sean will say. It's a bumpy ride on the track, as always, and the spruce wood is filled with shadows as the car heads toward our farm. When we come out of the wood, the windows of the house are dark, but there's a truck parked out front. It's Freddy's truck, and Freddy and Lily Soloman are standing on the path, waiting for us. I breathe out slowly; surprised by how relieved I am to see them. Sean pulls up and we all get out.

Before I can head over to find out where Lily and Freddy have been, Sean puts out his hand to stay me.

"Beet," he whispers, "it was *her*." He looks at me like he's begging me to understand. "Like it happened before. I couldn't sleep. I woke up from this nightmare where all I could hear was Marina Shaw, singing. I looked out the window and saw her with little Joseph. He was following her along the beach like he was under a spell. That guy Uist was there, too."

"So, what then?" I ask. "You left your house, with your aunts sleeping . . . just to help Joseph?"

"Yes." Sean says this like it's the most obvious answer in the world. And the thing is, looking at him, I know he means it. I know he didn't even think twice. He reaches out like he's going to take my hand, then draws back. "Look, I'm sorry I didn't tell you that my aunts were speaking to Marina. . . . I know they're busybodies, but they're not . . ."

"Evil?" I say, remembering my Mom's words, though I don't thank her for them just yet.

His blue eyes are pleading. "Beet, you have to believe me. I'm on your side. I brought you the article and—"

"The what?" Now I'm just confused.

"The article, in the envelope. I left it with your mother. Didn't she . . ."

And suddenly I go from confused to ashamed and stupid all at once. "She did. I just . . . I didn't open it."

Sean looks like someone smacked him in the face.

"I'm sorry. First I was mad, and then I didn't want to open it with Je . . ."

"With what?" Sean tilts his head, like he's confused, but I realize there's no way to explain to him what I was thinking, especially when I don't know myself. All I know is that we've wasted too much time already. Dawn is spreading across the sky with an orange glow, just like the morning Joseph was born, the air just as still. Mom and Dad will be home tonight, and what will we tell them?

Lily Soloman is coming toward us, while Freddy hangs back with Deirdre and Jeannine. Lily's face is serious and watchful as ever, and her voice is brisk.

"Sean MacInnes, let's get that car back to your aunts; then we'll head to the library." Sean looks at me just a second more, that same bewildered look on his face, then gets in the car and backs it up the swamp road before finding a place to turn.

I look around to find Lily watching me again, watching me watching Sean. "We have to talk," Lily tells me. "All of us." I know she's right.

There's deep, uneasy silence all around us. It makes me want to run away.

"And Beatrice," Lily adds finally. "Go get your fiddle. You're going to need it."

~

"She's not what you think she is," says Lily Soloman. She is sitting across from me in the back of Freddy's truck, with Jeannine and Deirdre beside her. Deirdre's face is a mask.

For the first time, I'm really looking at Lily. Her gray hair is done in a long braid, with the only lines in her face those around her brown eyes. I always call her old Lily, but in the pink morning light, I guess she's not that much older than my dad.

"Marina Shaw," she says. "I knew I'd seen her before. I recognized her at Poxy Point, and then again at the dance, but I didn't think it was possible. No one would think it was possible."

"Think *what* was possible?" Sean asks. Once he dropped off the Publicovers' car, the rest of us picked him up in the truck. He's sitting next to me now. Freddy hits a pothole, and we're jostled so that Sean ends up leaning against my shoulder. He backs away quickly—too quickly—and I'm surprised by a little pang of disappointment.

Lily pulls a folded-up newspaper from the pocket of her wool cardigan and hands it to me. It's the *Daily Transcript*, from Moncton, New Brunswick. The paper is dated April 2, 1900, but made of heavy stuff and barely yellow at all, nothing like the old newspapers that Dad uses to kindle the oil stove.

"The rag content in these old newspapers helps to preserve them," Lily explains. "And the ink stays true. They'd only just started printing photographs that year, or maybe the year before, but you can still recognize her."

On the front page is a picture of a woman in a white dress with a high collar, her hair piled on top of her head in a soft, old-fashioned style. But even in the morning light I recognize her face. Marina Shaw, with her pale skin and large upturned eyes. She's even wearing a curving seashell necklace, just visible at the bottom of the frame.

"Holy mackerel," Jeannine says, grabbing the paper away from me. "It's a relative or something, right? Has to be . . . I mean . . . *lorsh* . . ."

"Not a relative," Lily says. "The same woman."

For a moment, I don't even breathe.

"But this was fifty years ago," I say finally. "And Marina Shaw can't be older than her late twenties."

"Plus," Jeannine says, "the woman is named Marie Doucet." She points to the caption under the photo, but she has a kind of excited expression on her face. If I know Jeannine, and I do, she's got the edge of something, a story.

Freddy has just pulled up to the library. He cuts the engine. I search the sky for the birds that would usually be hovering nearby this time of the morning. There's not a one.

"Yes." Lily's voice is calm as calm, like she's talking about the weather or what she's going to have for dinner. "That's one of the names she's called herself."

"That's crazy. . . . You're crazy," Deirdre says, sounding angry and afraid at the same time. "Why are we listening to you? We need to find Joseph!"

"You're right, dear," Lily says gently. "And I can help you, but please hear me out."

Freddy steps out of the cab and comes round back to open the tailgate. He offers Deirdre his hand, but she gets out on her own. I follow her and put my arm around her shoulders, partly to keep her from bolting. Lily Soloman is right. We have to talk to one another, work together, to figure out what to do.

When Lily speaks again, her voice is kind as can be, but firm, too. She's looking straight at Deirdre. "Joseph is in danger. No doubt about it. But there's still time to save him." She holds out her hand for the newspaper, and Jeannine gives it to her.

"I saw this very picture once when I was a little girl. After what happened at the dance, I had Freddy drive me to Charlottetown, to the library at St. Dunstan's University, where they keep all the old Canadian newspapers."

"So that's why you and Freddy disappeared!" I practically squeak.

Lily Soloman speaks calmly, but the look on her face is the same I saw that night at the dance. "Yes, so I could find the picture. I needed to be sure. I needed proof."

"Of what?" Deirdre makes it a demand, not a question. Around us is the smell of sea salt, and something underneath it—roses.

"That Marina Shaw and the woman in that picture are one in the same. And that she killed my father."

CHAPTER TWENTY-TWO

April 2, 1900

Lily Soloman

CAP-PELÉ COUPLE FEARED DROWNED IN SPRING SNOWSTORM. Cap-Pelé fisherman Serge Doucet and his wife, Marie, disappeared yesterday after leaving their home to search for a beloved horse, which had broken free of its paddock as the April Fools storm beat down on New Brunswick communities from Moncton to Shediac.'"

Laura MacEachern looks up from the *Daily Transcript*, which is spread out on her sturdy kitchen table, alongside the tea and biscuits she's set out for Lily Soloman and her father, Jack. "It says here this Marie Doucet was last seen wearing a blue dress and a green silk shawl patterned with pink and gold starfish." Laura gives a little sniff. "Well, aren't we just grand?"

The MacEachern farm is in Donaldston, Prince Edward

Island, on a hill overlooking Tracadie Bay. The kitchen is warm and sweet smelling from baking. Through the window above the washbasin, ten-year-old Lily watches swallows dive after one another in the clear blue and cloudless April sky. The bay is now dead calm and glistening as if it never thought of a storm. Laura and her family have been a stop on Papa's peddler's route since before Lily was born. Traveling with her father these past three springs and summers since Mama died, Lily has gotten to know Papa's customers well. "Read the rest, please, Mrs. MacEachern," Lily asks quietly. Mama was teaching her to read before she died. After all these years, Papa still isn't good with English print, though she has seen the letters he writes in the beautiful curling script of his homeland.

Laura MacEachern lifts her round rosy face toward Lily and smiles. It's a smile filled with pity. Since Mama's been gone, Lily has gotten used to seeing this look on women's faces, especially if they have children of their own. Laura MacEachern has five sons. "God love ya," Laura says softly. "Where was I? Oh, here we are . . . 'Thursday's storm hit New Brunswick unexpectedly, causing particularly extensive damage in Cap-Pelé, including the wreckage of a number of small boats in the harbor, but Mr. and Mrs. Doucet's are said to be the only possible deaths. Considered a great local beauty who kept her youthful looks well into her forties, Mrs. Doucet had been failing physically in the months leading up to her going missing, and is said to have become desperately attached to the lost horse.' Laura stops reading, shaking her head. "Of all the foolishness . . ." She pours Papa another cup of black tea.

"And there's more." Laura winks at Lily and goes on, slowly. "'Among the many sad ironies of this story is the fact that Mrs. Doucet was herself pulled from a wreck seventeen years ago after a freak storm hit the Gulf of Saint Lawrence in November of 1883. She had been set adrift in a lifeboat and rescued off the New Brunswick shore. Readers may also remember that storm as the one in which Prince Edward Island shipwright Thomas Gray was killed, dealing a blow to the shipbuilding industry throughout the Maritimes.

"'Mrs. Doucet and her husband were perceived to have led a charmed if solitary life in the small fishing community of Cap-Pelé, but as many neighbors interviewed for this story were quick to attest, "In the end, the sea will have its own." Mrs. Doucet and her husband were childless, and Mrs. Doucet had considerable personal wealth in railroad stocks. A niece in Massachusetts is being sought to help contend with the legal and financial matters surrounding her disappearance.'"

Laura MacEachern lets out an exasperated breath. "She runs out into that storm after a pet. I mean, really!"

"I dunno, Laura." Papa takes a sip of tea and ruffles Lily's long hair. His voice is low, his hair and eyes, like Lily's, black against a face that is tan from weeks on the road. He places the blue-and-white teacup back in its saucer. "Some people are just animal lovers, I guess."

Laura just looks at Papa, her thin, dark eyebrows arching inward. "Some people are stupid as a bag o' hammers. . . . Oh, wait. There's even a picture of the 'great local beauty.' It's a wedding photograph, I think." Laura pushes the paper across the table to Papa and Lily, and Lily takes a look. She's only ever seen famous people's photographs in the newspaper, people like Queen Victoria or the Prime Minister or (once) a front-page photograph of the boy from Souris who won a spelling contest all the way in Toronto. That photograph was blurry and hard to make out, but not this one of lovely Marie Doucet. Every detail in it is clear, the pale hair piled thickly on top of the woman's head, her face framed in wisps of curl, the large eyes that seem to stare at Lily from right out of the newspaper page, and a sort of queenly half smile, as of someone who is used to things going her way. Lily can even see the thin chain around Marie Doucet's neck, and the pendant, a long swirling seashell.

Papa is staring at the paper now, his dark eyes wide and kind of far away. Outside, the swallows have disappeared. A gust rattles the kitchen window and goes still.

"Papa . . . ?" Lily puts a hand on his shoulder, gently, the way she does when she has to wake him early in the morning.

"They say that's the drowned woman, Laura?"

Laura nods. "What is it Jack?"

"She has the look of someone I know," Papa says quietly. A smile passes quickly across his face, as if he's remembering some brief long-ago wonder. "Someone I met when I was a boy." He takes a last sip of his tea, drains the cup, and his smile is gone. "Couldn't be, though. . . . The one I'm thinking of's been dead some seventeen years."

Papa stands up, holding out a hand to Lily. "Lily and I had

best be going. We're due in Charlottetown in two days, and I still need to stop off at Scully's on my way through Pleasant Valley."

"Well, all right, then, Jack." Laura places the dishes in the basin. "But I don't know how that child can ride with you in that cart all over Creation like she's doing."

"Lily's strong," Papa says matter-of-factly.

Lily beams. Papa pays her so few compliments, though she knows he loves her. She helps him stuff his samples back into the brown canvas sack he has brought in from the cart—red-and-white enamelware pots, serving spoons, a set of wooden bowls, a few books, and two black lacquered music boxes, "a perfect gift for the ladies." Then, casting one last look around the warm kitchen with its bright yellow wallpaper and smell of cinnamon sugar, she heads off to the MacEacherns' front door, after her father.

Laura sees them out into the soft blue April light. There's a chill in the air, and Lily pulls her mother's old Sunday coat around her shoulders. Laura gives her a light kiss on the cheek, hands her the newspaper. "Keep practicing your reading," she says, "and we'll see you when you come round in August."

Lily waves back at Laura MacEachern as the peddler's cart rolls slowly down the farm's track toward the Stanhope Road. "Careful with that child now, Jack. Watch out for fallen trees."

They camp that night in a clearing in the spruce wood near the entrance to Covehead Bay, Lily as sheltered as possible in the covered peddler's cart and her father in a tent under the trees nearby. The air is still, the cold as heavy as a block of ice, but that is not what's keeping Lily awake. It is restlessness. She has awoken many times during the night, disturbed by dreams of herself drowning while a faceless woman looks down on her through the rippling surface of the water, singing in a high, echoing voice, empty at its core, a big voice wrapped around hollowness. The song is still swirling around Lily's head when she wakes up for the fifth time, so it takes her a moment to realize that the voice is not only in her head. The singing is coming from the water, carried on a wind that is making the spruce trees shudder.

Pulling on her coat and boots, Lily gets up to follow the sound. It is early morning, and the old carthorse, Jim, tied to a birch tree about twenty feet away, is awake already, pawing at the ground and nickering softly. The flaps of Papa's tent are untied and Lily peeks in to find his bedroll undone and empty. The high, echoing tune returns with a gust of sea air through the trees. Lily turns to follow the music, hoping that Papa has gone that way, too. Spruce needles stick to her boots as she plods through the dark stand of trees toward the Bay. Many trees have been blown over by the gale of two days before, their ragged roots showing thick with mud and melting snow. Lily has to climb over one large fallen spruce after another, tree sap collecting on her bare knees. The air is as still as it was yesterday afternoon when they left the MacEachern farm. The waters of Covehead Bay, and beyond its barrier dunes to the Gulf of Saint Lawrence, are glittering silver, reflecting the early morning light so that Lily cannot tell where the sky ends and the water begins. From behind the last of the trees Lily scans the beach for the source of the strange music she still hears.

On the shore, interspersed with the delicate tracks of the snipe and plover that chase the waves in and out, are hoofprints leading out into the still half-frozen waters of the bay. Ice cakes, thick and blue white, bob on the calm waters, occasionally bumping into one another. On one of these small ice islands, the one closest to the shallows, a pearl-gray horse with a silver bridle stands silently as gulls circle its head, mewing and occasionally diving at it, beaks wide and sharp. Like the ice, the horse's mane is bluish white, its coat so shiny it almost glitters, a ghost of a horse against the morning sky. Only one thing about the picture seems solid—beside the horse's front hoof, a dark pile of what look like rags spreading out from the ice to float in the glistening water. The air smells of cold and salt, and rotting flowers.

Lily stops at the water's edge, trembling. The music is coming from her left, about fifteen yards down the beach, from a sandstone boulder lodged at the edge of the low water mark, covered in tangled kelp, all yellow and rust brown. An old woman is hunched against the boulder, water rippling thinly above the hard, red sand around her swollen blue-veined feet. The sound from Lily's dream is now a harsh, beckoning hum, a sound like a smell, like dead fish lying in a market bin. Slowly, Lily turns from the sight of the horse and moves closer. The woman's long gray hair hangs about her shoulders like eelgrass, bleached dry by the sun, covering her face so that the eyes are not visible, only the cheeks, lined and pale, and a mouth open in a hard, thin-lipped "O" as the tune she is singing grows louder. From the old woman's shoulders hangs a green silk shawl patterned with starfish. Like the woman from the newspaper, Lily thinks.

"Mrs. Doucet." Lily's whisper is lost in the sound of the music that has set the air around her whining. She shakes her head. Not Mrs. Doucet. Of course not. This woman is much older than her forties, even a ten-year-old can see that.

"Hello?" Lily calls out. She waits a minute, two, three, but the woman does not answer or look up. As Lily tries to decide whether to move closer or run to find Papa, the woman starts to shake there on the sand. Lily takes a step backward, the hairs rising on her arms. Mama shook like this, right before she died. Lily remembers it, a shudder that went through Mama's body from head to toe and filled the room first with panic, then stillness. Unlike Mama, though, the old woman does not go still after her fit of shaking. Instead, the movements grow fiercer, more convulsive; the old woman jerks and rattles, legs sticking out straight, arms flailing. The hum of the music becomes a sound like rushing water, then like waves crashing on the shore, as the woman's body swells and stiffens into an almost-standing position, her pale, engorged face thrown backward. What looks like a jet of clear water shoots out from her mouth like a fountain, bursting straight upward, its storm-like music filling Lily with nausea and dizziness so overwhelming that she falls to her knees. Then the music changes, becoming a high-pitched call, like a lament played on a fiddle, and the body collapses onto the hard sand as well, surrounded by the retreating tide.

As Lily watches, sand sticking to her palms, the jet of water reshapes itself into a figure of clear green, swirling first into the shape of a seashell, curled and pointed, then gradually taking form as something else, something human—a woman made of clear green glass. That figure changes, too, becoming no longer clear but first opaque, then solid as flesh. A woman, young, naked, her skin white as porcelain, has taken shape beside the crumpled body. The music is now rippling from the young woman's open mouth in echoes as big and hollow as in Lily's dream. Lily covers her ears with trembling hands, and watches. The woman is tall, her long hair flowing around her body as if it were still made of water, like a picture Lily once saw of a beautiful goddess sailing to shore atop a scallop shell, with angels all around her. No angels here, though, just the strange woman, her eyes large, upturned, and as clear green as the water that just formed her. Around her neck she wears a silver chain with a pendant in the shape of a seashell, smooth and twisting outward to a point. The woman closes her mouth, ending the music, and leaving in its place the sound of tiny rippling waves. Her lips curl into a placid, slightly sneering smile. It's the smile of the bride from Laura MacEachern's newspaper, Marie Doucet young again. She stoops to wrap herself in the starfish shawl, now lying beside the corpse of her ancient used-up self.

"Well done," this new Marie Doucet says, her speaking voice hard and flat as wet sand, green eyes fixed on a point behind Lily's head. The sharp angry cry of a gull rises behind Lily, and she turns to see the bird hovering just above the familiar pearl-gray horse. The animal, less glittery now and more solid, is standing close by at the water's edge, having dragged to shore the pile of dark rags Lily saw earlier on the ice. With a swift movement the silent creature shakes its hoof free of the rags, which drop heavily onto the sand, then moves slowly along the beach toward where Marie Doucet is standing. The tide has reached its lowest ebb now. Just beyond the low water mark, where the drop-off begins, something large and dark is floating in the deep blue along the edges of the thick, scattered ice. A quick cold breeze rises, turning the tide inward. Inside of Lily, in her stomach, in her chest, a small secret emptiness has begun to spread.

Marie Doucet is now wrapped completely in the green shawl, her long blond hair floating around her in the newly risen breeze. She takes a step toward the horse, then stops, looking for the first time at Lily. For a second, the woman's eyes flash darker green, as if the sea were showing its depths. "How old are you?" the flat voice asks.

"Ten," Lily whispers, her own words echoing the emptiness inside her.

The woman turns away. "Nothing to fear from ten," she says to herself, or maybe to the horse. Lily cannot be sure.

"Come," Marie Doucet says to the horse, taking hold of its silver bridle. The animal follows her away down the now-silent beach. Lily watches them go a long time before she can bear to look closer at that pile of rags, the dark thing in the water.

When she finally does look to see Papa's ruined wool coat lying in the sand, Papa's bloated face floating above the shadow of his drowned body, all Lily can do is sit, and let the emptiness that's been growing inside her swallow her up.

When Laura MacEachern reads the paper on Tuesday, the front page will be crowded with stories: of an elderly woman found drowned, the death of a peddler, and his orphaned daughter's sorrow.

CHAPTER TWENTY-THREE

June 21, 1950

Beet MacNeill

The library is really just one room, neat and narrow, lined mostly with kids' picture books and red leather-bound encyclopedias, with three great big tables in the middle and a desk by the door. There's also a storage closet where Lily Soloman keeps old newspapers, along with labeled crates of town records, deeds and letters and stuff. Right now, most of those are piled on the center table, where we're all gathered together, listening to her finish her sad, terrible story.

"The woman in the newspaper, I saw her myself, standing over my father's body. I've seen the woman—*this* woman—twice since then, once when I was still young, in Charlottetown, and now again here in Skinner Harbour. And I've heard her voice . . ."

"Like at the dance," Jeannine says. "The song . . . like . . ."

"What song?" Deirdre breaks in. She's shifting in the hard wooden chair, looking ready to bolt. "What are you all talking about? Why are we sitting here? Joseph is out there!" I understand her fretfulness. How's a mother supposed to sit around when her baby could be just anywhere, hurt, even . . . I can't even say it. I'm scared for Joseph, too, but I know Lily's trying to help us.

Still, I am wondering why I had to bring my fiddle.

"We can save Joseph," Lily tells Deirdre in that calm, no-nonsense voice of hers. "But you all need to know what we're up against."

Freddy's been standing behind his aunt this whole time. Now he pulls out the chair next to Deirdre and sits down beside her.

His voice is quiet and steady when he talks to her. "Deirdre, listen to me. You'll understand once you hear it all."

"But he could be . . ."

"He isn't," Freddy says. "Not yet." He rests a hand on Deirdre's shoulder. "There's still time, but we have to listen now." His dark eyes stay on her face. "Please trust me."

Deirdre looks at him a minute, then nods and sinks back in her seat.

The clock on the library wall says seven thirty in the morning; outside the high windows, the town is moving. Cars and trucks rumble by on the way to the docks; across the street, Mr. Lavangier is opening up his store. I'm thinking of Gerry's ghost in the garden and how Deirdre heard his fiddle playing the night Joseph was born, and about all the strange things that have happened since then.

Lily looks around the room and goes on. "That song of hers, the one some of you have heard, it has been around a long time. And so has she. We've been searching through some records and old newspapers in the storeroom."

"We?" Deirdre says.

Lily nods toward Sean and he blushes for no apparent reason.

"I wasn't sure what we were looking for at first either," Lily goes on, "except that it would have something to do with Marina Shaw. But . . . well, listen for yourselves."

The room is rosy with the last of the dawn light. Lily riffles through the pile and hands me two sheets of thick yellowing paper, attached with a wooden clip.

The first letter is written in old-fashioned, perfectly slanted script. I read out loud:

Matthias Batchelder
Skinner Harbour
County King's
Prince Edward Island

His Honor
Lord Sebastian Stephens
Lieutenant Governor of Prince Edward Island
Government House
Charlottetown
6 August 1820

Your Honor,

On the 23rd of July there arrived in this port from Glasgow, Scotland, in the barque Polly, *eighty-five immigrants, destined to join their friends in Stanhope, P.E. Island, but that smallpox having made its appearance among them, they have been detained in quarantine at Perry Point in the neighbourhood of Skinner Harbour. During the course of the outbreak, twenty-three passengers were lost.*

The quarantine now being lifted, I have been authorised by the Provincial Government to forward the survivors to their original destination and to ensure that they are delivered into the hands of their friends.

While relatives of the orphaned children are en route to meet the Polly *at Skinner Harbour, one young woman in the party remains without assistance. She is Mrs Morag Ferguson, widow of Captain John Ferguson, who is believed to have gone overboard in delirium from the sickness. His body has not been recovered. Mrs Ferguson has herself made a miraculous recovery but is left without acquaintance on the Island or anywhere in the Dominion.*

I am instructed by the Mayor and Board of Skinner Harbour to request you send an emissary to collect Mrs Ferguson. It is hoped that she may find lodging in the neighbourhood of Charlottetown until she can orient herself and decide whether she wishes to return to her homeland or begin a life here among us.

Mrs Ferguson is not without funds to pay for such assistance, as her husband, Captain Ferguson, left her well set up, in the sum of three hundred pounds. What she is most in need of now are friendly faces and the comfort of Christian fellowship.

I await your word and rely on your disposition.

Sincerely,
Matthias Batchelder

"The captain's wife survived." Deirdre's face is full of worry, but she's keeping her voice calm. It's drafty in here, and she is sitting with her legs curled under her skirt, Freddy's old gray sweater draped over her shoulders. "But the captain . . ."

"Read Stephens's reply, Beet," says Sean, and Lily smiles at him like the two of them are partners in some scheme.

The next sheet of paper is in a different, bolder hand, with an official-looking seal at the top:

Matthias Batchelder
Skinner Harbour
County King's
Prince Edward Island
20 August 1820

Dear Mr Batchelder,

We are in receipt of your letter regarding the troubles

besetting the Polly *and the case of Mrs John Ferguson. We are pleased to inform you that Mrs Ferguson has been offered assistance by Mrs Alice Winchester, a widowed lady of the neighbourhood of Charlottetown, until such time as Mrs Ferguson should choose either to continue the process of immigration or return to her native soil. The shipping company representative, by the name of George Bixby, will arrive in Skinner Harbour in ten days' time, to assist Mrs Ferguson in her journey to Charlottetown. On behalf of the Crown, we offer condolences to Mrs Ferguson and all surviving passengers and crew of the* Polly.

Sincerely,
Sebastian
Lord Stephens
Lieutenant Governor of Prince Edward Island

Freddy has gotten up from his chair and is half staring out the window.

"Who was Morag Ferguson?" I want to know. "What does she have to do with finding Joseph? With any of this?"

"There's one more thing." Sean takes a long breath and looks straight at me. "Remember I told you, Beet? Miss Soloman . . . Lily . . . had a photo of my mother from when she was in school to show me, and I was helping her look through the newspapers. I had brought that box of stuff home. Well, that's what was in the envelope I left for you—one of the newspapers."

That sense of stupidity and shame washes through me again, for not trusting Sean, for thinking . . . What was I thinking?

I open up my fiddle case, take out the envelope, and tear open the seal. The newspaper inside is dated 12 August 1820, and printed on the same heavy stuff as the photo Lily showed us in the truck. Sean points to an article in the center column. The print is bunched close together with barely a space between words, but I read it out loud as best I can:

> **Montague, Prince Edward Island. The arrival of the ship, *Polly*, on the eastern shore of the Island, has led to reports of strange events. The ship has been quarantined off Perry Point (Skinner Harbour Town) for several days, amid reports of passengers and crew having been stricken with the smallpox. The disease is thought to have appeared shortly after the ship made port at Glasgow, Scotland, before its ocean journey. The quarantine of the *Polly* has led to some apprehension for the safety of people on land—especially in Skinner Harbour—and residents in the area have been asked to avoid approaching the ship.**
>
> **Disease is not the only cause for concern. Recent events related by passengers and crew of the *Polly* may only be described as fantastical. The crossing from Scotland was much rougher than usual for the season, and many crew tell of freak storms preceded by what they describe as strange "unearthly" singing. According to Dr. Neil MacKenna of Stanhope, brought on board to treat passengers in part because of**

> **his knowledge of their Gaelic language, patients claim to have sighted a being known as the *each uisge*, translated in English as "water horse," a sea monster of Scottish folklore which they say has been following the ship from her port of origin on the Hebridean Island of South Uist, Scotland. The passengers describe the *each uisge* as a fine-looking horse that lures unsuspecting people onto its back before transforming into a hideous beast that plunges its unsuspecting rider into the water, there to devour him. Needless to say, government officials have dismissed such talk as the superstitious ravings of a backward people. The singing is another matter, however. Respectable farmers and fishermen from both Skinner Harbour and nearby Georgetown have recently reported the voice of an unseen woman, a soprano in full song, echoing on the waters of the Northumberland Strait in the vicinity of the *Polly*. On at least two separate occasions, this singing is said to have preceded instances of rough weather, high seas, and near drownings.**

By the time I'm done, Jeannine is practically jumping out of her seat. "Beet, that's what you saw!"

"Saw, Beatrice?" Lily fixes those eyes of hers on me, but Jeannine answers before I can get in a word.

"The *each u* . . . whatever. Beet saw it last week. There's a picture of it in one of the books you gave me, but they call it something else."

"Kelpie," I say. "But it's supposed to be a river creature. . . ."

"Does it look like this?" Sean opens his black book. He has drawn a horse-like monster, right at the surface, with bulbous eyes, covered in seaweed, like the creature in Jeannine's library book, but with more detail. Then he looks at me, speaks just for me to hear. "This was what I was trying to tell you, at your house, when . . . when we argued." His voice is speeding up again. "I didn't put it all together, not until the other day when I saw that monster in the water. When I . . . my aunts and I . . . were at your house, I tried to tell you . . ."

I want to say I'm sorry, but it's not the place.

He turns to the rest of the group. "I saw it from the bank near my aunts' house, just after . . . after Beet's birthday." His voice gets quieter, just for a second, but then he speaks up. "I was sitting on the bank, drawing the sunset. . . . So beautiful, the colors changing so fast . . . Anyway, the creature surfaced and stayed there, not hiding at all, until I finished, even with gulls flying round it, trying to shoo it away. It was like it was posing."

And it's true, the eyes seem to be staring out from the page, planning. Drawn from life, not just imagined like in a book, the creature is almost as scary as what I saw in the Cardigan River. I'm shaking all over now.

A beam of early sun shines through the library window, lighting up Freddy's face. He turns from the window and stares slowly around the table at all of us, lastly at Deirdre. She looks back at him, that worry in her eyes again, but she doesn't move, and he doesn't say a word.

"Holy . . . well . . . just holy!" Jeannine breaks the silence, eager as a hunting dog. "The immigrants thought they saw the creature *and* they thought they heard music, strange music surrounding the ship. A woman's voice."

Lily nods. "It all happened at the same time. The captain's wife who made a miraculous recovery from smallpox, the 'unearthly singing,' and the immigrants' stories about the water horse."

A sharp gust of wind rattles the windows then quickly fades. Outside, gulls fly by in a flock, quarrelling as they go. Meanwhile, Jeannine is sitting straight as Sunday, smiling her head-of-the-class smile. "We know of at least three times when a beautiful singing woman and the water horse have shown up together, and someone always drowns—the captain, Lily's father, and now Beet has seen Marina using her voice to control Uist. A water horse creature and unearthly singing reported at the same time, just like now—"

Lily Soloman breaks in, speaking as carefully as crossing a stream. She waves Freddy over next to her. "There's no way of knowing for sure, but it seems as if the woman we know as Marina Shaw is the same one I saw step out of that shell of a woman's body when I was a child. She may even be the captain's wife from two hundred years ago."

Jeannine might just burst with satisfaction, by the look of her. "That means that Marie Doucet and Marina Shaw are the same woman, and probably even—"

"Sarah Campbell," I say. "That would explain how she looked so young for so long. Plus Mom says she always wore that seashell necklace, the one Marina has now. Mom thought Marina stole it. Remember, Jeannine?"

Jeannine nods.

Sean is closing his book and looks about to say something, but Deirdre beats him to it. She's calm, but her voice is angry. I don't think I've ever heard her angry. "This is all just a story. How does it help us find Joseph? How do we stop that woman from hurting him?"

"The creature." Jeannine's eyes are wide now. "The creature ties them all together."

Sean struggles with the name. "The *eck us* . . . um . . ."

"*Each uisge*," Lily Soloman says, pronouncing the words "ach ushka." "Water horse, kelpie. Whatever they called it, Beatrice, you and Sean are not the only ones to have seen it."

She looks from me to Freddy.

"I saw it," Freddy says. "Or him . . . and Marina Shaw. I saw them together. And I think Gerry did, too. I think it's why he's dead."

CHAPTER TWENTY-FOUR

June 17, 1950

Freddy Soloman

Freddy Soloman arrives at the Cozy Hall, delivering eight bottles of bootleg from Norm Gotell's still, plus a cooler of sandwiches and molasses cookies for the late-night dancers. The cheerful notes of "Whiskey in the Jar" are coming from the brightly lit windows of the hall; the sound of stomping feet and the flickering of shadows makes the building itself seem to dance. Freddy has never been a good dancer; his mother died too early to teach him. But it does not really matter to him anyway. The only one he would want to dance with is home, alone with his old friend's baby, although Freddy will not mention that part when he tells this story later on.

Freddy stoops in the shadow of the truck to tie a battered shoelace. Though the sky is a blaze of sunset orange, the churchyard is in shadow, placing Freddy in darkness. The music has gotten fainter inside the hall, and Freddy hears a female voice singing somewhere near him—a deep, low song, like an incantation, not right for dancing at all. Not right for anything, Freddy thinks as the vibrations surround him and little by little the fiddle playing inside the hall fades away, swallowed up by the woman's singing. Hidden from view, Freddy hears the hall stairs creak, followed by voices coming from the same direction. Dizzy, he sits down on the dusty ground beside the truck.

As the speakers reach the bottom of the stairs, Freddy can see their shoes under the truck: a man's shoes caked in mud and a woman's soft kid-leather slippers, all wrong for Prince Edward Island clay. Freddy does not recognize the man's voice, which echoes as if he were speaking across a wide body of water. The language is different, too, although it has rhythms he has heard before, years ago, from relatives who were already very old when he was small. The man is asking a question.

"It has to be now," the female answers in English, and that voice Freddy knows right off, soft and flat calm as a windless day. Marina Shaw. There is something else in her voice this time, though, a halting, measured quality, as if she has been climbing a steep hill and needs to stop for breath.

"It is not time," the echoey voice replies. A breeze stirs the birches in the churchyard to Freddy's right, making their leaves whisper.

"You more than anyone must know: there is no exact measurement for the timing of the tithe. Such things are wives' tales.

Like my mother's." A sneer creeps into Marina Shaw's voice.

"But it's only been a year since the boy . . . since the last tithe." The stranger's words have almost a pleading quality. He trails off, and for a moment no one speaks at all. Up in the hall, the music has not started again. "A brave boy, too," the stranger continues. "Tried to save his friends. It was a shame to take him."

Freddy's knees hurt from staying in the same position too long, but he wills himself not to move. What boy? What tithe?

Marina Shaw's voice goes sharp. "Since when do you feel shame, creature?"

There is another pause.

"He was, after all, your child." The answered words float, then sink in the suddenly dead air. Inside, at the dance, the band begins to tune up again. There is a note from the piano, sweet and clear. Freddy feels tears pricking his eyes. He blinks.

"Yes, and carrying him kept me in the last body too long, made me dependent on that ignorant fisherman. It was weeks after the boy's birth before I could make the change, and even then I had to return and raise him. And now after a year, I am already weakened. Look at my hands, the veins in them swelling. I can feel that girl's music pulling the youth from my body."

The man answers slowly, his voice deeper and almost reverent. "Yes, she has weakened you. Her playing has great power. I felt its pull."

Freddy's eyes are filled with tears now. The sky above is blue black. On the Island, night does not creep in. It falls like a curtain.

"This body is sick already, and I do not wish to die with it." Marina Shaw's voice has lost its haltingness now, its tone gone from flat to hard as January ice. "The tithe must be soon, the solstice. Spring tide will give me power. In four days."

"Where?" The word seems to come from far away.

"The place they call Poxy Island." Marina Shaw almost laughs at the name as her soft footfalls retreat across the clay lot. "Remember, creature, we are bound to each other."

Freddy stays still for two, three minutes longer and listens to the breathing of the man with the echoey voice. Then the man steps into the pool of light that grows and shrinks with the glow from the headlamps of a passing car. Still hidden, Freddy has just long enough to see that it is Mr. Uist. His handsome face is tilted toward the flickering light of the windows, where earlier there was sweet fiddle music and the stomping of so many feet.

As Freddy watches, something happens. At first he thinks it is a trick of the shadows, but what he sees next leaves him gasping. Uist turns toward the churchyard, his pale face seeming to elongate and darken while his arms narrow and stretch outward. His fingers fuse together and flatten, pawing at the air in a frantic motion. The transformation becomes faster as Uist's upper body rears back, the skin on his long face now covered in glossy fur as his eyes widen and darken and slip to the sides of his head. Soon Uist is an animal rearing up on hind legs—a horse the color of clouds in the night sky. The creature lowers its face, shakes its mane, and lands on its front hooves.

Its eyes flash red, and for a moment, Freddy imagines it has caught sight of him. He keeps as still as if he has never moved in his life. Then the horse that was Mr. Uist turns and gallops off on almost silent hooves, leaving Freddy to the sounds of the crowded hall and Leo Jenkins's boys calling out for whiskey.

CHAPTER TWENTY-FIVE

June 21, 1950

Beet MacNeill

That's the most words I've heard from Freddy Soloman at once, maybe ever, and the whole time he's talking, he's pacing back and forth like a dog in a ditch. I add my part about Mr. Uist and the monster in the Cardigan River, and Sean talks about seeing Joseph with Marina and Uist from the Publicovers' window. Afterward, the room is quiet just long enough for me to notice that there still aren't any birds singing, not even the crows and jays that are usually waking the world long before this time of the morning. Outside the library's high windows, the sky has gone from pink to pale blue, and dust fairies are floating in the beam of light that falls across the table. When Deirdre turns to me, there are deep shadows under her eyes.

Freddy looks at Deirdre, pleading. "I wouldn't have gone. I wouldn't have left you alone, except, she . . . it said they were waiting for the solstice. I never would have—"

"I know." Deirdre's expression is kind. "It's okay. I know." But then her voice goes hard. "That creature killed Gerry . . . for *her*." The sun from the window is shining right into Deirdre's face, but she doesn't seem to notice. She doesn't even blink. I know how she feels, even though I keep my anger inside.

"And we have more than just pictures now," Jeannine puts in. "Marina's own words say how long she's been alive. Because of . . . what's the word?"

"A tithe." Freddy keeps pacing, talking almost to himself. "They kept talking about a tithe."

"Her payment," Sean says simply. "Her magic relies on a blood sacrifice, and she's made a deal to keep paying it in exchange for her youth and beauty."

Lily sneers a bit. "Such as they are."

Jeannine gets a look on her face now, right smug, like she answered all the questions correctly on a quiz, but it passes quick. Mostly she seems scared. Like we all are. "See, Beet. I *told* you. It's a deal with the Devil. She made a deal with the Devil for eternal youth."

"Well, not quite," Lily says. "I have been collecting stories like this ever since I lost my father, from people, from books. My life's work, you might say. It is true that most of them have to do with the Devil—"

"Like in my book," Jeannine interrupts. "That Scottish story . . . you know . . . Tam Lin! The fairy queen has to sacrifice a human to Hell every seven years."

Lily takes a breath. "Yes, yes. But this time, from what Marina said to Uist, it seems as if her tithe is to the sea itself."

"'The sea will have its own. . . .'" Deirdre's voice is hard. We all look at her. "Some of the fishermen say it. If you were meant to drown, you drown." I've heard that expression, too, and it's always scared me. It scares me now.

A shadow passes over Sean's face. "My mother used to say that," he says, mostly to himself. "I never knew what it meant."

"But Marina always manages to get someone to take her place!" Jeannine is speaking slowly, her hands tapping the table as she ticks off names. "Gerry's dad, Lily's father, Gerry, too, from what Freddy tells us. . . ." Her face goes white.

Outside, the sky gets just faintly darker, but it passes quick, like a small cloud has flitted across the sun. Deirdre says one word: "Joseph." She says it quiet, but it's a scream all the same.

Freddy stops pacing, sits down beside Deirdre, and takes her hand in both of his. He looks only at her, talking fast.

"Deirdre . . . please. We won't let that happen. If what I heard is true . . . whatever Marina is planning, it's for the spring tide. That's not until tonight, hours away. I told you, we have time." He looks down at Deirdre's hand in his and lets go, then gets up and starts pacing again.

Lily's sharp eyes soften when she looks at her nephew, and

she gives just the smallest hint of a real smile. "The spring tide," she says thoughtfully. "The highest tide of the month. And a solstice spring tide, too . . ."

"I don't understand," Sean says.

"Me neither," Jeannine adds. "It's only been a year since Gerry was killed. Why does she want to take Joseph now?"

Lily is starting to pack up the papers on the table. She hands Jeannine her book. "Remember, there's never an exact date. That's just for stories. Humans are always looking for patterns. Always three wishes or twelve princesses or seven, ten, twenty years between each tithe, but we already know that the deaths that involve Marina do not come on regularly."

"That's true!" Jeannine almost squeals. "They come after a storm, or the smallpox, or something natural."

Lily nods. "The sea, the body, nature, they don't run like clockwork machines. It seems there is only a point up to which they can be controlled, or counted on, even for someone as powerful as Marina. She has a new body, but it is still only a human body. It can still become ill. If it does, or if there's a baby, she has to pay her tithe earlier or later than she wants. She told Uist her body was failing."

Sean speaks quietly again. "When my mother was dying, before she even told me she was sick, I knew there was something wrong because of how she had to stop and catch her breath, how pale she was, a hollow look in her eyes. It was all just a little bit different, and there was . . . a shadow . . . a shadow over her.

It's the only way I can explain it. But I've seen the same thing in Marina Shaw. I recognize it."

Looking at Sean now, I think of my own mom. I sure don't know what I'd do without her, sour as she is. I remember what she said about Sean, too, being alone in the world, needing a friend, and I feel ashamed again. I try to catch his eye, but he seems to be somewhere else.

Lily goes on. "That she must pay the tithe now means danger to Joseph, but it is also good for us. It shows us her weaknesses. She can't stop her body from sickening."

"But she can raise the wind," I say. "And she can make a storm stronger."

Jeannine cuts in, her eyes bright. "And with the makings of a storm already out in the Gulf, she'll have even more power . . . especially tonight, the highest tide of the month *and* the first day of summer, all at once." She takes a breath and looks at Lily.

"But there's something against her this time," Sean says.

"Yes," Lily says. "Marina's power is in her music." She turns to me. "But, like all else about her, it is not absolute. At the dance, Beet, you weakened her hold on Uist, on the creature. I could see it. He stood and watched you play for a long time." I can see Uist's face looking up at me, and I shiver. I'm starting to understand.

"You've got power, too," Sean adds. "Until she showed up the other night, Uist couldn't tear himself away from your music. I was watching." I think of the drawings in my bureau drawer and smile at him.

"And she was weak after," Freddy says. "When she was talking to Uist. She kept sayin' she was weak and that's why she needed to do a new tithe."

There's a lump in my throat all of a sudden, or maybe it's been there all along, since that morning in the rose garden. "By the river. Gerry's tune came through the trees, the tune he played in the garden the day he died, the one Deirdre and I heard. . . ."

Deirdre draws in a sharp breath, and right away I feel guilty. I never told her that I had heard Gerry's tune that same morning. I never told her that I saw him in the garden.

"I'm sorry, Deirdre," I tell her. She doesn't say anything, but she manages a smile.

"The tune is what saved me," I go on. "Uist could have killed me as that creature, and he didn't."

Lily nods. "There is a strong bond between Marina and Uist but it's an old, old bond, more than a hundred years that we know of, and probably much more. It's as if he . . . it . . . is some kind of servant to her. I can't imagine how it started, but what matters now is that the bond is fraying, and music may help to break it."

"We have to challenge her with music," Jeannine agrees. "That's why you wanted Beet to get the fiddle."

"Good girl." Lily pats her hand. "Marina will be going to Poxy Point to perform the tithe tonight, from what Freddy heard. To stop her, we need to break the connection between her and

Uist. Marina sang up the water horse with her voice. She controls him that way. It's her gift. If our music is stronger, we'll get the control."

Lily and Jeannine are talking to each other like there's nobody else in the room, like they are planning a party or something, and it makes me mad. I look back and forth between them. "But I can't play like . . ."

"Like Gerry." Deirdre's voice is steady, the scream gone from it. "Play like you, Beet. Keep thinking of the dance."

"But that was me with Dad, Les, and Lou behind me. . . ."

"You have to try," Lily says, placing the old letters and newspapers carefully back into their boxes. She's right, of course. I know she is. "What's more, you have to do it soon. The spring tide is at quarter past seven tonight."

The calm in the air around us, the birdless silence, is beginning to bear down on me. Outside the window, more clouds have formed. Freddy picks up one of the boxes and Jeannine hops up to get the other.

"There's one more thing I don't understand," Jeannine says. "Joseph is just a baby. If Marina had had the time to raise Joseph, I could see . . . but the others all seemed to be willing victims in some way."

"Willing, yes," says Lily. "But not necessarily for Marina's sake. I think her plan is to lure someone else into the sacrifice."

"Someone?" Freddy says, sharp-like. "Who?" And then I know who, and my heart sinks.

Deirdre has gone silent and is sitting so still you'd think she was never going to move again. Now she gives Lily a look of understanding. Lily holds out a hand to her, and she takes it.

"It's me," Deirdre says quietly. "The sacrifice is me."

CHAPTER TWENTY-SIX

July 20, 1820

Morag MacDonald

Morag's hair is long and clean and golden, with a hint of red in it, like sun on the sea. She tosses the hair back from her pale, sharp face and walks lightly to the river, two empty buckets in her hands.

"Ann MacLean won't wear that blue dress to another dance," Morag says out loud, to the empty fields. "Serves her right, for dancing with John Ferguson all night. He's to be my husband. . . ." She gives a short, cold laugh. "When he sails for America, it's me he'll take with him."

Morag climbs over the rocky field on small, lovely feet, the same ones that tripped Ann MacLean into the peat fire at last night's dance. "Poor Ann." Morag smiles to herself that smile that hardens her beauty. "I'm sure her hair will grow back."

As Morag nears the crest of the hill, not yet within sight of the river, an odd sound brings her out of her thoughts of the fine clothes she will buy in Boston or New York. It is a dull, steady, wet thud, repeated over and over again, like someone beating a small dead animal. Rounding the hill at last, Morag spies what's been making the sound. An old woman in a ragged dress, its color all run to faintly purplish gray, squats by the river with her back to Morag. Beside the woman is a pile of clothes. She takes a dress from the pile, blue as the one Ann MacLean wore to the dance, and stained with blood. The old woman dips the dress into the river water, releasing the blood from the fabric in a cloud, then takes it out and slaps it against a large gray rock five, six times before putting it aside for another dress, this one of white lace, like the one Morag dreams of wearing when she marries John Ferguson, the young sea captain. As the old woman slaps the white dress against the rocks, the blood that stained it spreads until the whole dress has changed to a sickly brown.

"The *bean nighe*," Morag whispers, frozen to her spot on the hill. "But I thought she was just a story." Morag's mother has told her about the *bean nighe*, the Little Washer by the Ford, who squats by the river washing the clothes of those soon to die. To see her means your own death is near, Morag's mother has assured her, but Morag never paid any attention to the ignorant woman with her foolish prayers and superstitions, and is only waiting to leave their filthy crofter's hut with its dirt floor and straw roof and make her way, somehow, to America. She sees now that her chance has come, and that perhaps her mother has been right, for once.

"She hasn't seen me yet," Morag says to herself, then laughs softly. If one can catch the Little Washer before being seen, death can be averted, and more than that. . . . Morag sets down the empty pails in the grass and takes from her wrist the thin iron bracelet, engraved with the sign of the cross, that her mother has given her for protection. On her small, silent feet, those capable of tripping a dancing woman into a fire, she approaches the *bean nighe* from behind, holding out the bracelet.

"Old woman!" Morag says sharply as she nears the river. "Old woman, turn around."

The *bean nighe* gives one more slap to the dress she is "cleaning" and turns slowly toward Morag—who barely holds in a gasp. The woman's hair is greasy and straight, with a bald patch at the crown from where she has pulled it out. Her eyes, in her round and strangely pale face, are yellowed over with cataracts and ringed red as if from weeping, but with a glint of green around the pupil.

"So," the *bean nighe* says through a mouthful of broken teeth. "So, Morag, you have found me first." Her voice is flat and hoarse, like someone who is done with crying, and she has an accent, too, as if the words she speaks are foreign to her.

"I'll have my wishes, old woman," Morag demands, still holding out the bracelet. "I've caught you, and I'll have them."

The *bean nighe* gives Morag a look both weary and sly. "Well, what are they, then?"

"I want to go to America."

"Lord Selkirk's ship leaves South Uist port in a month. Captain and Mrs. John Ferguson will be on it."

"John Ferguson," Morag spits, and goes on to her next wish without thanks for the first. "I want a singing voice better than Ann MacLean's, so beautiful that it . . . it charms the waters."

The *bean nighe*'s grin shows more of her broken teeth, but she says nothing.

"Do it, old woman."

"It's already done. Now what for the third and last of your wishes?" Behind the *bean nighe*, the sun is beginning to set on the river flowing westward into the North Atlantic.

"Beauty," says Morag clearly. "I want beauty."

"But you already have . . ." The *bean nighe*'s tone is flattering, wheedling. The setting sun bleeds its light into the water, like the stain from the soaking clothes.

"No, no, I want it forever. I want to be young and beautiful always."

"Ahhhh," the *bean nighe* says in a satisfied tone. "Now, that wish is not mine to grant. There's a price for that wish."

"I'll pay it," says Morag quickly, impatiently. "What is it?"

"A tithe. A tithe of blood to the sea. Each cycle of twenty years, sometimes more, sometimes less, you must lead a willing soul into the sea to drown. When the sea receives its tithe, your youth and beauty will be restored to you. Without it, you will age just as other women, and lose your looks just the same."

"But how will I get someone to drown for me?" Morag asks

desperately, though she will not hesitate to pay the price if she can.

"You have your beauty," says the *bean nighe* in her flat, hoarse voice. A silver chain glints at the old woman's neck, like a thick braid. "And your voice, a voice to charm the waters is what you wanted. Try it now. Sing."

Morag begins. What comes from her mouth would not charm anything; even she knows that. She stops and turns to the *bean nighe*, angry. "Old woman, my voice sounds exactly the same." The air is still.

"You have to step into the water," says the old woman, her flat voice rising slightly. A breeze sends a ripple across the water. "Step into the water and sing."

Morag removes her shoes—they are brown and shabby, and she hates them—and does as she is told. As the tiny incoming waves lap at her feet, she begins again to sing. What comes out of her mouth is as dull as it has ever been, but behind her someone else is singing. The old woman. It is one note at first, then many notes together, coming from deep in the woman's throat. Morag has heard music like this before, at funerals, but something makes it different this time. Funeral music is sad, and there is no sorrow in this music. She tries to copy what she is hearing. She feels dizzy for a moment, as the still evening air shivers again and the surface of the river begins to shake as if stirred by invisible hands. Morag stops singing, draws in her breath.

The *bean nighe* stops, too. "Keep singing," she urges, her voice the slap of bloody clothes on rocks. Her hand is grasped around the silver chain at her neck. "Step farther into the water."

Morag hesitates and begins singing again, feeling the old woman's voice as if it were coming out of her own mouth. It's happening, Morag thinks, and visions of America, of dresses and adventures, appear in her mind. Something seems to rise out of the now-churning water.

"Keep going," the old woman urges her between breaths of strange song. Slowly, the head of a horse appears, then its neck, its shoulders. A horse, but smaller and sleeker than any Morag has seen. Gray like the river, it rises slowly toward Morag until it is standing only three feet from her. Its long, slender legs are still half submerged, its head bowed.

"The water horse, the kelpie!" Morag exclaims. "Mother was right about it, too. And now I've called it to me with my voice." She laughs and turns to the *bean nighe*, who has come close without her knowing. There's a seashell hanging from the silver chain at the old woman's neck, curved inwardly and spiked, becoming infinitely smaller. The old woman's thin lips curve like the edge of a fishhook.

"Yes, with your voice."

Morag holds out her hand to touch the creature's mane, and its long—longer than normal—neck. The horse's mane is wet to Morag's touch, and so sticky that she can't release her hand. She pulls at it with her other hand, and now they are both stuck, entwined in the gluey fibers as in a trap. Morag feels a panic inside her.

From behind her comes the old woman's voice again, flat and full of contempt.

"Didn't your mother tell you not to touch the water horse when it is wet?"

The horse rears back as Morag again struggles to get free. "But . . . but . . . ," she sputters.

"But your wishes?" The *bean nighe*, who is not the *bean nighe*, who is older by far than that story, laughs, fingering the silver seashell pendant. "Who told you I could grant wishes?"

Morag tries to dig her feet into the river bottom, to stay put, but she can't find any purchase. She lifts one leg to kick the creature away as its body elongates, serpent like, its eyes deepening to red, its teeth getting longer, longer. Now her skirts are caught, glued to the kelpie's black scales. She is screaming, calling to her mother, to God, to anyone. "Please, please help me!"

The kelpie throws back its scaly head and roars, its teeth jagged and yellow. Morag is lifted momentarily out of the river before the creature dives, dragging her struggling deeper and deeper into the suddenly roiling water. On shore, the old woman smiles. Lord Selkirk's ship sets sail in a month, and she will be on it.

CHAPTER TWENTY-SEVEN

June 21, 1950

Beet MacNeill

It's midafternoon but feels like nightfall, and still not a bird in the sky, not a sound but the waves and the channel marker, clanging deep and slow. We're standing on the shore of Poxy Island, with Dad's lobster boat anchored as close by as possible. The tide is rising and there is a good quarter mile of choppy water between us and Poxy Point. It hasn't started to rain yet, but the wind, cold as late November, shears through my damp pant legs. Freddy's standing beside me; I can see a curved knife—like the kind you use to gut fish—sticking out of his jacket pocket, in a leather sheath. Next to him, Jeannine is dressed right for once, or at least warmly, in a yellow Sears catalogue raincoat with little flowers all over it, a kerchief covering her hair.

A little farther down the beach, Deirdre and Sean stand

facing the water. Lily Soloman is standing in the stern of the lobster boat, steady despite the rolling waves, her gray hair fluttering around her face. She volunteered to stay behind with the boat, since outside of Freddy and me, she's the only one who can pilot it, and as she said, "There may be a need." I have my fiddle, its case wrapped in an old raincoat to keep it dry until it's time to use it. Mom and Dad weren't back from Rollo Bay when we came for the boat (small favors) so I've left them a note saying that we all went out early. I just have to hope they don't ask *where* we went, though if things go wrong, I guess I'll have a lot worse things to worry about than Mom's temper.

Poxy Island is all over gulls. They are roosting on the rocky beach, dozens of them, their feet tucked under their fat bodies, their heads turned in different directions, still as a painting except for where the breeze ruffles their feathers. Bird droppings are splattered white and almost glowing on the red rocks and sandy shore of the little island. The wind is still picking up slowly, but below its whisper is another low sound, that song of sinking and drowning, Marina's voice coming through the trees, and I fight off that flicker of dizziness that comes with it.

"Beet," Jeannine whispers (it feels as if we should whisper). "Do you hear that?"

I reach out for her hand and squeeze it. Dizziness washes over me for just a second as the tune—mixed with the wind—rises and falls and almost disappears. "It's coming from the other side of the island. The Strait side."

There's a thicket of black spruce covering most of the island. Freddy points toward a partly grown-over footpath. "Through there."

Deirdre steps forward first and we follow her toward the trees, picking our way through the crowd of gulls. As we go into the spruce wood, single file, the wind dies down and Marina's song becomes easier to hear. It isn't far to the other side of the wood, but it's hard going with Marina's voice reaching into my head. I need to walk more slowly to keep my balance. Slows Jeannine down, too. Even Freddy looks green. Sean puts out a hand like he wants to steady me, but I shake my head. It's not to be mean, though. I just need to be strong, like Deirdre. Only Deirdre walks straight and quick, like she doesn't hear Marina at all, or doesn't care. The gulls are everywhere even as the ragged black trees bend in toward us. Gulls are nesting right on the branches. Mosquitoes swarm around us, too, the farther we get into the woods, and without the sound of the birds, their buzzing is loud as a sawmill on a Tuesday afternoon. Still, it's not loud enough to drown out Marina's call.

The path opens up a bit to a clearing, all strewn with old rusty spruce needles and broken branches. The needles make the wet ground right slippy, though the smell of them perks me up a bit. At the center of the clearing is a circle of sandstone grave markers, overgrown with tall grass and wild blueberry bushes. The names on the markers are gone, if there ever were any, except on one great granite stone in the middle of the circle. The top and sides are covered in moss, but these fading words can still be seen: "Here lie the crew and passengers of the HMS Polly, from South Uist, Scotland. Dead of smallpox. Interred here July 31st, 1820. Tread softly." A list of mostly Scottish names follows: MacLean, MacDonald, Ferguson, even MacNeill, and I won't deny the sight of it shakes me.

"John Ferguson," Deirdre says out loud, but her voice is like a ghost's. "The sea captain."

A fat gull sits atop each grave, all as quiet as judges, and there are more birds spread out in the clearing. They turn their heads toward us, eyes like small shiny stones. Above us, thunderclouds are gathering, and Marina Shaw's voice is closer now, just beyond these trees, on the Strait side of the island. A flash of lightning fills the clearing for a moment, then there's a pause and the rumble of thunder, maybe five miles away. The gulls don't stir a speck.

This time it's Sean who gets us moving again. The path goes on past the graves, downward through the trees to a low bank hung over with sideways-leaning spruce. Through the opening in the trees, the Strait can be seen, and the gray sky above it, too. To get to the beach, we have to climb down carefully, placing our feet on tree roots and the flat places on red sandstone boulders. I slip a couple of times and have to grab on to Jeannine.

Sean gets to the bottom first and helps the rest of us down. The beach on this side is rocky, and it, too, is covered in gulls sitting quietly, waiting. I never knew there were so many gulls in the world. Some are brown and speckled, some white with wings gray like the sky above us, some with black heads, some black winged and big as cats—the minister gulls. I find myself looking for the one with the crooked beak, but he's not with them.

On this side of the island, the water is moving in slow swells, and the almost fully high tide meets the red rocks that stick out above the surf. The waves hit the shore, splitting off in different directions at the island's tip, folding over one another, a rip tide. Still, despite the gray of the sky and the lightning just a moment ago, the sea is far from wild. There are rocks, boulders, on the beach, much more so than on the landward side of the island, but the water washes over them in a smooth sweep, and the air is as still as the quiet, curious gulls that surround us. It's then I realize that I haven't heard Marina's song since we began to climb down the bank.

"Where is she?" Jeannine says out loud, but Deirdre puts a hand on her shoulder to quiet her. As we step forward along the length of beach, the gulls start to move, slowly, to let us through. In the strange stillness that surrounds us, I do hear what sounds like a gull, a loud and angry gull, but it's nowhere that I can see. I spare a glance at Sean and catch him watching me, too, but there's not time to think about the look in his blue eyes.

About one hundred feet to the left of us, the bank becomes a gentle slope where the trees meet the water. Marina Shaw—or whatever her name is—steps out from a grouping of trees. She is barefoot and bare legged, wrapped in her starfish shawl, a green brocade dress beneath it that reaches just past her knees. The air around us is heavy, dull as the dull gray sky, flat as the speaking voice that comes from Marina Shaw's hard, smooth, white, beautiful face.

"So you've come." Marina's lip curls in a sneer. Her eyes are on Deirdre.

"Where's my baby?" Deirdre's voice is shaky at first, but she takes a deep breath and goes on more steadily. "I've come to offer myself for the tithe."

Freddy moves to stand beside Deirdre, and the quiet gulls close in around them.

"But you have to agree to our deal first." Freddy's voice is strong as I've ever heard it. Deirdre smiles at him and reaches for his hand.

Marina Shaw's green eyes flash bright bitterness, but her words are dull as mud. "Deal? You have nothing to bargain with, and I have . . . the child." I hear that cry again. It's a gull for sure, but something else, too, high-pitched. . . .

"But you need a willing sacrifice," I say. I have to talk loudly to get her to take her eyes off Deirdre. "So we're here to offer you a contest."

Sean steps closer to me, and Jeannine puts her skinny arm around my shoulder and sticks out her pointy chin. "That's right," she says. "A *music* contest."

Marina lets out a dry sound that is probably meant to be a laugh. "Let me guess. You think this girl's music can turn the waters against me. And if you can, I forego the tithe. I seek my sacrifice elsewhere."

"No," Deirdre says. "You stop looking for sacrifices. You give up and live out the rest of your body's natural life, then die like everyone else has to."

There's that almost-laugh again, Marina choking on her own meanness. "And whose idea was this? The old woman's? Yes, I remember her, that weak child who couldn't save her father. And now she sends more children to fight *me*." I feel my heart hardening with a feeling worse than anger or fear. It's hatred. I hate Marina Shaw, or whoever she is, for what she did to Gerry and all the others. Who knows how many?

Then she eyes Sean for a moment. "And what would your aunties say?" He doesn't answer, just takes another step closer to me, and that small gesture is enough to keep the hate from overpowering me, to remember the happy girl in those drawings, the girl he sees. Marina Shaw raises a perfectly groomed eyebrow.

"You foolish people with your superstitions and stories. Do you know how long I've lived? Don't you think I've heard all these fairy tales? Do you think I don't know what you are trying? As if no one has tried before." Marina Shaw smirks. "That's not the way things really go." Still, there's a quaver in her voice, even if it is ever so slight. I'm not sure anyone *has* tried before, not with her, anyway. Her hand goes to her seashell necklace and tightens around it. The incoming waves spread across the hard sand like a bridal veil, fall back, then spread forward again. The air smells of spruce needles and salt and rot.

"Well, if you don't agree to the contest, no one is getting into that water for you willingly." Jeannine says this, and she's got her hands on her hips now, too. The look in her eyes is pure Mom.

"Look," Sean whispers to me. "Look how she holds on to that necklace." Jeannine nods; she's seen it, too.

Marina Shaw smiles, and it's like a scar across her face. "I think you will, when you see where the child is." The air is still not moving, and that one far-off gull has gotten louder. "Follow me, won't you?"

She turns without another word and makes her way toward where the bank juts out into the Strait. The sound of the gull (and the something else) is coming from that direction. Deirdre and Freddy follow, holding hands, with me behind, the wrapped-up fiddle still under my arm, and Sean and Jeannine beside me. "I don't like this," she whispers. I don't either, not one bit, but I have to keep my focus.

We don't have to go far before I see it: a low, flat sandbar about twenty feet from shore, just the other side of the point of land, where the waves meet and cross and move apart again like dancers. On the sandbar is a wooden lobster trap, the square kind, big enough to fit ten adult lobster . . . or one year-old baby. And now I know what I've been hearing. It's the crooked-beaked gull pacing back and forth on top of the trap, and Joseph inside, crying and calling to us. He's still out of reach of the rising tide, but it is inching forward with each wave, eating up his time. The minister gull is flapping its wings and squawking at something that floats low in the waves beyond the sandbar, at the drop-off: two bloodred eyes, swollen, set above a tangle of bleached horse hair and kelp—the creature from the Cardigan River, the water horse. The memory of it comes back to me in a terrible rush, but I push it away.

Deirdre has gone pale and trembling, but her eyes have steel in them. Marina Shaw's face is hard as marble.

I hand Jeannine the fiddle.

Deirdre doesn't even look in Marina's direction. Instead, she takes Freddy's other hand. They've been friends their whole lives, and maybe that's what I hear in her voice now. "Get my baby, Freddy. Keep him safe." All he does is nod, but as he turns toward the water, there are tears in his eyes. Deirdre speaks to me next, just one word: "Play." Then she's gone, into the water.

Jeannine has already unwrapped the fiddle and hands it back to me. At the same time, Marina starts singing, her voice a high, clear, hungry trill. I back up to shelter under the leaning spruce. There's worry in my heart, but I raise the instrument to my chin anyway and draw the bow across the upper strings. I start with tunes I know well, "Maiden's Prayer," "Old Joe Clark," even "Pop Goes the Weasel." Around me the gulls are silent, staring. Marina's tune moves like the tide, rising, falling, turning in on itself, pulling everything along with it, into the sea. Her voice billows over me, and so does a quick urge to throw myself into the water. As if he knows this, Sean puts his hand on my shoulder long enough for the feeling to pass, though I know it could come back easily. The water starts to bubble and boil against the rocks. I don't shake Sean's hand away.

Freddy is at the end of the point, wading out to where Joseph is trapped. He looks toward Deirdre, who is swimming toward the creature with the red eyes. When she reaches the drop-off, she disappears for a moment beneath the waves, but then I see her, hair floating as she treads water about twenty feet away from the waiting creature.

Marina's song rises higher and higher until it seems like something other than music, other than human. The wind has risen with it, spinning, lifting sand into my face. I lose my tune for a moment; the notes lose their truth. But I keep going with "Whiskey in the Jar," the tune that had them all dancing at the Cozy Hall—it seems so long ago now. The waves are capped with white; Marina's song becomes a shriek of laughter as Deirdre sinks under them once more.

Freddy reaches the sandbar just as the waves break with a crash against the shore. He uses the knife he brought with him to cut the ropes of the trap. As the water rises ever higher, the black-backed gull hovers over him, on the wind, nagging.

Just as I switch to the whirling, happy notes of "The Dusty Miller," tapping my feet on the hard, wet sand, Jeannine points to the sandbar. The creature is sitting lower in the water than before. Its eyes seem less red, its head smaller, and it has turned away from Deirdre, toward the shore, toward us. Jeannine calls to me above the wind. "Something is happening, Beet. It's listening . . . to you. It's listened before."

Sean's hand is still on my shoulder. He gives me a light squeeze. "Keep going!"

Freddy has got Joseph now and is holding him in his arms; the baby has stopped crying and buries his head in Freddy's shoulder. The reversing waves hit Freddy hard, shattering into tiny droplets all around him, but he does not let go of Joseph. The water horse sways back toward Deirdre, moving forward in time with Marina's tune, in rhythm with the rolling waves. Marina's voice swirls higher and higher now, lifting the tide into the beginnings of a whirlpool. I feel faint again as the music pulls me toward its hollow center. I fight it, and so does Freddy. He grips Joseph as they stumble forward out of the water. Freddy falls and rolls onto his back, always keeping the baby safe, then lies there a moment, not letting go. Jeannine gets to them first, followed by the mottled-winged gull, flapping and hollering. Jeannine wraps the baby inside her coat. She joins me and Sean by the bank as Freddy heads back into the water. The wind blows and blows, making its own sounds, shrill as the voice that called it up, but wilder, too, without plan or purpose.

Then comes the cymbal crash of thunder overhead, and the sky opens; raindrops pierce the surface of the Strait like needles through skin. The water horse creature with the bloodred eyes is twelve feet from Deirdre now and moving fast, as the sea spins and spins around them. Freddy fights the current to put himself between Deirdre and the monster. He's treading water, his wet hair in his face. Then the sea swells again, and they are all hidden from my eyes.

Marina's song keeps turning in on itself, repeating itself, like merry-go-round music. The undertow feeling washes through me again, the panic of drowning, and worse, that feeling that life itself is empty, that maybe drowning is a good idea. Next to me, Sean has started trembling, just slightly. Sheltered by the trees with Jeannine, Sean, and Joseph, I am safe from the worst of the rain, but my fiddle is creaking with the dampness of the air, the sound so far from true that I might as well not be playing at all. On top of that, the wind, the sea, and Marina's twisting tune make it so I have to strain just to hear myself. Still, I go through the motions. What else can I do?

Despite the roaring air all round us, despite the spinning, empty pull of Marina's song, the gulls stay as calm as judges, sitting still on the sand or riding the rolling water. Except the minister gull. He's pacing at my feet, squawking so loud that I do have to stop playing, if just for a second. When I do, I notice what I should have been paying attention to all along: Joseph, in Jeannine's arms, crying again, the tears rolling down his cheeks and meeting at his tiny chin. He's crying for his mother in little gasping sobs that swell and fall away and swell again, repeating like the waves, like the pull of Marina's voice.

But also not like it.

Joseph's shoulders rise and fall with each sob, as they did

that day in my room, when I almost had Gerry's tune. The rise and fall come slowly, a quiet sadness, not one that says, "Look at me. Feel sorry for ME!" It's a father sitting by his child's hospital bed with his head in his hands, a widow alone in an empty church, past raging, but not past weeping. Watching Joseph, I can hear the tune in my head, exactly as it sounded on that morning in the rose garden. The tune Gerry played for me, that saved me at the river. Gerry's tune says, "Good men drown. Terrible things happen, and who knows why?" It's sorrow too deep for whining and whinging, a sorrow that comes to everyone and keeps coming, an old sorrow, old like the sea, as salt as tears. Sorrow like falling water, worrying the rocks until they are smooth. Marina's voice will never sound like that, with all its hollow beauty. Hollow because her heart is hollow, wooden horses going nowhere, circling an empty space. But Gerry's tune is *full*, not just of sorrow but of love. It's full of Deirdre, out there now, facing that monster to keep Joseph safe; full of Joseph weeping in Jeannine's arms; full of me, and Mom and Dad, and Freddy and Jeannine—their loyalty. I can hear Lily in it, too, Lily who never forgot her father, who lived so long alone and reached out to Sean in his loneliness. And Sean's there, his blue eyes watching everything, making beauty from what he sees. I can feel Gerry's music now, welling up behind my own eyes. "Keep going," it sings, "in spite of your tears." In spite of the rain. In spite of a creaking fiddle.

Next to me, Sean has let go of my shoulder and is singing,

slow and sad, and suddenly I can see him as that lonely boy at his mother's deathbed, and there's an ache in my heart for him. He looks at me, and even in the rain, I can tell there are tears in his eyes.

I close my own eyes and draw the bow low across the strings.

CHAPTER TWENTY-EIGHT

Long ago

The Sea God

The sea god has answered to many names and takes many shapes: sometimes a man, sometimes a horse like those that grace the prows of the ships that set sail from Carthage and Tyre, and sometimes a monster, red-eyed and rough-scaled, as he is now, lying low in the water and waiting. In times of distress, of famine or war, the people occasionally seek to placate the sea god with sacrifice, tossing their children from the cliffs or chaining them to rocks that will be covered at high tide. He has dragged many such sacrifices with him beneath the waves, though he rarely sends the asked-for blessings.

The sacrifice this time is young, not a girl perhaps, but young still, with long yellow hair hanging down her back and eyes that glint green against her pale, perfect skin. Her gown is the purple reserved for the priestly class, dyed from the shells of the sea snails that live in abundance along these shores. Unlike the sacrifices brought to him in the past, this one is not weeping, nor pulling at the chain that trails out from beneath her purple gown as the tide rises and the water covers more and more of the platform, ready to swallow her up. Instead, she sings.

Her beautiful face is hard, but she sings a song so soft and alluring that it draws the sea god farther in toward shore. Around him, he feels the waves rise and fall, just slightly, but to the rhythm of her voice, high and clear and haunting. Hidden within the bell-like notes of the song is a command.

The woman has always been able to call things to herself with her voice. Even mortals can have magic, and this is hers. Her mother taught her long ago how to lure in ships that sailed close to their island home, that the sailors might wreck themselves on the rocks and give up their treasure for salvage. With her mother, she has dressed in the feathers of seabirds and called the ships to her. Her mother has told her stories about the sea god, that to take a part of the sea god is to steal his power. If she can bind him, he will give her what she wants most. He will answer her questions. He must speak the truth.

The woman looks out onto the sea, but the creature is not visible. She sings the song her mother taught her, its words older than time, as old as the sea before her, calm and sparkling in the sun. Only once has the song failed, and only in the face of another song—a stronger one, that which trapped her mother and took away her power, so that she is nothing now but a washerwoman living in a shack.

The sky is as bright blue as the precious stones brought by sailors from Egypt, and the sea breeze carries with it a scent of salt and decay. A shadow falls between the woman and the sun. It is a young man, dark-haired and handsome, his eyes blue black like the darkest parts of the sea. He pulls himself up on the rock while she sings on as if he were not there. He falls asleep beside her, a dog at a widow's feet, and as he sleeps she takes out the knife that she has hidden beneath the folds of her dress. Her mother brought it to her in the night, after the priests left. The sun has begun to dry the man's hair, and though it is slightly sticky in her hands, she is able to hold a lock of it long enough to cut it off with the knife.

Around her neck is a silver chain with a pendant shaped like a sea snail's shell. The pendant can be opened by a clasp at the top. She springs the clasp and places the lock of hair inside, closes the pendant, then rubs her hands together to remove the rest of the stickiness. Then, slowly, she uses her knife to rattle the lock on the metal cuff that holds her ankle. All the while, she continues to hum her strange, ancient song, sending ripples across the water like breath.

In his dreams, the sea god is falling into the depths of the sea, too weak to stop himself, his power drifting away. He awakens to see the woman in the purple gown. She is sitting beside him in silence, her green eyes steady upon him, but she is no longer bound to the rock. The tide has risen almost to the foot of the cliffs above them, and there is a crumbling stone staircase that leads up to the top of the cliff. The sea god sits up slowly but can move no farther, held by some invisible chain.

"We are bound together, creature," the woman says. Her voice when she speaks is strangely flat. "You must answer to me now."

The sea god lifts his hand to his head, feeling the small bald patch where she has removed the lock of hair. Then his eyes fall on a silver shell pendant hanging from her long white neck. He reaches out a hand to snatch the pendant and return to the water, dragging this arrogant child-woman with him as he goes. Instead, he is seized with pain like a dagger cutting through his arm.

The woman's laugh is like winter.

"You see," she says. "And I know you must speak truly. Tell me what I want to know, and I will set you free."

Sea birds call from the cliffs, and above their heads the sun beats down harshly, burning this human skin of his.

"Ask," he says.

"How can I live forever, be young forever?" Her eyes are wide with greed. She is not the first to ask him this question. The sea god exhales slowly before answering.

"No human can live forever, only the gods."

Her reply is swift and sharp. "Then how can I become a god?"

The sea god is still young and handsome in this form but

burning in pain from within. He struggles not to answer. He looks off toward the empty horizon where birds are diving for their meals, white flashes against the blue sky. The salt air dries his throat.

The young woman's face is eager though her voice remains calm. "There is a way, isn't there?"

The sea god speaks slowly. He must get back into the water. "There is a way to be *like* a god."

"Tell me."

"Gods are made by tribute."

"Liar." The woman spits out the word. "I have seen the priests give tribute. I have seen them burn children, for good harvest, for safe voyage. The sacrifices make no difference."

The sea god's eyes, bleary from the heat and salt and sun, scan the cliff's edge, where someone is standing, dressed in white. "Tributes must enter the sea willingly. Like the mothers who fling themselves in after their dead children, the lovers who try to save each other from the priests' flames. Those are the tributes that are accepted. If you can lure someone to the sea, to die there willingly, you will keep your youth and beauty, for a time."

"When, when must I do this?" The woman's fingers close tightly around her locket. Behind her the person in white—it is a woman, small and plump, with straw-colored hair coiled around her head—is making her way down the cliff steps.

"There is no set time," the sea god says. "You will know because you will start to age. Your body will again become subject to time and illness. Not all tribute is equal, and there is no calendar for the tithe." A breeze rises, hot as a dying breath. He reaches out his hand. "Now release me."

The young woman laughs, clinging to the necklace.

"You cannot lie, creature, but I can. I will need your help if I am to gather my sacrifices."

The sea god feels his eyes flash red, but he speaks calmly, as to a child. "This will not end as you think. You may command me for a time, perhaps even a long time. But it will end badly. The sea will have its own."

"It will have its own, creature." The young woman's green eyes narrow at him. "But it will not have me."

The plump woman with the straw-colored hair has reached the bottom of the cliff steps and is running along the narrow beach toward the rocks. The sea god sighs.

"And who will you trade this time for your . . . eternal . . . youth?" he asks. "Remember. They must go willingly."

"Oh. She will." Her green eyes darken almost to black. "A mother will do anything to save her child."

She flicks her hand at him.

"You may return to the water, but do not go far."

The sea god slips off the rock, transforming as he does into his true shape. He lies in wait now, just beneath the surface, his bloodred eyes scanning the shore. The woman in white has reached the edge of the water and is wading toward the stone platform, her gown floating up around her. The sea god can make out her face now, and beneath its roundness and soft lines he can see a hint of the features of the woman who has just entrapped him. The older woman is calling and calling, a name he cannot quite hear, while the sea god's new mistress stretches out upon the platform, her pale face turned upward toward the sun, and starts to sing.

CHAPTER TWENTY-NINE

June 21, 1950

Beet MacNeill

Marina sings out a note that's true as death and high enough to shatter a teacup. Her voice cuts through me, almost taking my balance again, but I dig my feet into the sand and hold on, closing my ears to Marina, the storm, to everything except the tune I hear in my head. I just think of the rose garden and seeing Gerry's ghost, my big cousin, my friend, who died before he ever saw his baby's face. My heart fills up with that moment I realized he was gone from us. When I open my eyes, Joseph is still crying. His little lip is quivering, his chest moving up and down like he can't catch his breath. I match my playing, the rhythm of it, to the rise and fall of his sobs. My own tears are falling now, too, and I use them to feed the tune, a short up bow for each tear that falls, like taking in breath, as my right foot taps out the tempo on the wet sand. Then a longer note on the down bow, a slow sad sigh. It's a lament I'm playing, and my whole body echoes with it. I follow the waves of grief up and down the tune, letting them go, like they've been held inside me this whole year, which they have.

Sean is singing not two feet away from me. He's pouring his everything into the tune, like he knows it by heart, and his kind blue eyes are shining. It makes me proud to have him next to me, him and Jeannine both.

Before I can wonder how that's possible, I hear someone playing along with us.

"Boy!" Joseph's eyes are round as moons and his lip has stopped quivering. He bounces up and down in Jeannine's arms, pointing to something in the corner of my vision. "Boy, boy, boy!" When I turn, there's Gerry, just where the black-backed gull was a moment ago. He's wearing the same clothes as the morning he died, and his face is just as grave. Still, the tune flows from his fiddle, steady and sad, like blood from a broken heart. Together we play, and I feel the wind die down for a second. Marina must, too, because a shadow passes over her narrow face and she grips her necklace until her knuckles turn white. She starts to sing even stronger now, whipping the wind up into a gale that lifts bits of seaweed and driftwood to spin around us. Jeannine backs up against the bank as close as she can while Joseph keeps calling, "Boy! Boy! Boy!" The rain is picking up, falling in fat drops that splatter on the sand. Even in the shelter of the bank, I know what all this damp is doing to my fiddle, but I hold on, matching Gerry note for note as best I can.

Beside me, Sean's blue eyes are wide. He stops singing just long enough to shout, "I know him! I've seen him before!"

Then Sean takes up the tune again. He's not the best singer in the world, but his soul is in it, his good soul. The notes ring in the salt air. They wrap themselves around Marina's cold, shrill warble.

Beyond the shore, Freddy is treading water, facing the monster. If he wanted to, he could touch it, just reach out and touch its vicious, scaly face. In fact, he's moving in that direction. Deirdre, too. Marina Shaw's green eyes flash and her voice rises in a whir that cuts at my inner ear, making me wobble so it's all I can do to stand up straight. She keeps singing and the creature moves closer to Freddy, its head rising from the water as it opens its long, jagged mouth. I want to scream "No," but I have to keep playing. I use my fear for Freddy in the tune, a long, trembling note on the up bow, then down in short strokes as Gerry and I play together, fighting to calm the wind as Marina fights to raise it. Beyond the sandbar, Deirdre is struggling against the rolling gray water. She reaches for Freddy's hand just as he grabs the coils of the monster's seaweed mane. Then they disappear once more, Freddy, Deirdre, and the water horse, behind a sea swell as tall as a man.

Tears fill my eyes again, but I keep following Gerry as the tune begins to shift, and the long up and down notes of the lament give way to the rhythm of a waltz, one two three, one two three. Around us, the gulls have started calling and mewing in time with Gerry's playing. The rhythm pulls Marina's song with it, slowing it down, slowing down the whirling wind. There's a hiss in Marina's voice now, like she's emptying of air, but Gerry's and my tune is *filling up*, with the sounds of other voices. Sean's voice, but others as well. Other instruments, too, all kinds. Beside Gerry now stands a man in his thirties, dressed in fisherman's boots and a mack. He has Gerry's same freckles and wild hair and is playing a fiddle, too, his sad blue eyes trained on Marina the whole time. She doesn't stop singing when she sees him, but she takes a step back, holding on to her necklace with both hands now. The strings on my fiddle are loosening just slightly, but I focus on the sounds around me, and bow the strings to that one-two-three rhythm.

Beside me, Sean's singing has become a wail. My heart hurts for him, and I put that pain into my playing, too.

One by one, where the gulls were a moment before, more ghosts appear on the sand, adding to our music, all in different ways. There's a tall, dark man with a long, tattered coat and sad brown eyes like Freddy's. As the man's scarred hands clap out the rhythm of our tune, the expression on Gerry's face changes just slightly to the beginnings of a grin, that little smile he used to have, not quite big enough to show dimples. The spirits of the smallpox victims come next—men, women, and children, with pale, wrecked faces, singing together in a kind of mournful harmony. There's an older woman, too, in a long, white gown, hair coiled on her head like the ladies in schoolbooks about ancient history. She sings in a soprano as strong as Marina's, but with a sweetness to it, like she's singing to a baby. As more and more people join us, they add layers to the tune. We sing and play together, and the music starts to move quicker, turning and turning against Marina's. We're playing a jig now, but with an undertone, a low trembling whisper. It's the music of real feeling—sadness and grieving and fear, but happiness, too, spinning, dancing happiness, and love. And as our tune grows and grows, the winds die down even more. Marina's hollow singing is becoming just one strain within the rush of music surrounding me. Her pale face tightens up as she fights to keep her song going, and her eyes have a lost look. She goes on singing, though, squeezing that pendant of hers like she's breaking a bird's neck. My eyes search the water for Deirdre and Freddy.

Beyond the sandbar, Freddy's hand has gotten tangled in the water horse's oily mane, and the creature is pulling him out toward open water. The waves out there are still coming fast and hard as fists, but Deirdre hasn't let go of Freddy's other hand. Then the creature makes its dive, Freddy and Deirdre along with it, and my fiddle comes apart in my hands. I let out a wail of my own as Marina's song becomes a trill of gloating laughter, cutting into the harmony that Sean, Gerry, and the others have built up around us.

"Deirdre!" I'm roaring now. "Freddy!"

Jeannine steps out from the shelter of the bank, closer to Marina, keeping Joseph's face turned from the water and the empty space where his mother used to be. "Keep going, Beet! If you can't play, sing!"

There's not much I can say for my singing voice, but I know

she's right. I grab Sean's hand and join him and the others, the whole beach full of people—men, women, and children—playing and singing and tapping their feet. I lift my voice in a kind of tiddle-tar-tum, holding the notes as best I can. Then that sharp gust of air rises up, like the one we felt that time out clamming, when Joseph got lost on the beach. It's that quick burst of air that means the tide is turning, outward this time.

Still singing, Marina moves nearer to the edge of the water, like she's chasing that tide, and raises both hands to the clouds.

"She's let go of it!" Jeannine calls out over the music as it rings around us. "The necklace!" She darts forward, still holding the baby, and grabs the twisting shell from Marina's white neck, breaking the silver chain. Marina's song becomes a scream.

Jeannine stands in front of Marina, holding the necklace over her head and yelling. "Come and get it, you Devil!" I follow Gerry with my voice as he and the other fiddler (Uncle Angus? It has to be Uncle Angus!) slow the tempo to a lullaby. The wind dies down with it, and the waves stop battering at the rocks beyond shore. The rain just ceases, like it was never raining at all, leaving a soft, silken breeze across my face. For a moment all I can hear is Gerry's tune, mine and Gerry's, and the chorus of voices of the dead all around us. The tune becomes a whisper, and I let my voice fall away. Only Sean is left on the last note, his face full of sorrow. Then he stops and looks around like he's forgotten where he is.

There is another sound on the air now, though it takes me a moment to recognize it: the *ticktickt ick* of a motor, coming from around the sandstone outcrop. Then Dad's lobster boat comes into view with Lily Soloman at the wheel. She cuts the motor and the boat slows, floating on the diminishing waves.

As Lily weighs anchor, Marina opens her mouth again, not singing this time, just calling out roughly, "Uist!" But all I care about is what I see next. Deirdre is making her way toward shore. Alone, she limps out of the water, her wet dress covered in red sand whipped up by the tide, her arms and legs beaten and bruised. On the beach, the spirits of the dead part to let her through.

"Uist!" Marina calls again, almost like she's pleading. Deirdre reaches Jeannine and takes Joseph in her arms, kissing his curly hair. Behind her, a man's head surfaces near shore, dark wet hair covering his eyes. At first I think it's Freddy, but then Mr. Uist rises out of the water, naked to make a nun blush. His eyes are still red and swelling, but as he makes his way up the sand—toward Jeannine, not Marina—they change to dark brown. He stands in front of Jeannine and reaches out his hand. Then everything goes silent as a sick room.

As all around us the seas and the winds die down to a pure stillness, Uist speaks in a voice like running water. "That belongs to me," he tells Jeannine, who is doing everything she can to look at his face and nowhere else. She drops the necklace into his hand, blushing the whole time. Beside me, Sean is shivering. I squeeze his hand and smile.

The beach is still crowded with ghosts, silent and still, their eyes on Uist as his bare feet become hooves, and his legs the hind legs of a horse. Deirdre holds Joseph closer to her, and I step forward to take Jeannine's hand, trailing Sean with me. Then Uist turns toward Marina and, in one motion, grabs her arm before she can call out. As he dives, pulling Marina with him into the now flat, calm water, his body lengthens and grows scales. Uist drags her under the surface once he reaches the lobster boat, and that's when she starts to scream. For a moment, we hear her voice coming from under the water, shrill with the first emotion I've ever heard in it. Fear. Then there's a gurgle. Then nothing.

As Jeannine, Sean, Deirdre, Joseph, and I stand on the quiet beach, I see the man in the tattered coat gaze out across the water toward Lily, now standing in the stern of Dad's boat. She raises her hand to him as, one by one, he and the other specters that surrounded us become a flock of gulls once again. The birds turn their heads toward us, eyes gleaming, the water lapping gently at the shore. Then, quick as a wink, the gulls are rising from the beach. We duck and cover our heads as they turn in the air, as a group, and fly out over the water, across the Strait toward Nova Scotia. All but Gerry Campbell, who stands before us in his wet clothes, the fiddle at his side. He looks at his son, bouncing up and down in Deirdre's bruised arms.

"Gerry?" Deirdre whispers it, her eyes wide, while Joseph reaches out toward his father, pointing and laughing.

"'Ook, Mama! 'ook! Boy!"

Sean stares in wonder. He whispers to me, "I know him. I saw him the night my mother . . ." He stops suddenly and looks around, like he's remembering something, or someone.

"Freddy . . . ," Jeannine whispers.

There is no sign of him, but in the water, just past the almost covered-up sandbar and moving shoreward, a trail of blood can be seen.

"Oh, no." Jeannine says it so quietly, it's almost as if I hear her in my head. In the silence, the tide billows forward and pulls back again. Jeannine begins to sniffle, and Deirdre holds tighter to Joseph, who is quiet as can be.

My eyes stay on the water, where a shadow is moving beneath the cloud of blood. Freddy's face comes out of the water, his eyes closed, his mouth gasping for breath.

The trail of blood follows him as he reaches shore and struggles toward us, bruised and beat up and holding his bloody right hand against his chest. In his left hand he holds his fish-cutting knife. The clouds are thinning above our heads. Deirdre turns from Gerry to Freddy as Jeannine pulls the kerchief from her hair and wraps Freddy's hand the best she can. He gives a sad smile that makes me know he sees Gerry, too. The two young men look at each other for a moment, nodding once, before Gerry's gaze moves to Deirdre. Tears are falling down her face, but her eyes are sparkling, and she smiles at him. No one speaks, not a single word. It doesn't even feel like I'm breathing. Then Gerry's eyes light on mine as he lifts the ghost of his fiddle to his chin to play one last perfect note. I raise my hand to him, and it's shaking. "Oh, Gerry," I whisper from my full heart, like on the day I saw him first in the rose garden. "Oh, dear Gerry. Goodbye."

Then Joseph cries out, "Bye, boy! Bye!" I look at him quick, but when I turn back, the black-backed gull has taken Gerry's place and is already hovering above us. In the air is the faint sound of a new tune, a true jig, but with a hint of the one Gerry played in the rose garden on that morning that seems like yesterday, and like a hundred years ago, too. The gull stares at us for a moment and then wheels away on the breeze. I glance toward Lily Soloman, and even from here, I can see the look of peace on her face.

On the still, quiet beach, the scent of roses kisses the salt air, and far-off seabirds call.

CHAPTER THIRTY

August 20, 1950

Beet MacNeill

It's taken almost two months to get Marina Shaw's last scream out of my head—Marina Shaw, or whoever she was. I don't know how many times she changed identities over the years and centuries, or how far back her lives go—but from the look of those gull ghosts on the beach, it was farther back than just arriving here from Scotland. I'll never know the whole story, but I do know that it's over now. I haven't felt the undertow since that day on Poxy Island, not even in my dreams. And I haven't seen Gerry either, although that gull comes around sometimes, peeking in the window or balancing on the rose garden fence.

Jeannine and I start at Montague High School in two weeks, though Jeannine is more excited about that than I am. Joseph seems to be growing overnight, his head reaching higher than the porch railing now. He can say more words than just "Mama," "Boy," and "Bird," too. He says "Beet," and "cookie," and "Freddy." Freddy comes by all the time to play with him and see Deirdre. She smiles when he visits, and sometimes they take Joseph on walks by the beach. Other times just the two of them go. Gerry set her free that day on Poxy Island.

"When's he going to ask her to marry him?" Mom asks, really to herself as she sets out a plate of biscuits on the porch table. The sky-blue pink evening stretches out all around us, and the breeze is like a kitten cuddling up against me.

"Soon enough," Dad says, then turns to me. "How's Jeannine taking it?"

"Oh," I just laugh. Dad's always behind on the news and gossip. "She's after Gordie MacLean now. Got his own truck and a head full of curly blond hair."

"Somebody ought to watch that girl," Mom sniffs. I'm not worried about Jeannine, though. She's got too much to her to get mixed up with Gordie MacLean. She's just looking. Told me she's thinking of going to school to be a Mountie or policewoman or something. She read about it in the *Guardian*. I haven't the heart to tell her they don't let in girls, not for police duty anyway, but who knows? Jeannine's the type to make them change their minds.

Sean is going back to Boston today, and then back to that school in New Hampshire, where he'll live in a dormitory and play sports and wear a uniform. He came by with his aunts to say goodbye. I gave him a new sketchbook; that other one was pretty crammed, after all. We promised to write, and he will send me drawings now and again. The Publicovers are already planning to have him back next summer.

He walked with me out in the rose garden before he left, just the two of us, and it was the first time I've felt happy there since Gerry died. He talked about his neighborhood in Boston and the Public Garden they have there with swan boats and with weeping willows and busking musicians everywhere, and how he always used to go there with his mother. I told him about Gerry and all our adventures. Before Sean had to go, he made a move like he wanted to kiss me. So I kissed him first, long enough so that he won't forget me. I was quiet for a long time after he left, just looking at the roses and thinking.

There's going to be a dance in September, raising money for a new library. It was Lily Soloman's idea, now that she has decided to stay on there full time. Mom is making me a dress to wear onstage, and more important, she and Dad surprised me with a new fiddle. Well, it's not new, really. They found it at a church sale and Dad fixed it up for me, polished and re-stringed and everything. They never pressed me about the old one either. I thought Mom would flip her lid about it for sure, but she didn't. It's like we have an understanding now, Mom and me. She can still be right sour, of course, but it's different somehow.

I watch baby Joseph on the lawn with Freddy, rolling in the grass, running, chasing birds. Deirdre looks so happy. Even though I haven't seen Gerry again since that night, once in a while, I think I hear him playing his fiddle. It's a new song, though. Quicker, brighter, like you could swing to it. I'm trying to learn it for the dance. When they ask me where I learned it, I'll say I had it from the sea.

AUTHOR'S NOTE

While *The Coming Storm* tells the story of a Scottish Canadian girl and her friends, and touches on the experience of settlers and immigrants, it is good to remember that Prince Edward Island has a long history of human habitation. The Island's first people are the Mi'kmaq, who arrived at least twelve thousand years ago to the place they named "Epekwitk," often spelled "Abegweit," meaning "something lying in the water." The Lennox Island and Abegweit First Nations call the Island home to this day, and their culture continues to thrive there.

ACKNOWLEDGMENTS

To my young readers, remember that when a dream finally comes true, there will always be people to thank. I am grateful to my agent, David Dunton, at Harvey Klinger and my editor, Reka Simonsen, at Atheneum, who gave my manuscript their precious time and who are just lovely people. Thanks also to Justin Chanda, Kristie Choi, and everyone at Atheneum whose input made this book better and better—especially associate director Jeannie Ng and copyeditor Clare McGlade, who caught all of my many mistakes; and artist Tran Nguyen and book designer Greg Stadnyk, who created just the cover I imagined.

Thanks to my early readers Kate Burns, Julie Cremin, Gabriella Gage, and cousin-brother Michael Cremin; and to loyal friends and listeners Alana Caron, Rachel Bernier, Judy

Costello-Cloutier and Monique Samuels, Juliette Mastroianni Warhurst, Emily Smith-Sturr, Karen Durant, Sarah Borchersen, Paul Thur, Alyse Bithavas, Lou Caron, Monika Ille, Laura A. Seel, and Valerie Bolling.

My love and appreciation goes out to colleagues and friends at Boston University's College of General Studies, including Natalie McKnight and Davida Pines, who value fiction writing, and Megan Sullivan and Donna Connor at our Center for Interdisciplinary Teaching and Learning for supporting my student researchers. Thanks also to Sally Sommers-Smith, who answered all my questions about fiddle playing, and Rayhme Cleary, who set me straight on some aspects of Syrian-Lebanese culture. Love to all my students, especially researchers Alyssa Garcia, Yael Bermudez, Emeline Antunes, Arjun Anand, Anushka Singh, Noah Pereira, Kiara Reagan, and Michelle Nguyen.

The Somerville Arts Council and the Massachusetts Cultural Council provided grants that gave me time to write. Thanks to the wonderful people at the Somerville Public Library and the Melrose Public Library, and to everyone at Bloc Café in Somerville, Massachusetts, where this book was mostly written. Thank you to my writing teachers the late Jeff Kelley and Morse Hamilton, and to Madame Eveline Naggar, a fourth-grade teacher like no other. To TC, Patsy, and Pat, don't give up.

All my gratitude to my many long-time friends from the International Conference on the Fantastic in the Arts. Theodora Goss and Daryl Gregory provided empathy and good advice. The great Gina Wisker gave me a platform. Thanks as well to the tsunami of support that is Derek Newman-Stille, and to P. Andrew Miller, Judy Collins, Graeme Wend-Walker (who knew), and so many others. To my Northern brother, Greg Bechtel, and my transatlantic sisters, Anya Heise-von der Lippe and Isabella van Elferen—there are not enough thanks in the world.

Love and gratitude to my extended family of Hansens, Gages, Laverses, Cremins, Pizzellas, Gibbses, Brazzells, Dragos, Amazus, and Kemmetts—my cheerleaders Maureen and Albert Cremin; my siblings, Charles, Michele, Laura, Charlotte, Matthew, and Gabriella; my two sets of parents—Charles Hansen Sr., whose stories and memories made this book better; my beloved Mama Linda Hansen and Papa Bill Gage; and my mother, Mary Cremin, who made a better world for her children through love and sheer force of will. Finally, thanks to my children, Dominic, Angelina, and Veronica, and my husband, Brian Kemmett. Their love is my most precious thing.